Kate L. Mary

Copyright © 2014 by Kate L. Mary
1st edition July 2014
2nd edition March 2015
Edited by Emily Teng
Cover art by Jimmy Gibbs
ISBN: 978-1500257743

For my biggest cheerleaders: Erin, Sarah and Tammy.
Thanks for loving Axl and Vivian as much as I do!

ACKNOWLEDGMENTS

Broken World has been a long time coming. I love zombies, and thanks to the recent success of a little show on AMC called *The Walking Dead*, they've become very popular. As soon as I started writing I wanted to get a zombie story out there, but it's a hard sell for agents and publishers, so I put it off. When I finally gave into the ideas swirling around in my head, three books poured out of me along with the concept for several more. And I fell in love with these characters.

I want to give a huge thanks to my three good friends Erin Rose, Sarah McVay and Tammy Brewer-Moore for loving these books and being overwhelmingly supportive. They really are the biggest cheerleaders when it comes to Axl and Vivian.

Thanks so much to the other first readers of this book: Jeremy Mary, Russ James and Lisa Terry. I appreciated all your enthusiasm and critiques. Thank you also to Meredith Tate for helping me track down the last few pesky typos that reviewers kept complaining about. After reading through this book hundreds of time, there were a few that just kept hiding. Hopefully between the two of us we've found them all!

To my editor, Emily Teng, who worked so hard on the revisions while I was still with my former publisher. I appreciate your focus and the fact that you did your best to get answers for me. Thanks for doing such a good job and for your professional behavior!

Of course, I have to thank Robert Kirkman and AMC for bringing about the popularity of zombies. Anyone who knows me at all knows I am in love with *The Walking Dead.*

And to Daryl Dixon, the zombie apocalypse messiah who somehow manages to make women swoon while being covered in dirt. You are amazing and I never get tired of seeing you kick some zombie ass.

Thanks to my family and all my friends, and every person who loves zombies as much as I do. I hope you all enjoy this series as much as I love writing it, because I don't plan on stopping any time soon!

Chapter One

The Car Sputters when I maneuver it into a space, but it doesn't die. Not yet, anyway. The small orange light screams at me from the dashboard—*check engine*. Ten hours, that's how long I've been on the road. I didn't really believe this piece of shit would make it all the way to California, but I'd hoped it would at least get me halfway there.

I squeeze my eyes shut and rest my forehead on the steering wheel, right between my clenched fists. The orange words dance across the back of my eyelids. Even with my eyes closed I can't escape them. They taunt me. *Check engine*. They may as well be *you failed*. That's what it feels like.

I jerk the keys out of the ignition and grab my travel papers off the dashboard, shoving them both in my purse. Leaving the papers behind would get my car broken into for sure, plus I'll need them if I run into a cop. If my papers get stolen, I'll be stranded.

The diner is the type of place I would normally avoid. It's nothing more than a truck stop really, probably fifty years old or more. I'm sure the walls are coated in grease, and the bathrooms most likely haven't been cleaned well since the late eighties. It's full of truckers and white trash. People who remind me of the life I ran from. But I don't have a choice. I have to pee, and this is the only route open that leads to California.

The inside is exactly the way I imagined it. Old booths with cracked seats covered in duct tape, the walls brown and grimy. The grease invades my pores and nostrils the second I step in. It goes down into my lungs and coats them in a thick, oily film. I want to get in and out of this place as fast as possible.

I've only taken two steps when a man stops me. He's big and round, and his face is red and sweaty. The pits of his shirt are stained an ugly yellow-brown color that smells as bad as it looks. Even over the grease and cigarettes his pungent odor burns my nostrils. He also has a gun strapped to his chest.

"Papers." He holds his hand out expectantly. His face is hard.

My heart pounds as I pull the papers out of my purse and hesitantly hand them to the man. Hopefully, he actually works here and he's not robbing me. I hold my breath while he slowly unfolds them, then exhale when his eyes narrow on the fine print. His mouth is pulled into a tight line when he nods.

He folds the papers in half, snapping his fingers across the crease before handing them back. "Welcome." It sounds more like a death sentence than a welcome.

I return his tense smile and shove the papers back in my purse. "Where's the bathroom?"

He tilts his head to the right, but doesn't say a word. I nod and head in the direction he indicated, keeping my eyes down, trying not to meet anyone's gaze. I don't need to look at the people to know what expressions they wear. It's the same everywhere. Fear, frustration, hopelessness, and loss. It's how things have been since martial law was declared six weeks ago. And I'm tired of it. I have my own worries. I don't want to see the despair in other people's eyes, don't want to focus on anyone else's problems.

The bathroom is empty, thankfully, and just as dirty as I imagined it would be. I squat over the toilet, trying my best not to touch the seat. The pressure in my bladder is agonizing. I'd started to think I was going to have to pee on the side of the road.

A sigh of relief whooshes out of me when I've finally relieved myself. I pull up my skinny jeans and head out to wash my hands. The mirror hanging above the sink is cracked and filmy. I can't make anything out other than my tangled blonde hair. I work my fingers through the knots and look away from the mirror. Doesn't matter how I look. There won't be anyone to impress on this trip.

I wash my hands and shake them dry before heading back out into the diner. No way am I eating here. It would be a waste of time. Plus,

I have no desire to sit and breathe in this grease-filled air. But coffee is a must. I want to make it at least another four hours before pulling over for the night.

A woman in her fifties stands behind the register. She wears the same uniform as the other waitresses: orange dress with short sleeves and an apron that probably used to be white. The entire thing is now splattered with food and grease, old and worn just like she is. Her hair is short and jet black, the kind of color that only comes from a bottle, and the creases on her face are so deep they're probably just as full of grease as the walls of the diner. Her arms cross over her chest and she shakes her head, frowning at the man in front of her.

"Please, I'm begging you. I was on a business trip when this all started. I've been stranded for weeks trying to get home to my family. I've spent every last penny I had on my physical and a car. I'm starving." His voice is desperate, begging. Same story, different person.

"No credit," the woman says. She won't budge. Why would she? People like her are making a killing off travelers. A few weeks ago, she probably barely made enough money to live on. And now…well, if this all blows over, she'll be comfortable.

The man pleads for a bit longer and I shift from foot to foot, waiting for him to get the point. I should have some sympathy for him. I should. But if I felt bad for every person I passed who was desperate and running out of time…if I did that, I wouldn't be able to keep going. I'd sit down on the floor right here in the middle of this diner and never move again.

The television mounted on the wall catches my eye, and I tune the man out. It's an old tube TV and the reception is awful, but the news is on. Maybe there will be an update on the virus.

"…travelers are advised to display their papers at all times and to keep to approved routes. Anyone who is found traveling on closed highways or without papers will be arrested immediately and held until martial law has been lifted.

In local news, police are still on the lookout for two men responsible for robbing several convenience stores in the St. Louis area. They are described as two white males in their mid- to late-twenties and were last seen traveling in a dark blue SUV. They are considered armed and dangerous…"

"That's it," the woman at the counter says, making me jump. She nods to the armed man at the door, then turns to me. I guess she finally got tired of listening to the desperate man. "What can I get you?"

Her gaze holds mine. Both of us avoid looking at the man as he's dragged from the diner. Neither one of us bats an eye when he screams for mercy. Begs for help. My throat constricts, burning a little at his cries. But I can't give in.

"Coffee," I say. "To go."

She nods and turns away, not even bothering to ask me if I have cash. She shouldn't have to. Not with the giant sign over the register that says *Cash Only*, and not after the screaming man was ripped from the building.

I lean against the counter and close my eyes for a second. My shoulders slump and my limbs feel weighed down, like they're made of lead. I feel a hundred years old, not twenty.

When I open my eyes, my gaze locks with a man a few booths away. Everything about him screams redneck. From his flannel shirt, unbuttoned to reveal his wifebeater and beer belly, to the bulge in his lower lip. His upper lip curls and his eyes go over my pin-up body. He nods in approval and raises an eyebrow. He's in his thirties, probably getting close to forty, and he's hard. Like he's been dealt a rough life and didn't have an issue giving some back. I've known men like him. Hell, I've dated men like him.

There's another man sitting at the table with him, but his back is to me so I can't tell what he looks like. Probably more of the same. The first man grins and picks up a soda can, spitting into it. My stomach churns. He gives me the creeps.

I turn away when the waitress comes back carrying a cup of coffee. "That'll be five bucks."

I dig my nails into my palms. "Five dollars? What do you think this is, Starbucks?"

She purses her lips and both her penciled-on eyebrows pull together. "I know this ain't Starbucks, but I also know there ain't another place to get a cup of coffee for 'bout fifty miles. And that's if you're goin' east. If you're headin' west, it's further."

I'm going west, of course.

I rip the cup out of her hand as violently as I can without spilling it and slam a five-dollar bill on the counter. "Don't expect a tip."

I turn on my heel and walk out of the diner, keeping my eyes straight ahead so I don't have to look at the redneck again. His eyes bore into me as I go.

I make it three more hours before the car sputters and starts to slow. That's all. My foot slams on the gas pedal, but nothing happens. The wheel is stiff as I turn it hard to the right and pull to the shoulder. A car blares its horn when it flies by. I probably got the finger, but my vision is too clouded by tears to know for sure. It's over. This is it.

The entire car jerks when the engine sputters, then dies completely. I don't even bother putting it in park. There's no point. It's never moving again. I stare straight ahead. What do I do now? There's a sign about fifteen feet in front of me, announcing that the next check point is twenty miles away. I can walk or I can try to hitch a ride. Both are a risk. But then again, so is sitting here.

I grab my purse and pull out the photo, clutching it so tight the paper crinkles. Her blue eyes stare up at me, big and round. Innocent. Squeezing my heart and making my throat constrict. I just wanted to see her one time before it all ended. Just once.

A horn honks and I jump, almost dropping the picture. A car has pulled to the side of the road less than six feet behind me. My heart pounds and every muscle in my body tightens. Good or bad? I don't know. No one gets out of the car, and I can't see in.

My purse is still in my lap.

I put the picture back and pull out my gun.

Closing my eyes, I take a deep breath, then open the door and step out. It's a dark blue Nissan Armada. A monster of a vehicle. The windows are tinted so dark there's no way it can be legal. The outline of two men is barely visible through the dark windows, but I can't tell who they are or what they look like. And I have no idea what they're doing.

I take two small steps toward the car and the driver's side door opens. The redneck from the diner steps out.

"Well, hello there!" he drawls. His accent isn't southern exactly, more low-class than anything else. He keeps the door open as he steps away from the car, his own gun clutched in his right hand. "What a surprise. Thought I'd never see you again." He winks.

I tighten my grip on the gun and raise it to chest level. Steadying it with both hands. Aiming at the center of his chest. I'm a good shot.

He puts his hands up, but doesn't release the gun. "Hold on now, no need to point that thing at me. I just stopped to see if you was havin' car trouble."

The passenger door opens, and the other man steps out. He stays behind the open door but points another gun at me through the gap between the door and the car.

"I think you should put that down," he calls. He sounds younger than the first man, but their voices are similar. Same low-class accent.

"Just a precaution." I keep my gun up and my arm steady. "I've had lots of target practice, so don't think I don't know what I'm doing."

The first man nods and slowly bends down, lowering the hand with the gun toward the ground. "I'm just gonna put this down, and my brother is gonna put his down, and we're gonna have a nice chat. That sound good?"

His tone is condescending. Warm and fuzzy, but in a fake way. It puts me on edge. I shouldn't trust this man. I know it.

"Lower your gun, Axl. Come on out where she can see ya."

The man behind the door pulls his gun back and walks forward. He is younger than his brother, and taller. Where the first man is stocky with a beer belly, Axl is broad. His muscles strain against his flannel shirt. He's average-looking. Not unattractive and hard like his brother, more unassuming. Probably why his brother called him out. So I'd let my guard down.

I'm silent as the two men put their guns on the ground and take a step back. My eyes flit between them while I try to decide what to do. Axl's face is blank and he's silent, his hands casually at his side. His brother, on the other hand, grins at me with his hands still in the air. His smile is fake as my boobs.

"We ain't gonna hurt you," Axl spits out. His voice drips with irritation. Guess he isn't thrilled they stopped to help me.

"Why did you stop then?"

"I told you, darlin'," the first man says. "We was just checking to see if you needed help. That's all. I'm Angus, and this here is my brother, Axl. We're travelin', just like you. Thought we'd help out."

"Nothing's that simple these days." I flex my fingers around the grip of my gun.

Axl rolls his eyes and turns toward his brother. "I told you this was stupid. Let's go."

"No, no. She needs help. It's obvious." Angus turns back to me and smiles in what I'm sure he thinks is a charming way. It's not. "We just wanted to help ya out. That's all."

I study them for a minute longer with the gun still aimed at Angus's chest. My knuckles start to ache. These two rednecks may be my only option. "Where are you headed?"

"California." Angus flashes me a big grin.

Sighing, I lower the gun. Shit. "Me too."

This makes Angus smile even bigger, and I have the urge to shoot him anyway. There is definitely something creepy about this guy.

"Well then, we'll just travel on up there together," Angus says. Another smile.

"You'd give me a ride?"

"Sure would. Can't leave a young lady out here all by herself. It's a dangerous world." Angus winks and his eyes sweep over my body, just like they did in the diner. I shudder. He's dangerous.

"I'd pitch in for gas and anything else we needed." I cringe at the pleading in my voice. Not sure if there's any sense in hiding it, though. Angus knows I'm desperate, like everyone else on the road.

He smiles again. "Sure you will."

Angus picks up both guns on his way to the Nissan. "Help her with her bags, Axl." He doesn't even glance at his brother. It's an order. He is definitely at the top of the food chain here.

Axl doesn't blink. Not that I thought he would. He heads toward my car. Axl doesn't frighten me or put me on edge like his brother, but maybe he should.

I open the back door and give him a strained smile. "Sorry about the gun."

He nods, but barely looks at me. "Understandable."

Axl grabs both my bags without so much as a grunt and heads back to the Nissan. I gather my meager belongings as fast as possible since I don't want them to drive off with my stuff. I jog to catch up with him. Angus catches my eye. He gives me another one of his smiles and I do my best to return it. I'm sure mine is even less convincing than his.

"You're in the back," Angus says, but he isn't talking to me. He's talking to Axl.

My stomach twists into knots, but I climb in the passenger seat anyway. I should argue, say I'd rather be in the back so I can get some sleep. But I don't want to cause problems. I have to get to California. Emily is there.

Chapter Two

Angus pulls onto the road, and I barely look at my piece of junk when we drive past it. Good riddance.

"So you gonna tell us your name or what?" Axl asks from the backseat.

"Vivian," I say. "Vivian Thomas."

Angus gives me that creepy grin again. "So where you comin' from, *Vivian?*"

The way he says my name sends a shudder through my body. Not to mention the fact that his eyes haven't once focused on my face for more than two seconds.

"Kentucky. Outside Louisville."

He laughs and shakes his head. "You thought that piece of shit was gonna get you all the way to California? I've seen some desperate folks the last few weeks, but that takes the cake."

"I had to try," I say flatly.

"What's in California?" Axl leans forward.

There's a straightforward vibe in everything he says, unlike his brother. Angus tries to make every word out of his mouth sound light and teasing. Smooth. He's anything but smooth.

I turn to face Axl, really studying him for the first time. He's got to be twenty-four, maybe twenty-five. His hair is longer than his brother's, which is buzzed, and it looks soft and feathery. A nice dirty blond. He has a one-inch scar on the left side of his chin, almost reaching his lips, and his eyes are a startling shade of gray. Dark.

Stormy like a rain cloud.

"My daughter." Axl's eyes have me so mesmerized that the words are out before I realize it. I press my lips together and silently curse myself while twisting the strap of my purse between my fingers. That was stupid.

"Then what's in Kentucky?" Angus asks.

I pull away from Axl and look straight ahead. Can't get away from the truth now. "My life. Where I was living."

Angus raises an eyebrow. Might as well just go for broke. Who cares if they know? If this really is the end of the world, what does it matter anymore?

"I grew up in California. I moved to Kentucky when I was eighteen, but before that I had a baby I gave up for adoption. I haven't seen her since she was born. I just figured with everything that's going on I should go meet her. She's four now…"

Angus purses his lips and nods. "Makes sense. You have any problems gettin' travel papers? Hear it's hard."

My heart drops to the floor. I twist in my seat to face Angus.

"Don't you have papers?" My throat is so tight that the words are barely a whisper. I have family in California, that's the only way I was able to get travel papers. It was easy, once I paid the $500 for my physical and the $400 for my papers. Anyone without family is screwed. They're not allowed to travel

Angus laughs and narrows his eyes on my face at the same time. "Don't worry. We ain't infected."

"Where are your papers then?"

Axl leans forward, practically sticking his face between the seats. His mouth turns down slightly in the corners. "We got papers, they just ain't quite legitimate. But we ain't infected." His words ooze annoyance, but I don't give a shit.

"I want you to stop the car." My body shakes. This isn't how it ends for me. Being murdered by a pair of rednecks is one thing, but the virus is another.

"Calm down," Angus growls. "We got a physical and we were clean. We just didn't have any reason good 'nough to drive 'cross the country. So we had to purchase some papers." He narrows his eyes at me even more. "Under the table."

He's lying. I don't trust a word that comes out of his mouth. Not with that monkey grin he keeps flashing me.

I face Axl. For some reason I believe those stormy eyes will tell me the truth. "You swear? I can't get sick. Not now."

Axl nods, but Angus answers, "We're clean."

My heart is still racing. Should I trust them? I twist my purse strap tighter around my finger. The weight of my gun presses on my legs. It helps keep me from panicking. I don't have another option. Who else is going to give me a ride?

"What're you so worried 'bout?" Axl's voice is tight. Why is he so irritated by my presence? "They got this thing contained anyways. Saw it on the news."

Angus laughs and shakes his head. "That's my kid brother, always lookin' on the bright side."

I shift in my seat so I can see Angus, even though the bulge in his lip makes my stomach churn. He spits into an empty soda can and wipes his mouth on the sleeve of his shirt.

Swallowing against the bile in my throat, I say, "You don't think it's contained?" Obviously I have my doubts or I wouldn't be on this trip, but I'm curious what other people think. There are a lot of rumors out there.

"Hell no, it ain't contained," Angus barks at me. "If it was contained do you think they'd be makin' us see a doctor before lettin' us travel? And what about this martial law bullshit? If this thing was even close to bein' contained, why wouldn't they just lock down them cities? Why put the whole country under martial law?" Angus spits so violently I'm afraid he'll miss the can. Thankfully, most of it hits the mark. Only a few drops stain his hand.

He has a good point.

"The news said they haven't had any new cases outside the locked-down areas. Not since they declared martial law six weeks ago."

Angus studies me with one eye, the other one on the road. "You gotta know I'm right or you wouldn't be on this here trip."

"I wanted to see her, just in case." I shake my head. I don't want to talk about my daughter, not with this disgusting redneck and his brother. "What about you? You obviously don't have family or you would have been able to go get papers. Where are you going?"

"We're gettin' the hell away from the virus. That's where we're goin'," Axl says.

I look him up and down, trying to size him up. He's hard to get a read on. "Thought you believed the government?"

He shrugs. "Don't hurt to take precautions."

"That's right." Angus nods. "Hell yeah. No way anyone is gonna tell the James brothers they can't drive to California if they want."

"Got that right," Axl says.

For a brief second the exchange strikes me as sweet: them against the world. Then it hits me. What would they be willing to do to stay together? A shiver runs down my spine and I grip my purse tighter. Gun or no, getting in the car with these two probably wasn't one of my better ideas.

The world flies by in a blur. It almost makes me dizzy how fast it all disappears. Angus plays with the radio, constantly changing the station. He finds a song he likes and leaves it on long enough for the song to end before he starts searching again. This thing has a six-CD changer. Why doesn't he put a CD in? I doubt he has an iPod; he doesn't really seem like the type. I have one, but there's no way my taste in music is the same as his. I picture him as a Billy Ray Cyrus type of guy. Not exactly my speed.

In the back, Axl starts to snore. He's stretched out across the seat, looking cozy. I'm jealous. My eyelids are heavy and the constant flipping of the radio is oddly soothing.

"I've been awake for about fourteen hours now," I say with a yawn. "I'm going to have to get some sleep."

"Go on ahead." Angus doesn't even glance my way.

He still makes me nervous, but maybe he isn't as disgusting as I originally thought. Maybe he just likes to put on a good show for other people.

"Thanks." I grab my jacket off the floor and roll it into a ball, so I can use it as a pillow. The fabric is stiff and scratchy, and not the least bit comfortable, but even before I close my eyes the world starts to drift away.

Emily is in front of me. I haven't seen a picture of her since she was nine months old, but I know it's her. She has my golden blonde hair. My real hair, not the bottled stuff. And my eyes. They are big and round, soft brown and turned up slightly at the corners.

Her mouth morphs into a wide smile, and she dances across the room, singing a silly song while she spins. It's a dream. I've been having the same one for weeks now.

She sees me and stops. Her small face lights up. She smiles, revealing a dimple in each cheek. Just like me.

"Hi." Her voice is soft and musical. It breaks my heart. A tear rolls down my cheek but I'm too shaken to wipe it away.

"Hi." I take a small step toward her.

"Wake up!" she screams at me, her voice deep and masculine.

My eyes fly open and a small sob bubbles up in my throat. I cover my mouth with my hand as I turn my face toward the window. My cheeks are moist from tears and I quickly wipe them away. I don't want Angus to think I'm weak.

"Check point," he says.

He's not looking at me. His body is tense and he grips the steering wheel tightly as the car slows. I don't blame him for being nervous. He should be if his papers are fake. Hopefully they don't slow me down. I have to get to California.

"Axl!" The words comes out like a growl.

His brother shoots up in the backseat. He sputters and makes sounds that are probably supposed to be words. They are not.

A road block is set up in front of us. Four military vehicles and a group of heavily armed soldiers. The automatic weapons in their hands make my throat tighten. It's not the first checkpoint I've gone through, but it still makes me nervous. I have too much at stake.

Only one car is ahead of us. The tension in the Nissan swirls around us, threatening to suffocate me. I play with the hem of my shirt and lean forward, trying to get a better view. One soldier stands at the driver's side, examining a few travel papers. Four others obstruct the road, their guns aimed at the car. After a few minutes the soldier hands the papers back and waves to the armed men, who step aside and turn their guns toward us. The other car speeds away.

"Here we go," Angus says.

He pulls up and rolls down the window.

"Papers!" the soldier barks.

Angus hands them over without a word. I reach into my purse to get mine, but they aren't there. My heart beats against my ribcage and little beads of sweat break out across my forehead. Where are they? I *know* I put them here. When I look up, Angus grins at me with his eyebrows raised. The soldier has three pieces of paper in his hand. Angus went through my purse while I was asleep.

Axl sits forward so he can see between the driver and passenger seats, and I glance his way. Did he have anything to do with this? His hair is messy and his eyes are hazy from sleep. He stares back at me blankly. He doesn't have a clue.

"What business do you have in California?" The solider looks through the window. His eyes sweep over the three of us.

"Family." Angus sits up straighter, like he's trying to appear bigger.

The soldier frowns. "You have a different destination than the other two." His eyes bore into me, dark brown and intense.

"My car broke down. They were nice enough to offer me a ride." I'm shaking, but not from fear. I'm furious that Angus went through my purse.

The soldier nods. "You will stick to this route all the way to California, understand?"

"Yes, sir. We are law abidin' citizens." Angus's tone is too harsh. It sounds like an order.

The soldier's frown deepens, becoming exaggerated. "Route 66. That's it." He looks directly at Angus.

Angus's jaw tightens. He doesn't like being challenged. "We. Heard. You."

For a second the two men stare at each other, not moving, but eventually the soldier sighs and hands the papers back. "Move on."

Angus takes them and folds them up, shoving them on the dashboard. He nods to the soldier then rolls the window up.

"Asshole," he mutters once the window is secure. The soldier must be able to read Angus's lips, because his face darkens.

"Shut up, Angus," Axl hisses.

Angus glares at his brother in the rearview mirror but doesn't respond. The second the soldiers move, he slams his foot on the gas pedal. The tires squeal against the pavement as we speed away.

I dig my nails into my palms so hard I'm sure they'll draw blood. They're long and red, fake like the rest of me. My body shakes. I should keep my mouth shut. Angus is already pissed at being challenged by the soldier. But I can't. Not that I ever could.

"You went through my purse while I was sleeping?" I say through clenched teeth.

Angus barely glances at me. "So? I needed your papers for the roadblock."

"Don't you dare!"

Angus chuckles. "Or what? You'll shoot me? Better check your purse again, Blondie."

My stomach bottoms out and I dig through my purse. My gun isn't there.

Now I'm really shaking. "I want it back!"

My only warning is the tightening of Angus's jaw. His hand makes contact with my cheek and a crack echoes through the car. It catches me by surprise and I slam against the passenger door. My cheek stings and my ear rings, but I don't move. It's not the first time a man has hit me. I'm used to it. If he wants to intimidate me, he'll have to do better than that.

"Dammit, Angus!" Axl says.

"Shut up!" Angus points at his brother's reflection in the rearview mirror. His face is bright red and a little vein has popped up on his forehead.

Axl sits back, and Angus turns to me. "Now you listen here, girlie. This here is my car. You wanna travel with me, you play by my rules. Got it?"

We stare at each other for a second and I don't blink, but I'm stuck. He must see it in my eyes—the desperation—because he smiles. I dig my nails deeper into my palms, then face the passenger side window. Just a few days. Then I can get away from this asshole and never see him again.

"We're gonna stop for the night here soon," he says.

I shake my head and turn back to face him. Getting hit again would suck, but stopping seems stupid. "Why? There are three of us. We can drive straight through and get there in no time."

"My car, my rules. Remember?" Angus doesn't even look at me. He just grins. Like he enjoys bossing me around. Probably does. "Soon as we find a motel or area to camp we stop. I wanna get some real rest. Can't sleep with the car jostlin' around like this."

I sit back and cross my arms over my chest. There's no way I can win this argument.

Chapter Three

We don't find a motel, so we pull over and set up camp on the side of a road. Right next to a crumbling gas station that probably hasn't been open since the '60s. The parking lot is overgrown, covered in weeds that are soft and full. It's flat. The perfect place to set up a tent.

Camping on the side of the road probably would have been a big deal in days gone by. Just like the rabbit Angus shot for our dinner. But not now. Pretty much anything goes these days, as long as you have the proper travel documents.

The brothers are prepared for anything. They have equipment for camping, hunting, fishing. Pretty much any scenario that might come up. Like it really is the end of the world. It makes me think. Maybe I'm not so bad off with these guys. I don't have to trust them, or like them, but if I can get them to trust me… These are the kind of people you want on your side when the world goes to hell. These are the kind of people who will survive. Who will do whatever it takes to make it. That's not such a bad thing.

I haven't had much of a chance to talk to Axl, so I'm still trying to figure him out. Angus is an open book; there are no surprises with this guy. But Axl is interesting. He doesn't say much, but when he does he's blunt. Almost abrasive. When Angus barks orders at him he doesn't even blink. His brother is the boss. Probably has been his whole life, and he looks at Angus with a kind of reverence that's almost unnerving. Like he owes him his life, and he'll do whatever it takes to repay him. But it's clear just from watching Axl that he can handle himself. Angus shot the rabbit, but Axl skinned and gutted it. When he pierced the body with the metal spit he looked like a pro. He's probably done this a million times.

We sit around the fire in camp chairs. The brothers barely talk. Barely interact. But it's like they are hyperaware of each other's presence. I'm across the fire from them, and I get the impression it was set up this way intentionally. They trust me about as much as I trust them. Something that needs to change.

"So I think we got off on the wrong foot," I say as Axl leans forward and rotates the rabbit.

"You could say that." Axl glances at me briefly. Even in the light of the fire his eyes are stormy.

"Look." I inhale slowly while I push every last bit of pride down. It's the only way I'll be able to get the words out. "I get why you took my gun. I don't love that you went through my purse, but I get it. I pulled a gun on you, so I'm the one who started it. I want to finish it. Right here." I blurt it out all in one breath, before I lose the nerve.

"Mighty nice of you to say," Angus says. "But I ain't givin' you that gun back."

I dig my nails into my palms. "Fair enough. You just hold onto it until you feel like you can trust me."

He gives me a half grin, but it's there in his eyes. He has no intention of giving me that gun back. Ever. I'll have to work hard at getting him to trust me.

Axl will be easier, as long as I can keep his brother from hating me. He'll do whatever Angus says, but he's not as hard as his brother. Not quite.

"So I never asked where you guys were from," I say, taking a sip of my beer. The brothers have a cooler full of ice and Coors Light. They probably thought it was as necessary as the camping equipment when they packed their car. I'm glad they have it though, it's cold and having something in my hand helps me relax. I can pretend it's my gun.

"Tennessee," Angus says.

"Good riddance," Axl mumbles.

The rabbit must be done, because he takes out a knife and cuts a big chunk off it. He tosses it on a paper plate and holds it out to me.

His eyes hold mine when I take it from him. I force out a smile. "Thanks."

Axl serves his brother, then gets some for himself. I stare uncertainly at the plate in my hands. I've never eaten rabbit, but it doesn't smell bad and my stomach is growling. It probably tastes like chicken. I take a big bite. It's greasy and gamier than I expected. More like a chicken leg than a breast. It's not awful, just bland. But I'm too hungry to care.

"You have family in Tennessee?" I ask between bites.

Angus stops eating and glares at me. "What's it to you?"

"Just making conversation."

He purses his lips. "What about you, Blondie? You got family? You say you're goin' to California to see your daughter, but that ain't what your papers say."

I squeeze the beer can so tight the aluminum crinkles, echoing through the silence. Angus reading my papers hadn't even occurred to me.

"Who's Roger Clifton?" Angus grins like he just loves seeing me squirm.

I swallow and take a deep breath, trying to ignore my racing heart. "Roger Clifton is my father." I hold Angus's gaze. Just saying his name leaves a bad taste in my mouth.

"So what's the story there? Must be interestin' if it's got your feathers all ruffled like that." Angus takes another bite, grinning like a chimpanzee. A little bit of grease trails down his chin, and my stomach convulses.

"It was just an excuse to get me to California. I have no intention of seeing my father. But they wouldn't have let me go to see my daughter. She's not mine. Not legally." I try to relax, I really do. But I can't. Every muscle in my body is wound tight and all I want to do is dive across this fire and punch him in the nose for looking at me like that. So smug. So happy he's gotten under my skin.

"Look," I say as calmly as possible. "I don't like to talk about my father, but I'll tell you my story just so we can establish some trust. Just this once. After that, the subject is closed. Off limits. Understand?"

Angus gives me a mockingly sympathetic look. It makes me want to squeeze his neck until his eyeballs pop out of their sockets. My hand wraps around the can more tightly, and I pretend it's his throat.

"My father was….not nice to me. To put it mildly." I take a deep breath so I can get the words out. "He beat me. Often. I left the day I turned eighteen. He was passed out drunk, had just cashed his welfare check that morning. I grabbed his car keys and all his cash and walked out the door. Never looked back."

"Why Kentucky?" Axl asks. He's been watching me this whole time. His eyes are sympathetic, unlike his brother's.

"I just drove until I ran out of money. Kentucky is where I ended up. I found a job at a strip club, crashed on the couch of one of the other girls for a few months, and pretended Roger Clifton didn't exist. It worked just fine until all this started."

Angus sits up straighter with the rabbit halfway to his mouth. He wiggles his eyebrows at me. "Stripper, eh?" He gives me a big grin. "Maybe you could give us some entertainment."

I fight back a shudder. He gives me the creeps but I don't want to show it, so I laugh. "Maybe one night, if I get drunk enough. Not tonight, though. I'm too tired." I try to make it as casual as possible, and from the excited gleam in Angus's eyes, I assume he buys it. But I need to be careful with this guy. He's the type who would take any flirting as consent.

Angus goes back to eating, and I turn away. My gaze meets Axl's. He's watching me closely. Eating his rabbit while his eyes study me thoughtfully. Maybe he's the one I should be more worried about.

"We got no family," he says. "It's just Angus an' me." Angus glares at his brother, but Axl shrugs. "What? She shared. Only fair."

"What happened to your family?"

"Mom's dead. We got different dads—both of 'em are MIA. It's just been the two of us since I was seventeen." Axl takes one last bite. He tosses the rabbit bones over his shoulder and wipes his mouth with his sleeve.

These two are exactly like the men I grew up with. Angus could almost be my father. He has the glare down pat and the same hardness in the way he carries himself. Axl, on the other hand, seems different. He's more like one of the trailer park victims. Uneducated and blindly following in the footsteps of the men before him, never considering that there might be something better out there. That he might be better. He's not weak and he's not a follower, he just exists.

"How'd your mom die?"

"Does it matter?" Angus growls.

19

He spits into the fire and it sizzles, breaking through the silent night. A sudden shudder racks my body. It hadn't occurred to me how eerily quiet it was before now. It's scary how suddenly the world has changed. Terrifying.

"I'm turning in." Angus gets to his feet. "You take the first watch, Axl. You got plenty of sleep in the car." He turns and smiles at me. "Wanna join me? Bet we could both squeeze into one of them sleepin' bags."

I have to choke down a gag. "I got some sleep in the car. I'm going to hang out here for a while." Thank God I grabbed a few blankets as I was leaving my apartment. I got lucky.

Angus grunts. "Suit yourself."

He ducks into the tent, and I shiver. It's a good size, but I have no desire to be in there alone with him.

"You cold?" Axl gets to his feet. "You shoulda packed warmer clothes. That ain't the kind of stuff you wear travelin'."

He walks over to the car and opens the back door without waiting for an answer. When he comes back, he's carrying a flannel shirt. The quilted kind redneck men wear in the winter instead of jackets. I hate them. They remind me of my father. But the gesture is so sweet I take it anyway.

"Thanks." I flash him a smile while I pull it on. I am cold. I didn't realize it until now.

Axl moves his chair closer to me, then takes a seat. There's only about two feet of space between us now.

He glances toward the tent. "Sorry Angus hit you."

His tone is too blunt to be apologetic, but it still makes me feel good he said it.

I study him and try to figure out what he's thinking, but his expression doesn't give anything away. He stares into the fire, his fingers curled around the gun in his lap. He doesn't look at me and he doesn't say anything. He just sits there, slouched over and staring off into the distance.

"It's not your fault." I take a sip of my beer and wince when the liquid fills my mouth. It's warm. I set the can on the ground.

"He ain't that bad. Just Angus. It's the only way he knows how to be."

My mouth goes dry. This is the most I've heard him speak since they picked me up. I don't want him to stop. Maybe if I make small talk. "So what did you do for a living? Back in Tennessee."

"Construction. When I could get work." He still doesn't look away from the fire. "Shitty economy and all that. Made it tough."

That explains the muscles.

"So you stripped? How was that?" He finally looks at me, but his face is expressionless. Just like his voice.

"Paid the bills. Got me away from my dad." I shrug. My mouth feels like it's full of cotton. I grab the beer again. Who cares if it's warm?

He stares into the fire like it holds the secret to life or something. "Must've been tough. For datin', I mean."

"The kind of guys I dated didn't really care," I say dryly. It's an understatement, really. They were the kind of men who bragged about my job. Even brought their friends in to see me. I've never been married, but I bet if I were that old saying would prove to be true. I'd probably end up with a husband just like my dad. Lord knows those are the kind of guys I tend to go out with.

His stormy eyes search mine. "People should come with warnin' labels."

I laugh. It's so sharp and bitter that it surprises even me. "No kidding. What about you? You have a girlfriend, ever been married?"

He guffaws. "Hell no. I'm only twenty-two. I ain't gettin' tied down to no woman at this age. Maybe later. Maybe…" He grins, and I relax a little. Finally he's loosened up. "What 'bout you? You been married?"

"I'm too damaged." The firelight flickers off his face. It makes him appear more vulnerable, more his age.

He lets out a small sound, somewhere between a grunt and a sigh, and turns back to the fire. "We're all damaged. Even them people livin' in them fancy houses out there in Hollywood. Maybe they don't show it as much because they got money, but they got baggage. Same as you an' me."

I shake my head, but he doesn't look over at me. "I've known plenty of people who weren't damaged."

He takes his eyes off the fire and purses his lips, studying me. "Like them men that came to see you dance?" There's something strange in his tone. Disgust, bitterness. Something else I can't quite place.

"Like you've never been to a strip club?" I roll my eyes but don't look away from him.

"Never said I hadn't. But I'm as damaged as they come, never pretended to be nothin' else."

"What makes you so damaged?" He still hasn't told me what happened to his mom.

"My story ain't nothin' new." His hand clenches the gun in his lap a little tighter and he purses his lips, making him suddenly look more like Angus. "Dad left when I was a baby. I grew up in a trailer park, and my mom was a drunk. She spent her time either neglectin' me or smackin' me around. Nothin' that really gets a whole lotta sympathy these days."

"You want sympathy? Doesn't really seem like your style."

His eyes grow hard. Darker than before. Like the clouds that fill the sky right before a tornado hits. "Hell yeah, I want sympathy. My mom didn't pass me off to strangers and I wasn't locked in a closet to starve, but I been through plenty. I deserve it. I can't tell you how many times I had to make my own dinner, how many times I had to walk home from school in pourin' rain 'cause my mom was too wasted to remember she had a son. I've been bruised and neglected, and I deserve to have that acknowledged. Never got it, though. Social workers came, took me away for a few days, only to send me home soon as mom sobered up enough to show up at the office. My situation wasn't bad enough to warrant help." He glances over toward the tent. "Angus looked out for me, when he could. He was in juvie a lot, but when he was home he taught me how to be tough."

My stomach twists into knots, and a sour taste fills my mouth. It's a sad life if that's the only role model you have.

"I think your situation is worth sympathy," I whisper.

His eyes soften. A small smile tugs at his lips. "That says a lot, comin' from you."

I sit up straighter. "What's that supposed to mean?"

He tilts his head to the side and purses his lips again as his eyes pierce mine. I squirm. It's like he's reading my mind. Like he knows all my secrets.

"You got a little experience when it comes to baggage. If you're willin' to give me sympathy, that's somethin' at least."

He's smarter than he gives himself credit for.

My throat tightens. I swallow and jump to my feet. Talking about myself isn't something I usually do. "I'm going to get some sleep."

The idea of climbing into that tent with Angus is less than thrilling, but right now it seems better than sitting here with Axl.

Chapter Four

When I open my eyes it's still dark, but I'm alone in the tent. I'm still wearing Axl's flannel shirt. It smells like the outdoors. The brothers' muted voices drift through the canvas walls. That must have been what woke me. I pull out my cell phone and push a button so the screen lights up. It's only a little after four in the morning. Did Axl get any sleep?

I crawl out from under the blankets and pull my shoes on. Axl was right. I didn't dress for travel. All I have are silly shoes like these: three inch wedge heels with open toes. Cute, but totally impractical.

"Mornin' sunshine," Angus says when I crawl out of the tent.

They're sitting around the campfire chatting. That's it.

"Why are you up already?" I yawn as I drop into the camp chair next to Axl. "Did you get any sleep?"

"Some." He shrugs like sleep doesn't matter. "I don't sleep much."

I wonder why.

"You get enough?" His tone is still blunt, but there's a softness to it that wasn't there yesterday. Like having me around doesn't piss him off anymore. Good. Maybe we can be civil toward each other from here on out.

Angus looks back and forth between us, and his eyes narrow. "You two get a little too friendly last night after I turned in?"

Seriously? Axl's nice to me and Angus immediately assumes it's because we had sex. Right. Like I'd ever be into Axl. He's everything I've been trying to run away from. Well, not everything. It's not like he's Angus or anything, and he's good-looking, I guess. But still, I'm not going to sleep with the guy!

The longer I think about it the hotter my face gets. Angus is an ass.

I open my mouth so I can tell him to go to hell, but Axl beats me to it. "Shut up, Angus," he says.

"Don't tell me to shut up, you little prick. I got the right to know if you're screwin' her. I ain't gonna have you ditchin' me for some two-bit floozy just 'cause she was willin' to open her legs for you."

My whole body is hot now. I jump to my feet. "Back off, Angus. I didn't screw your brother and I have no intention to. Just like I have no intention of screwing you!"

Axl flinches. Why? Did I hurt his feelings? I didn't mean to, but I'm not going to let Angus cause problems where there aren't any.

That little vein on Angus's forehead pulsates. He and I stare at each other. The longer I hold his gaze, the bigger his vein gets.

Just when I think Angus is going to explode, Axl bolts from his chair. "Shhh! Did you hear that?"

My heart leaps to my throat. I clamp my mouth shut. What am I supposed to be listening to? Axl clutches his gun tighter and my heart—still lodged in my throat—pounds harder. Then I hear it. Footsteps. Definitely human.

"Who's there?" Angus pulls his gun from the waistband of his pants.

None of us move. My hands clench and I bury my nails in my palms. If only I had my gun.

"Don't shoot!" a quiet male voice calls. His voice shakes.

All three of us turn toward the sound. It only takes a few seconds before I make out the figure of a man walking toward us.

"Put your hands in the air and approach real slow!" Angus raises his gun.

Axl raises his too. He's tense, but calm. Whereas every visible muscle in his brother's body stretches tight. Angus looks like he's ready to explode.

"Okay. Just don't shoot."

The man steps forward with his arms raised high. He's tall and thin, lanky. It's hard to tell if he's a kid or a man. He has brown hair and a plain face. Forgettable. He's the kind of guy you'd see huddled over a desk at the library on the weekends with dozens of books piled around him.

The firelight glistens off the beads of sweat on his forehead. Why's he sweating? It isn't hot, so he's either very nervous or he's sick. The urge to run is so strong my legs twitch. I take tiny step back. As if a few more inches of space between us will somehow save me from the virus if he is infected. Right. A slightly hysterical laugh bubbles up in my throat, but I swallow it down. It almost chokes me. He can't be sick. He can't. Other than the sweat he looks fine. He isn't coughing or hunched over like he's weak.

The guy's eyes dart back and forth between the brothers. His hands shake. It makes me nervous. "I'm clean. I swear. Don't shoot me!" he says.

Not sure if I trust him. People aren't trustworthy. My life is proof of that.

"You got travel papers?" Axl demands.

The guy nods so fast he reminds me of a bobble head. "I do. I'll get them. Just don't shoot."

"Shut up!" Angus growls.

The man slams his mouth shut and slowly reaches into his back pocket. I tense, half expecting a weapon. But it's a piece of paper, just like he said.

"Here." He holds it toward the brothers with a shaky hand.

Axl steps forward and jerks it out of his hand. He unfolds it.

"They're real 'nough." He glances back toward the guy. "Where's your car, Joshua?"

Joshua shakes his head, and a bead of sweat runs down the side of his face. He swipes his hand over his forehead, wiping his brow. His eyes are huge. He's still shaking, but now that I've had a second to look him over, I don't think he's sick. He's so scared of the guns he's about to pee his pants. "I ran out of gas. There was no one to help. I've been walking since this morning and no one stopped."

"Where's he goin'?" Angus asks. He hasn't lowered his gun.

"Says Arizona." Axl gives the papers back to Joshua and looks at his brother. "Put the gun down. You think this kid's gonna overpower us?"

Angus grunts, but lowers his gun.

"Now what?" Axl asks his brother.

He's not infected. Turning him away seems like a shitty thing to do. "We could give him a ride," I say.

The brothers both look at me like I'm insane.

"You gonna volunteer our car like it belongs to you?" Axl says. All the softness from a few minutes ago has disappeared, like a puff of smoke on a windy day. Poof. "Angus an' me'll decide what we're gonna do with this guy."

Guess I'm back on the outs.

Axl shakes his head like I'm the dumbest person he's ever dealt with. It stings, but I shrug so he doesn't know. "Just an idea. Doesn't hurt my feelings."

He spits, which hurts even more. What did I do to piss him off so fast? Angus grins at me, of course. He's just loving how quickly Axl's soft side—what little there is of it—disappeared.

Our little spat doesn't affect Joshua, who suddenly looks like we just offered to give him the answers to the universe. "If you give me a ride, I can pay you."

"Is that right?" Angus says.

Angus must be dumber than he looks. What's he going to do with money if this really is the end of society as we know it?

"Exactly what you gonna pay me with? Your money's gonna be worthless when all this goes to shit." He waves his arms in the air.

Okay, maybe he isn't a total moron.

Joshua bites his lip. "I can buy you supplies. Food, whatever you need. Whenever we get to the next gas station."

"Ain't a bad plan," Axl says to his brother. "We're set on survival gear, but we can never have too much food and water."

Angus nods. "'Kay. You got yourself a deal. But I'm going to tell you the same thing I told sugar tits over there." He jerks his head toward me and takes a step closer to Joshua. "My car, my rules. Got it?"

Joshua bobs his head so hard I'm afraid it will give him whiplash. He looks ridiculous because his hands are still in the air.

"Have some self-respect," Axl says. "Put your hands down. Nobody's got a gun on you."

Joshua lowers his hands and shoves them in his pockets.

"You want coffee?" Axl asks me, barely glancing my way.

I nod, and he gets to work making coffee with a fancy-looking coffee maker. It's similar to something you'd see in a person's kitchen, only it says Coleman at the top and has a small propane tank at the bottom. It looks expensive.

"Takes about fifteen minutes," he says when he lowers himself into the chair next to Angus.

I take the third. Joshua stands awkwardly off to the side. He hasn't moved from that spot since he put his hands down.

"You're makin' me nervous," Axl says. "Take a seat."

There aren't any other chairs, so Joshua takes his backpack off and sets it down. He sits right on the ground and awkwardly crosses his long legs.

Angus watches Joshua wordlessly, spitting into his soda can every so often. I have to turn away. Watching him do that makes my stomach turn.

"So what's your story?" Angus finally asks.

Joshua shrugs but looks down, like it hurts to think about it. "Trying to get home. Just like everyone else on this road."

"Not everyone." Angus spits again.

Joshua cringes a little and looks away from Angus, toward the fire. "I lived in Baltimore, moved there four months ago. When this got bad I tried to leave, but we were already on lock-down."

I sit up straighter and so do the brothers. "You're from Maryland?" It's so close to New York. So close to where all this started.

"It was bad where I was. I can't imagine what it was like in New York."

"When did you get locked down?" Axl asks.

The shadows created by the fire cut down Joshua's face, drawing his mouth into an exaggerated frown. He reminds me of the Joker. "Eight weeks ago maybe. It was earlier than they're saying on the news."

I stare at him, speechless. The news reports said only New York was locked down that early. Everything else was open until martial law was declared. They lied.

"Shit." Angus shakes his head. "I told you them bastards was lyin' to us."

Axl's mouth scrunches up like he wants to spit. "Good thing I listened and we got the hell outta there when we could."

I ignore them and lean closer to Joshua. "What was it like?"

He swallows. "Bad. I know I already said that, but...I just don't know how else to put it. There aren't words. All nonessential businesses were shut down, hospitals were overrun, and they had to set-up temporary clinics in the schools. People were literally dying in the streets."

My stomach twists. "You said 'were.' So it's contained now?"

Angus and Axl stop talking.

Joshua sniffs. "No. It's not contained. It's more like everyone who was going to die from it already did. This thing is weird. Only about seventy percent of the population is affected by it. The rest of us are immune."

"So you're immune?" He must be. He has papers.

"Yeah. I passed my physical exam. And trust me, if I was going to get it, I would have." He looks up, and his eyes bore into mine. "I was at the hospital there in Baltimore, working in the ER."

"You're a doctor?" A big smile spreads across Angus's face. Once again he reminds me of a chimpanzee.

"First year resident. I saw it all first-hand, and let me tell you, it wasn't pretty."

My head pounds. I run my hands through my hair, then massage my scalp. This can't be real. "Has it spread then?"

"Yeah, it's spread. I mean, they're doing what they can. They've been cremating the bodies and putting cities on lock down, but it's an impossible task. No matter what they do, someone is going to sneak through." He sucks in a slow breath, like breathing is difficult. "This whole thing, the travel papers and check points. It's all for show. They know it's going to sweep across the country and there's nothing they can do about it. Seventy percent of our population is going to die from this virus. Whatever it is."

"How do you know all this? You're just some ER doctor, you don't work for the government or nothin'." Axl narrows his eyes at Joshua like he doesn't trust him.

Axl actually has a point.

"I understand your suspicion, and you're right. I'm nobody. But we had doctors from the CDC with us at the hospital. I became friends with a woman who worked for them. She got sick and told me all this before she died, so I could go see my family before it was too late. Just in case they're not immune." His eyes are damp and he looks away, clearing his throat. Probably doesn't want to cry in front of the brothers. Not that I blame him.

"I'm sorry," I say. I guess that's the good thing about not having any family to lose.

Joshua wipes his eyes with his sleeve while he looks us all over. "So you all passed your physicals, right? Where are you from, what cities?"

"I'm from the Louisville area," I say.

"Clinton, Tennessee. Not too far from Knoxville," Axl says.

Joshua frowns and rubs his chin like he has a beard or something. It's as smooth as a baby's butt, though. "I don't know about those areas. If you were from one of the northern states, I'd say you were safe. But I don't think Tennessee and Kentucky have been hit hard by the virus yet." He give us a sympathetic look. "I'm sorry, you'll just have to wait and hope."

A pit forms in my stomach, and I can't move. There's a seventy percent chance I am going to die. It should hurt less. I don't have much of a life, anyway. No family, few friends. What am I leaving behind? Nothing. But the pain in my chest is so intense it's like I've been hit by a car. It hurts like hell.

"Dammit!" Angus gets to his feet and stalks off toward the crumbling gas station. A string of profanity drifts back as he goes.

Axl looks the same as he always does. Resigned. At what point did he accept this is all he'd ever be? All he'll ever have. I wish I'd accepted it. Maybe it would make this moment easier.

"Coffee's ready." He stands up and grabs a few steel camping mugs. "Doc?"

"Sure."

Axl hands me a cup. He pours a second one for Joshua. It's hot, but I wrap my hands around it anyway. My palms sting from the heat. I can't find the motivation to bring it to my lips.

Axl sits back down and nods his head toward the now empty chair. "Might as well take Angus's chair, he won't be back for a while."

Joshua gets to his feet. His limbs are so gangly that it looks like they're tangled together. A bit of coffee spills in the process. He cringes and shakes his hand, then blows on it lightly.

"Shouldn't you go check on your brother?" he asks when he's safely in the camp chair. It's too small for him. He has to be at least six foot six.

Axl takes a drink of his coffee. "Naw. He just needs to cuss a little. Maybe break somethin'." As if on cue the sound of breaking glass shatters the silence. "Told ya."

I finally take my first sip. The coffee is surprisingly good. I pay attention to the camping gear for the first time. It's all top-of-the-line. The tent isn't huge, but it's nice and solid. The camp chairs aren't the cheap kind you buy at the grocery store. They're the expensive ones that have padded seats and a back that reclines. How did the brothers afford all this stuff? There has to be thousands of dollars' worth of equipment in the car. And the car itself is new. And nice. Leather seats, totally spotless. There's no way they had the money for this stuff. Axl told me he worked construction, when he could get work. Bad economy. That's what he'd said.

Axl's eyes meet mine and his eyebrows pull together. "What?"

I take another sip while I try to keep my expression as blank as possible. "Nothing. Just thinking." Who did I get in the car with?

He nods, but his stormy eyes stay on me. He doesn't believe me.

Chapter Five

Angus staggers back just as the sun peaks over the horizon. The knuckles on his right hand are cut up and bloody. He clenches and unclenches his fist like he's trying to makes sure nothing is broken.

We've already started breaking down the camp. Almost everything is packed into the car. Axl put up the third row of seats in the Nissan, but there's still more than enough room in the back for all the supplies the brothers have.

Axl sees his brother's hand and walks to the back of the car. He shakes his head and cusses under his breath. When he comes back he has a first aid kit. He thrusts it at Angus. "Better clean it. Don't wanna find out you're immune just to die from infection."

Angus grunts and takes the first aid kit.

When we're all packed, we pile into the car. Axl takes the driver seat. Angus insists I sit up front. He acts like he's doing me a favor, but he just wants the middle row to himself. Joshua climbs into the third row and lays down. He'll be asleep in no time. He walked all night.

I can't get the camping equipment and car off my mind. How did I not notice it earlier? They must have stolen it. There's no other explanation. And it would be the perfect timing, too. No one is really going to worry about looking for them. Not with this virus sweeping the country, killing most of the people exposed. Who would bother?

Not the police. Probably not even the person it was stolen from. They know it too, or they wouldn't be so casual. These guys may be uneducated rednecks, but that doesn't mean they're stupid. They are smart and they are resourceful. They know exactly what they're doing.

"So no brothers or sisters?" Axl says out of nowhere, breaking the silence hanging over us.

His eyes sweep over my face, and I shift in my seat uncomfortably. He runs a hand through his dirty blond hair. It's messy, but in a cute way. His looks grow on you, I guess.

"No. Just me. And I'm pretty sure I was an accident. At least that's what my dad used to say..." I don't want to talk about Roger. Why did I say that? His gray eyes dart my way. It's distracting and jumbles my thoughts.

"Sounds 'bout right. My mom used to say the same thing to me. She say that to you, Angus?" He looks into the review mirror, trying to catch his brother's eye.

"Hell no, she never said that shit to me. She knew better. Knew I'd give it right back," he growls.

Axl flinches and looks back at the road. I guess Angus was immune to their mother's wrath. Maybe he was part of the reason for it.

"Yeah, well, she said it to me. Lots." Axl's hands grip the steering wheel tightly and his lips purse. He and his brother do the same thing when they're thinking.

He's silent for a few minutes. His hands relax. "She was a bitch. Hit me and screamed at me. But I still cried when she died. Go figure."

"That's 'cause you're a pussy." Angus chuckles to himself.

"It's because she was your mom," I say.

Axl looks over at me. "Would you cry, if your dad died?"

"Not now. I'm an adult. But if it had happened when I was a kid, I probably would have."

He nods, but he frowns like Angus's words really bugged him. He doesn't say anything else. Neither do I. I still want to know how she died, but I'm not going to ask. He obviously has a lot of issues with his mom.

We drive in silence after that. I grab a paperback book out of my purse and read for a while. It's an erotic romance. The more I read the more I'm aware of Axl sitting next to me. So close I can feel his body heat. I squirm in my seat and finally slam the book shut. This isn't the time or place. After that I just stare out the window, letting the hours pass while I imagine how I'll feel when I see my daughter.

A yellow sign catches my eye. "Next check point sixty miles," I say to Axl, reading the sign as we pass it.

"We're gonna stop here though." He points to a building in the distance. "We're gonna need gas before too long. Who knows when we'll see the next open station."

I glance over my shoulder. Angus lounges in the middle row, flipping through a *Penthouse*. Seems like the kind of reading he would pick. Joshua is passed out in the third row. I can't even see the top of his head from up here.

The car begins to slow, and I turn back around. The building is a gas station/diner combo, and it's old. Like everything else on Route 66. Just before we turn into the parking lot, we pass a large, handmade sign. It's nothing more than a piece of plywood with words painted in sloppy, white letters. *Next Gas Station 80 Miles.*

The parking lot is packed. Cars line up at the pumps. It's incredible how many people are here, considering you can go for an hour or more and not see another living soul on the road.

A few cars have handwritten signs in the windows that say things like *Need Gas, Please Help*. It reminds me of the man from the diner. He was out of cash and nowhere near home. What happened to him?

"We're gonna get gas first." Axl pulls up to the back of the line. "Who knows when these stations are gonna run out. People'll really be screwed then."

"Not us, brother." Angus leans forward. "Even if we don't make it all the way to the coast we're prepared."

Axl nods and his eyes meet mine. I can't get all that expensive camping gear off my mind. His eyebrows pull together, but he doesn't say anything. Neither do I. Truth is, I'm not sure I care how they got their gear. Not as long as I make it to Emily.

We wait for thirty minutes. Angus goes back to reading his magazine while Axl and I sit in uncomfortable silence. He glances at me from time to time. He almost looks nervous.

Axl gets out when we finally make it to the pump, and Angus clears his throat. The sound is thick and phlegmy.

"You're not gonna screw my brother. Ya hear me?"

I twist around to face him. His expression is hard. I hold his gaze for a few seconds. His eyes are the same color as his brother's. How did I not notice that before? Only they're different. They are pure violence.

"I have no intention of screwing your brother. I already said that."

"Good, then we're on the same page. We been through a lot, and I ain't gonna let some whore stripper come in here and rip this thing apart. We're blood. Ain't nothin' stronger than that." He raises his eyebrows like he's challenging me.

The speech would be sweet if it wasn't so threatening. But there's nothing protective or loving in his words. I know his kind inside and out. It's all about control with him.

"Whatever, Angus." I turn back around.

He doesn't say anything else. The pages of his magazine crinkle. Guess he went back to his *Penthouse*. Gross.

Axl climbs back in and starts the car. When he pulls into a parking space, the sudden urge to get out of the car overwhelms me. Being in here between the brothers makes me feel like I'm trapped in a mine. Just a couple days. That's it.

The air in the diner is smoky and thick. There is one open table. The waitress who leads us there probably hasn't slept in a week. Her eyes droop. She has a thick raspy voice and an even thicker cough. Smoker.

"I'll grab you folks some water and be right back." She barely glances at us as we sit down.

Joshua and I take one side. The brothers take the other. Axl keeps his eyes on his menu, but Angus glares at me. He brought his can. How am I going to eat with him spitting in that thing?

Joshua can't sit still. He studies the menu for a few minutes, then glances up at Angus's hard stare. Then back down at the menu. Back and forth it goes. He makes me more nervous than Angus does.

Finally he jumps up. "I have to use the bathroom. If she comes back, I'll take a burger and fries." He hurries away without looking at any of us.

"What the hell is goin' on?" Axl asks as soon as Joshua walks away. He looks at his brother, not exactly glaring, but almost.

"Nothin'. Just had a talk with the stripper earlier. Wanted to make sure she knew she couldn't screw her way between us." Angus spits into the can.

35

Axl rubs the bridge of his nose like the conversation hurts his head. He's not alone. "Nobody is screwin' anybody. Just drop it, will you?" He won't even look at me when he says, "Tell him."

"Look, no offense, but you guys aren't exactly my type." Lumping the two of them together isn't really fair. Truth is, now that I've been around Axl a little more, I don't think he's a thing like his brother. But I want Angus to get over this and convince him I'm not interested. Because I'm not. I'm really, really not. "Men like you are pretty much the reason I don't date anymore. I have a bad track record. It usually ends up with me getting the shit beat out of me."

Angus smiles, like the sound of someone beating me up appeals to him. It probably does. Axl's stormy eyes flash. They are so similar to his brother's, but so different.

But do I detect a little bit of hurt in them?

Axl tears his gaze away from me and faces his brother. "There. Good 'nough?"

Angus seems to relent a little. His body relaxes. "Fine. Wouldn't want to make the good doctor uncomfortable or anythin'. We may need him."

Axl goes back to his menu. I actually agree with Angus. We have no idea what's going to happen. What if this is the end? Having a doctor in our group might be a good thing.

Joshua isn't back before the waitress, so we order for him. The second she's gone I get to my feet. "I'm going to pee."

The diner is crowded. I have to squeeze my way between waitresses and patrons, dodging trays and elbows. I bet they haven't had a crowd like this in here since the 1950s.

There's a line for the restroom. I stand at the back and dig through my purse until I find Emily's picture. She smiles at me, and my heart aches.

I didn't want to give her up, but I was sixteen. It wasn't safe in my home—if you could even call it that—and there was no way I could bring a baby there. It was just me and my dad. Mom had run off with a neighbor when I was ten. Not that I can blame her for leaving, but I do blame her for leaving *me*. She must have known dad would need a new punching bag if she left. She obviously didn't care. That hurts even more than the beatings did. That she didn't care about me.

I loved Emily the moment I saw her. She was so tiny and pink, and her face was all smashed in from birth, so ugly-cute like all newborns. I loved her enough to give her to the Johnson's. They sent me updates for a while. Nine months, to be exact. Then they stopped. I can't blame them. It wasn't an open adoption, and they never got a single response from me. Maybe they thought I didn't care. Truth was, it just hurt too much.

The woman behind me coughs on the back of my head. Hot, moist air hits my hair and brushes it forward. I start to turn around so I can yell at her, but I freeze. She's not the only one. Half the people in this diner are hacking their heads off. People slump over in booths, their breathing raspy and their faces bright red. A woman moans and shivers. She has on two jackets, but she still shakes so hard her teeth clang together. Her face is covered in sweat. The man next to her urges her to eat something. But he coughs too.

My stomach aches. I'm going to hurl. It's here.

I forget the bathroom and head back to the table. I have to pee, but I can do it on the side of the road. We need to get out of here. Joshua is back. The three men are tense. They look up when I walk over.

"It's here," I say, but they already know.

"We're gettin' our shit to go," Axl says.

He's pale. So is Angus. His face isn't as hard as it was before. Death tends to do that to a person. Turn them into spaghetti.

Even Joshua shakes, and he knows he's immune.

I sit down and wait, wringing my hands on top of the table. My hands tremble so hard that when I pick up my glass to take a drink, water spills everywhere. I set it back down.

"We still need supplies." Angus's voice is hollow.

"Why don't you and the Doc head to the convenience store and grab us some stuff? Vivian and me'll wait for the food," Axl says.

Angus gets to his feet, and I stand to let Joshua out. People cough on them when they go by. Angus clenches his fist when a man sneezes on him. But the anger melts away and all the color drains from his face. He walks faster.

"Guess we'll know soon," Axl says.

I nod, but I can't make my mouth work to say anything. My insides curl into a ball. They grow tighter each time I think about it. I should be relieved. Soon the suspense will be over, and I'll know whether or not I'm going to die. But I'm not. I don't want to die, and the thought of it happening makes me want to throw up.

Axl and I don't speak. We just stare at each other. The diner is amazingly quiet, considering how full it is. People cough. There are a few quiet conversations. Otherwise it's silent. Deathly silent.

"Thought the end of the world would be more dramatic than this," he finally says. It makes me jump.

I look around. It is the end. It's written on the face of every person in the diner. I'm sure it's on mine. "There should be chaos or panic. Something."

"Probably is. In the cities."

He's right. Here the people are too disappointed. They were so close. They passed their physicals and thought they were in the clear. That they were going to make it. Is that what's going to happen to me? The thought sends a shiver down my spine.

The waitress finally brings our food. Axl hands her a wad of money without even looking at the bills. He grabs my elbow and pulls me toward the door. I try not to look at anyone, but I can't stop myself. I meet the eyes of every person who coughs in my direction. They're defeated and hopeless.

I pee behind the building, and we leave. We eat in the car. The silence is so thick and painful I wouldn't be surprised if it swooped in and smothered us.

Chapter Six

I wake to the sound of Angus cursing. He's in the driver's seat. I'm not sure when that happened. His face is tight and red as he stares out the front window. The car slows down.

There's a police car pulled off to the side of the road with its light flashing. A cop stands in the middle of the street. He waves his arms, trying to flag us down. Another car is pulled over and two people stand next to it. My stomach tightens. Now what?

"Should we keep goin'?" Angus glances over his shoulder at Axl, who leans forward. His head sticks between the seats.

"No. You gotta stop."

"What if they're lookin' for us?"

"They ain't lookin' for us. Not in Oklahoma. Not with the virus. We ain't important right now."

I was right. They are on the run.

"What do they want then?" I've never heard Angus sound so tense. I guess only the cops scare him.

"Guess we'll find out," Axl says.

Angus pulls over and plasters a fake smile on his face as the cop approaches the car. He rolls the window down, and we wait.

The cop draws his gun and pastes a tense smile on his face. He's trying to stay casual. It doesn't work. "Hey there, folks. Sorry for bothering you."

"Not a problem, officer," Angus says cheerfully.

"Listen, we've got a couple over here having some car trouble, and my partner and I were wondering if you would be willing to give them a ride to the next checkpoint. It's only about twenty miles up the road, but we can't leave our post." His eyes dart toward the couple, then back.

His partner stands by the police car with a shotgun slung casually over his shoulder. Watching us.

"Once you get to the checkpoint you can drop them off and someone will help them."

Angus frowns and looks over his shoulder, and I follow his gaze. Axl and Joshua are just as rigid as Angus. There's something wrong here.

"Sure, officer..." Angus lets the word hang in the air for a brief second. "We can give them a lift. It's only twenty miles."

The cop nods. His face is tight. "Thanks."

He doesn't move, and he doesn't take his eyes off us. He just waves to his partner and stays where he is. Tension fills my body as his partner walks toward us. The two people trail behind him. They each carry a few bags. Axl hops out of the car and goes around the back of the Nissan so he can open the door.

When they walk by me I get a better look at them. They're young. Eighteen, nineteen. College students probably. A guy and a girl. He's big like a linebacker. Dark black skin, hair cut short, serious face. She's tiny like a child, probably only five feet tall. Indian. Long hair and big, round eyes that flash with terror.

Angus makes a grunting sound, and I glance his way. His face is even harder than before. Is their skin color is going to be a problem? He seems like that type.

"Yo, Doc!" Angus yells back to Joshua. "Climb on up to the second row so these new folks can have that there third row."

"Thanks for your cooperation." The cop finally walks away. He barely glances at us before going to the back of our car where his partner is. He never asked for our travel papers.

Angus looks back at his brother and murmurs a few racial slurs under his breath. I knew it. This should make for an interesting trip.

The couple climbs in the back, and Axl hops in after them. "Let's get the hell outta here."

The cop never comes back. He and his partner stand in the road behind us, talking.

I turn around in my seat and smile at the new arrivals. I'm on edge, but I don't want them to think it has anything to do with them. "Hi. I'm Vivian. This is Angus, Joshua, and Axl."

The guy nods, but muscles in his neck are so tight his head barely moves. "Trey. This is Parvarti."

"Where y'all comin' from?" Angus calls back.

"Cornell University," Trey says.

Joshua spins around. "New York?"

They both nod, but don't speak. Neither do we. My heart pounds and a million questions go through my head. I can't force them past my lips. I want to know. So bad. But I don't.

"Where you headed?" Axl's voice is strained.

"New Mexico," Parvarti says, speaking up for the first time. Her voice is soft and small, just like she is.

"Berkley," Trey says.

Joshua finally finds his voice. "New York isn't on lockdown anymore?"

Trey swallows a few times, like he has a tough time finding his voice. "No. Things broke up about a week ago. The military started pulling out. The place is like a ghost town. There are still cops around, but not many. They're like the ones that stopped you. They're trying to maintain an air of authority, but they're just around to keep the peace. They don't know what to do. Everything is breaking down. There's just...nothing." He stops and looks at Parvarti, who scoots closer to him. "When people started to leave, I decided to get the hell out. I had the cash to get me across the country, but no car. People started putting notices up in the coffee shop on campus, looking for travel companions. Parvarti had a car, but not enough money to get her home. So we teamed up."

"So you didn't know each other before then?" I ask. She took a big risk, driving a guy she didn't know across the country. Then again, I did the same thing. Desperation.

"No," she whispers.

"What 'bout your family?" Axl asks. "You been in touch with 'em?"

"My parents are okay. They said not a lot of people out that way are sick. Parv's parents..." Trey looks down at her and frowns.

"The last time I talked to them was two days ago. They were sick. I haven't been able to get in touch with them since." Her eyes fill with tears. Trey puts his arm around her.

Joshua takes his phone out of his pocket.

"What are you doing?" I ask.

"Calling a friend. He's a lab tech with the CDC. The doctor friend of mine who died was his girlfriend. He'll tell me what's going on." His expression is tight when he puts the phone up to his ear. "Hector! It's Joshua. Listen, the group I'm with just picked a few people up from New York. What's going on out there?" He frowns, listening to the man on the other line. His face grows more worried by the second. "No. That's not what Isabel said."

A pit forms in my stomach. I chew on my lower lip and wait for him to tell us something. Trying to guess what the other man is saying just by Joshua's expression makes me want to scream. It's not good.

Joshua's face crumples and his shoulders slump. "That's it, then. This is the end." He shakes his head and listens a little longer. "Somewhere in Oklahoma." A pause. "It's all the way out there? There's no stopping this, is there?"

I can't look at his face anymore. I already know what he's going to say. He's going to tell us it's worse than they originally thought. That the government has no solutions. That I now have more than a seventy percent chance of death.

"Okay, thanks. I'll talk to you later, man." He lowers the phone and I turn back around. "It's bad."

"No shit," Axl says. "How bad?"

"Right now they're saying more than seventy percent of the population will be affected."

"How much more?" I whisper, twisting my head just enough that I can see him.

Joshua looks at me. "Eighty. Maybe eighty-five. There are speculations that it's some kind of man-made virus. Hector said there are rumors the government created it, that it somehow got out. But there are other rumors that there was a terrorist attack in New York. No one really knows for sure, and they probably never will."

"How do you know all this?" Trey asks.

"I'm a doctor. I worked in Baltimore and the CDC was there. It's a long story, but the short of it is this: you're immune."

Trey sits up straighter, but he keeps his arm around Parvarti's shoulders. "What do you mean?"

"You were in New York this entire time. If you weren't immune you'd be dead by now. How many of your friends got sick?"

"More than half," Trey says, so quietly I almost can't hear it.

Tears stream down Parvarti's face. "There's no chance of getting better?"

"No." Joshua's voice is firm. He doesn't even try to cushion the blow. "If you get sick, you die. If you don't, then you're immune."

Parvarti starts to cry harder, and Trey pulls her close.

I face the front. I'm hollow inside, almost resigned. There's no way I'll be immune. Deep down, I know that. How could I be? Nothing else in life has gone my way. Why should this?

No one talks for a while, and eventually Parvarti's crying stops. I'm glad. I should feel more sympathy toward her, but I don't. At least she knows now, before she gets all the way home.

We finally reach the checkpoint. If we didn't already know it was hopeless, we would now. There are still armed soldiers, still military vehicles, but it's nothing like the last one. The soldier who walks up to us has his gun strapped to his back instead of in his hands. His body isn't stiff like the last guy we saw. Only two soldiers block the road. One of them coughs.

"Papers." His voice isn't firm like the soldier at the last checkpoint. This guy's face is red and he has beads of sweat on his forehead. He turns his head away and coughs. He's sick.

Everyone passes their travel papers forward, and Angus gives them to the soldier, who barely glances at them before he hands them back. He's just going through the motions at this point.

"Stick to Route 66," he says, then turns away from us.

The other soldiers step aside, and Angus drives by. "Damn."

My throat is tight. I can't speak. The car is so silent it reminds me of a tomb.

Angus tosses the papers my way. "These are probably useless now, but just in case."

They fall on the seat and on the floor. I gather them up. I'm too drained to be annoyed.

"Guess we're stuck with you two." Angus looks in the rearview mirror and shakes his head. He purses his lips like he just ate something sour.

I completely forgot we were supposed to drop Trey and Parvarti off at the checkpoint.

"You can drop us off at the next motel," Trey says. He still has his arm around Parvarti, and all the muscles in the face are taut.

Parvarti pulls away from him. "No. You need to get home, Trey. Your parents aren't sick." She digs through a bag and pulls out a handful of money. Her hand shakes when she thrusts it forward. "We can pay you."

"We're going to California anyway." I focus on Axl. Angus would never agree to give them a ride.

Axl turns to Parvarti and Trey without even consulting his brother. "Put your money away. We'll give you a ride. You gotta pitch in. Help out when we camp and all that."

"Not even gonna talk to me 'bout this, Axl?" Angus glares at me, but I don't back down.

"How's it hurting you? We're going there anyway!"

Angus stares straight ahead. He mutters a few racial slurs just loud enough for me to hear them. I glance toward the backseat. Thankfully, it doesn't look like Trey and Parvarti heard.

Chapter Seven

Angus slows down and pulls up behind a black Honda Civic. A tent is set up about twenty feet from the road. Two chairs lay on their sides next to what used to be a fire, but no one is in sight. A couple huge black birds fly overhead, slowly circling the tent.

My stomach tightens, and I tear my eyes away from the tent, focusing on Angus. "What are you doing?" I have a bad feeling about this.

Angus doesn't turn the car off. He sits there with his lips pursed, staring out the window. He doesn't look at me, and he doesn't answer.

Axl leans forward. "What're you thinkin'?"

"I'm thinkin' that we may be able to find a few supplies." Angus catches his brother's eye in the rearview mirror. "You got your gun?"

Axl holds it up.

"Why do you need a gun? It's just a campsite," Parvarti says.

"Protection." Axl rolls his eyes.

"You ain't livin' in the same world you was a few weeks ago, darlin'," Angus says. "Things are 'bout to get real 'round here. Just wait."

Trey and Parvarti look at Angus like he's insane, but he's right. People are desperate. That makes them unpredictable.

He moves to the door, but stops and turns toward me. His lips are still pursed and he studies me for a few seconds. The hair on my scalp prickles. I can't read his expression. What's he thinking?

"You were serious 'bout being a good shot?" he finally says.

My heart races. Is it possible that he's going to give me my gun back? "No point in having a gun unless you learn how to shoot it."

Approval flashes in his eyes. "I can trust you not to blow my head off?"

"As long as you don't give me a reason to."

He chuckles and bends down, reaching under the front seat. When he sits back up my gun is in his hand. "Here. Why don't ya come with us? Give us a hand."

I wrap my fingers around the gun. Just having it in my hand makes Angus seem less threatening.

"Everybody sit tight," Angus calls as he opens the front door and steps out.

I hop onto the dusty ground, and Axl climbs out of the back. His gun is held tightly in his right hand. He raises it to chest level as we walk. Angus is more laid back. He keeps his gun tucked into his waistband, pulling his shirt up just enough to make it visible.

"Anyone here?" Angus calls out as he approaches the car.

Axl walks on his brother's right, keeping his gun up. His eyes dart around. My heart pounds and I tighten my grip on my own gun.

Angus goes to the driver's side and looks in the window while Axl goes to the passenger side. A thick layer of dust coats the car. It hasn't been driven in a couple of days at least. Angus tries the front door while I look through the back window. No one is inside, but there are boxes. Even a case of bottled water.

"It's locked on this side," Axl says.

"Same here." Angus frowns. "Let's check out the tent. Maybe we can find the keys."

I've only taken two steps toward the tent when it hits me. A heavy, putrid smell that makes me gag and causes my stomach to lurch. I stop and turn my head, coughing and breathing in slowly through my mouth as bile rises in my throat.

Axl stops next to me. "You okay?"

I nod and swallow. "Yeah. I'm alright."

Angus rolls his upper lip in disgust. "Come on."

The tent door is open. It blows back and forth, flapping in the breeze. I cover my nose when we get closer and try to fight the nausea. The last thing I need is to get on Angus's bad side again. Not after he just gave my gun back.

We're two feet from the tent when something inside moves. All three of us stop dead in our tracks. My heart jumps to my throat, and I drop my hand from my nose, wrapping it firmly around my gun.

Angus grabs the gun out of his waistband and looks over at his brother. "You hear that?" he whispers.

Axl nods. None of us move. A scratching sound comes from inside, and it may be my imagination, but I swear something brushes up against the side of the tent.

"Anybody in there?" Angus calls out, a little louder than necessary.

No response. Then more movement.

Axl takes one hand off his gun. He points to his brother, then over toward the tent. Angus nods, and they both look back at me. I nod and raise my gun. Angus tucks his back in his waistband. He takes a step forward. Axl and I follow, both of us hold our guns tightly in our hands. Aiming right at the door to the tent.

More movement. Something is definitely in there.

My heart pounds when Angus stops. He glances back at Axl, then reaches forward. The door flaps. Back and forth. Something inside scratches against the ground and brushes against the side of the tent. This time I'm sure it's not my imagination.

I tense and move my finger to the trigger, automatically checking to make sure the safety is off. My heart pounds in my ears. Angus reaches for the door. He doesn't look back at us, but he holds his right hand up, extending three fingers. Slowly he lowers one, then another. When he gets down to one I suck in a deep breath. He jerks the door back. Something flies from the tent.

"Damn!" I yell, taking my finger off the trigger as I jump back. The giant bird swoops by my head, screeching at me as it soars into the sky, joining his friends.

"Thought you were gonna shoot," Axl says with a grin.

It's the first genuine smile I've seen out of him. He has a dimple in his right cheek.

I laugh. My heart is still pounding as I put the safety back on. "I almost peed my pants."

Axl laughs and looks back at the tent. Angus stands there with the door pulled aside, peering in. I catch a glimpse of what used to be two people and squeeze my eyes shut, gagging. They are very dead.

The birds and other animals have gotten to them.

"Think it was the virus?" Axl asks.

The canvas rustles as the brothers step inside, but I turn my back to the tent. The images of those poor people will be burned into my brain for the rest of my life. I couldn't even tell if they were men or women. There was just nothing left…

A sleeping bag unzips. Something rustles around inside, like Angus and Axl are digging through their belongings.

"Don't see any other injuries. Just what the animals did," Angus replies.

I can't listen to them, so I tuck my gun into my pants and walk over to what used to be the fire. They're still inside when I carry the camp chairs back to the car.

"What was in the tent?" Trey asks.

"Two people. Or what was left of them, anyway. Looks like the virus killed them. Animals took care of the rest."

"What now?" Joshua asks.

I shake my head and glance toward the tent just as the brothers step out. "I think they were looking for keys to the car. There could be some useful things."

"You're just going to steal their stuff?" Parvarti looks so young and innocent.

"We're not stealing it. We're scavenging." I sigh. I hate to be harsh, but she needs a dose of reality. "Look, Angus is an ass, but he's right. Things have changed. Maybe it's temporary. Maybe things will get better. But if not…" I shake my head and turn away. Angus and Axl step out of the tent and head toward the Honda. "Just think about it," I say over my shoulder.

I stop in front the Honda just as Angus unlocks the front door.

"Open the trunk," I call.

He nods and the trunk pops open.

"Jackpot."

There are two boxes full of canned food and two suitcases. These people were prepared. Grunting, I lug the boxes out of the trunk and drop them on the ground, then turn back to the suitcases. They aren't small. It takes a minute to wrestle the first one out. It's wedged in pretty good, and I have to pull on it with all my strength. It finally jerks free, and I stumble back a few steps, dropping it to the ground.

"You need help back there?" Axl calls out.

"I'm good." I lean down to unzip the suitcase.

It's full of clothes. Women's clothes. They aren't pretty, but that doesn't matter in a post-apocalyptic world. Hopefully, I'll never need to wear them. For now, I'm going to hang onto them. I dig a little more and find a small bag of toiletries—always handy—and a couple pairs of shoes. Something I do need.

I pull out a blue-and-white Nike and look inside. An eight. I'm a seven and a half, but a little big is better than nothing. I sit on my butt and pull off my wedge heels, then shove them in the bag. I'm not ready to completely give up on the idea of pretty things, so I'm keeping them. I find some white socks and pull those and the Nikes on. My feet hurt less already.

Once that's done, I zip the suitcase back up and inspect the second one. I open it before I drag it out. Men's clothes, just like I thought it'd be. I throw it on the ground next to the other one. Shoved behind the suitcases are a couple of blankets. They're thick and flannel, exactly what we need. I toss them on top of the boxes, and the trunk is empty.

I head over to the passenger side, where Axl digs through the car. A case of water and another box of food sits on the ground. This one is full of snack items: chips, bags of cookies, granola bars. Things like that.

"Find anything good?" Axl asks me.

He has a purse in his lap. I pick up the wallet and my hands shake. Do I want to know who this woman was?

"Suitcases with clothes, couple boxes of canned goods and some blankets." I don't look at him. I stare at the wallet in my hands.

"No money in there," he says. He looks up from the purse and his eyes narrow on me.

"I was just curious who she was."

He nods like he understands. Probably does. No way Angus would.

I flip the wallet open. Her picture stares at me from her license. Amy Winston, born January 26, 1976. Lived in Peoria, AZ. Must have been where they were headed. Where were they coming from?

"You two 'bout finished?" Angus calls.

I toss the wallet on top of the purse and head to the back of the car. Angus stands there with a duffle bag slung over his shoulder and a toolbox in his hand.

"What'd you get?" he asks.

"Clothes, mostly. Figured we'd take them since we have plenty of room. Just in case we end up needing them."

He frowns. "Try to cut it down to one suitcase. We're gonna need some more survival gear."

He's right. God, I hate that he's right.

My gun digs into my hip when I kneel down and unzip both suitcases. But I get busy sorting the clothes.

Angus walks away, and Axl comes up behind me. I glance over my shoulder just in time to catch him checking out my ass as he picks up the box of food. My cheeks burn. I look away before he realizes I saw him.

It doesn't take long to go through the suitcases. I keep anything that looks warm. It's fall, and if things don't get sorted out before winter, we're going to need them. I get to my feet just as Axl comes back to get the second box. I end up leaving my wedge shoes, which hurts less than I expected it to.

"Got everything?"

I nod and walk toward the car. "Do you think we're overreacting?"

His eyebrows pull together. "Hard to say. All the lyin' is what bothers me. If things ain't that bad, why are they hidin' so much from us?"

I stop and turn to face him. "Where'd you guys steal the car?"

He inhales sharply. "Who says we did?"

"I figured it out. You just confirmed it this morning when the cops stopped us. I don't care. I'm just curious." Guilt tugs at me, but I can't give in to it. Things are different now.

Axl sighs. "Swiped it from my boss. The guy was a prick."

"What about all the gear? You steal that from him too?"

"Damn," Axl mutters. "We didn't hurt no one, understand? We held up a few convenience stores, outside St. Louis. They're rakin' in the dough right now. Everybody buyin' gas. We took the money and bought as much survival gear as we could."

There was something on the news about that. When I was at that diner.

"Is it gone?" It would be nice to have enough money for gas and food, as well as some more gear. Who knows if we'll come across another abandoned car anytime soon.

He narrows his eyes. "Why?"

"I'm not going to steal it from you. I just want to know what we have to work with."

He studies me for a second and then nods. "We still got some. Enough to get us more supplies and gas."

I start walking again. "Good."

Chapter Eight

We stop in Texola for the night. It's right before you cross from Oklahoma into Texas, hence the clever name. We pass a few houses—some boarded up, some not—and a few doublewides that may have been recently inhabited. But the town mostly consists of empty, crumbling buildings from the 1950s or earlier. There are no lights on in the buildings we pass, no streetlights in the town, no cars, and no people. It's terrifying. For a moment I imagine this is what the future has in store for us. Driving through abandoned city after abandoned city for the rest of our lives.

If we're immune.

The sun is low on the horizon and the sky is a bright shade of orange. We set up camp outside what used to be a bar. There's a colorful sign on top—hand-painted decades ago—with an odd-looking cowboy sitting on top of a horse. The words Water Hole #2 are painted next to him. It's boarded up, just like most of the other buildings we passed.

"You guys can handle this?" Angus walks up to us with a shotgun in each hand.

Trey steps away from the gun. "What are you doing?"

"Huntin'," Axl snaps as he takes the shotgun his brother holds out to him. "You wanna eat, right?"

"We have canned goods," Joshua says.

"Don't waste that. Save it for later, in case we have a night when

52

we can't shoot somethin' to eat." Angus spits on the ground at Joshua's feet.

Joshua and Trey look at each other, but neither one looks convinced. I'm not surprised. I bet neither one of them has ever missed a meal. They've probably never eaten something that didn't come from a grocery store or a restaurant. I have. Plenty of times.

"You're going to kill an animal?" Parvarti asks meekly.

Angus's face is red. He's on the verge of losing it, so I step in. "They're right. We have to be smart about this. Take precautions."

Joshua bites his lip and stares at me for a second. Then he nods. "Yeah. That's what we have to do." He turns back to Axl and Angus. "Go hunt, we'll set up camp."

Axl raises an eyebrow and looks Joshua up and down. "Can you start a fire? Set up a tent?"

"I can," I say.

Angus nods approvingly. "That's right. Trailer trash. Helluva life, but it makes ya tough." He turns and starts walking. "We'll be back. Shouldn't take long."

Axl follows his brother, and for a second, I don't move. My insides boil. No one knew I was trailer trash except the brothers, and if it had been up to me it would have stayed that way. I've worked hard to distinguish myself from people like them.

Get over it, I tell myself. *You're just as good as they are.*

Right. The doctor, the two students from Cornell. I'm a stripper who was raised in a trailer park. I'm a walking cliché.

"Let's get this fire going," Joshua says, breaking through my thoughts.

"Yeah." I walk over and help arrange the wood, breaking some of the sticks Parvarti collected into smaller ones for kindling.

"You're not trailer trash," Joshua says.

I keep my eyes down, focusing on getting the wood to light. "Yes I am. I'm just not redneck like they are."

The fire catches and I stay where I am for a moment to make sure it doesn't go out. It doesn't. Trey is struggling with the tent. These three are going to be in trouble if this really is the end of the civilization.

"Why don't you get the camp chairs out of the car?" I say to Trey. "I can do the tent. I helped with it last night." It's a lie, but he doesn't need to know.

He smiles gratefully, then jogs off to the car. Parvarti follows him. She doesn't say much. I'm not sure if it's because she's shy or if it has to do with the fact that she just found out her parents are dead. Only time will tell.

When the tent is up, both Trey and Joshua wander off to call their families. Parvarti sits next to me and stares into the fire silently. She wears Trey's sweatshirt, and it makes her look even more like a child.

"So you and Trey seem to have gotten close," I say. I want to make conversation, but I'm afraid to ask anything about her life. She seems pretty shaken, and the last thing I want to do is remind her that her parents are dead.

"He's been great to have around. I was worried about traveling with him. Going across the country with some guy I didn't know was scary, but I had no other options. If I didn't have him..." A tear slides down her cheek, and she stares at her hands.

I look out into the darkness, toward the sound of Trey's voice. "He seems to like you."

To my surprise, she smiles. "My mother would die—" Her hand goes to her mouth and she lets out a little sob.

My heart aches. I don't know what it's like having a family you actually love, but it must be horrible to lose something like that. I want to tell her to remember the good times, to be thankful she got to experience it. Not all of us do. But something like that wouldn't make sense to her. Not now, maybe not ever.

"I'm sorry about your parents," I whisper.

She wipes the tears from her face. "Me too. I just hope it wasn't too bad."

"Are you still going home? Maybe you could go with Trey. His family seems to be healthy still."

She looks up at me. Her eyes are huge in this light. "What about you? Is your family sick?"

"I don't have any family. Not really."

Her eyes grow bigger. "How did you get papers?"

I tense, and I look toward the fire. I should tell her, I know about her parents. "I do have a father, in California. Hell, maybe I have a mother too. Who knows? Either way, I'm not going to see them. I just used them as an excuse. I'm going to see my daughter. I gave her up for adoption four years ago and I just...I just couldn't let the world end without seeing her. That's all."

"Do her adoptive parents know you're coming?"

"I guess. I put a letter in the mail the day before I left. I didn't have a phone number for them, so I couldn't call. No email. So, as long as the postal service is still running they'll know. If not, then I guess I'll be a surprise."

Footsteps echo through the dark night. I turn. Axl and Angus are back.

"Where's everybody?" Angus asks, flopping down in one of the camp chairs.

"Talking to their families," I say.

Axl tosses something on the ground in front of the fire. "Came 'cross this mother on our way back. We got a few squirrels too, but this guy'll taste real good."

It takes me a moment to figure out what it is, and when I do even I turn up my nose. "An opossum?"

"Gross," Parvarti says.

"Sorry, your highness," Angus says. "We're fresh outta filet."

"It'll be fine." I'm trying to reassure myself as much as Parvarti. Opossums remind me of giant rats. Not exactly appetizing.

She starts to calm down until Axl takes out his knife to skin the animal. At the first sight of blood she's on her feet, heading off into the darkness. Probably in search of Trey.

I turn away, and my eyes land on Angus. He's fooling with his gun. It's the first time he hasn't had a soda can in his hand since he picked me up. "You run out of dip, Angus?"

He glares across the fire. "What's it to you?"

Axl chuckles. "Don't get him started. He's been bitchin' 'bout it all night."

"Better to get yourself off the stuff now," I say. "Where are you going to get dip when the world ends?"

"There'll be lots of it. No one's gonna raid the gas station lookin' for dip. They've got more important things to look for. Things we've already got."

He has a good point, but I won't give him the satisfaction.

Joshua walks up and falls into the chair next to me.

"How's your family?"

"Not good." He shakes his head. "My mom and brother are sick. So far Dad doesn't have any symptoms, though. Hopefully he's at least immune."

"I'm sorry, Joshua." I pat his arm.

He looks like a giant kid in that chair. All slumped over with his gangly legs stretched out in front of him. If only there was something I could say to make him feel better.

"Sorry, man," Axl says, standing up.

He's finished skinning the poor animals and has the spit securely through their bodies. He sets it over the fire and adds a few more pieces of wood, no doubt trying to get the flame a little higher. His hands are covered in blood.

"You're good at this," I say, staring at his hands.

He tries to wipe them off on an old shirt, but it doesn't exactly do the trick.

I grab a bottle of water and hold it out to him. "Here, clean your hands off."

"Don't waste water on your hands!" Angus shouts.

I roll my eyes. "It's not a big deal. We'll just save the bottles and refill them next time we stop somewhere. In the bathroom sink or something. Free."

Angus crosses his arms. "You sure you're blonde?" I give him the finger, and he smiles. "Anytime, Sugar Tits."

He makes my skin crawl, but at least he's started joking with me a little bit. It's gross and awkward, but it's better than the evil glares he was giving me before. And it got me my gun back. I guess he sees me as one of them, now that we have a few wealthy, educated people in our group.

Trey and Parvarti walk up. She's so tiny next to him; she only comes up to his chest.

"Your folks okay?" Axl asks.

Trey nods. "So far."

There are only two empty chairs. Parvarti takes one of them, which leaves Trey standing. Axl kneels next to the other one, and I don't think Trey wants to rock the boat.

"Take a seat, man," Axl says, tilting his head toward the chair. "I'm cookin'."

Trey sits down and studies us, chewing on his bottom lip. "I've been thinking about this virus thing, and I think you guys may be overreacting. I get it. Things may be rough for a bit, but you're acting like this is the breakup of our society." He shakes his head. "I just don't think it's going to be that bad. Even if only fifteen percent of the population survives, that's still got to be somewhere around forty million people, give or take. That's nowhere near the end of the world."

He has a point, right? That's a hell of a lot of people. But...
"Okay, say that's true. Say forty million people survive this thing. How many people in the government?"

He shrugs. "We have no way of knowing that."

"Exactly," I say. "So even if half the people in authority positions survive, which is being generous, how long before they can figure out who is actually in charge?"

He bites into his lip harder. "Weeks, maybe months."

"And what happens in the meantime?" Parvarti asks.

"Chaos." Axl turns the spit. "Anarchy. Lootin' for supplies, killin' for survival. Anything goes."

I nod. "So by the time the government gets its act together we've lost how many more people? Not to mention how spread out everyone will be."

"What will folks do about work and money? Who's gonna tell us all that?" Angus pipes in.

Trey swallows and sits back. He frowns and stares into the fire. He probably doesn't love being out-thought by a couple rednecks and a piece of trailer trash.

"Okay," he says. "But we still have forty million people."

"Sure. And a hell of a mess to clean up. We just passed two bodies today out in the middle of nowhere. Imagine what the cities are going to be like. Eighty-five percent of the population dropping like that—" I snap my fingers. "It's going to be a while before things get even close to being normal again. Maybe never."

"A new kind of normal," Joshua says. "Makes you wish you weren't immune." He slumps down and stares at the ground like he wishes it would swallow him whole.

Something else I hadn't thought about. The people who won't be able to deal.

Chapter Nine

I wake up shivering, and just opening my eyes makes my temples pulse.

It's still dark outside, and the rhythmic breathing of the others fills the tent. My head pounds with every breath they let out. I swallow and wince. My throat is tight and raw, and my lips dry. I press a shaky hand to my forehead. My hands are cold and clammy, but my face is on fire.

I'm sick. I'm going to die.

My body trembles and tears pool in my eyes. I'm not going to make it to her.

I roll onto my side. Every tiny movement hurts, deep in my bones. Even laying still is painful. I ache from head to toe. Axl is next to me, sleeping soundly. Should I wake him?

I reach under the jacket I'm using as a pillow in search of my phone. My head pounds like my brain pulsates. When I finally find it, I press the button and the screen lights up. It's almost six. The sun should be coming up soon. I look back at Axl. Every inch of my body aches with fever. I can't wait.

"Axl," I whisper. I reach out and gently touch his hand.

His eyes fly open, and he half sits up. When his gaze meets mine in the darkness, he lays back down. His eyes flutter shut. "What?" he mumbles.

"I'm sick." I say it as quietly as possible. I don't want to bother anyone else.

His eyes open again. Slowly this time. But he's wide awake now. "What's wrong?"

A small sob breaks out of my chest, burning on the way up. I shake my head. "My head is pounding, my throat is sore, my body aches all over." I swallow and cough slightly. "I'm not immune."

He frowns and even in the darkness his eyes give him away. He's thinking of himself, and Angus. But he doesn't say it out loud.

He sits up and grabs his shoes, pulling them on. "Can you walk?"

I nod and climb out from under the blanket, wincing. It's like someone is digging their fingers into my temples and the base of my skull. Every move makes the pressure mount. I get to my feet, but my legs quiver and the worlds spins. I have to sit back down.

Axl unzips the tent and steps out. He turns back and holds his hand out to me. I crawl toward him on unstable limbs. When I reach the opening, he bends down and picks me up, swinging me into his arms like I weigh nothing. It hurts. Everything hurts. I lay my head on his shoulder and close my eyes. He smells like the outdoors. Just like his flannel shirt did last night when he let me wear it.

"Damn, you're burnin' up."

He sets me in a chair next to the fire. The air is chilly, like a cold front settled in while I was asleep. I shiver so hard my teeth chatter. I open my eyes. Trey is by the fire.

He frowns and watches me closely with his hands shoved in his pockets. "What's going on?"

Axl takes his shirt off and lays it over me. It's the same flannel shirt he gave me before. "She's sick."

Now he wears nothing but a white undershirt. It's dirty. Someone should wash his clothes. Maybe I can do it later. I close my eyes for a brief second, trying to clear my head. Nothing makes sense.

I open my eyes and they meet Trey's. He doesn't say anything, but he doesn't have to. He knows I'm dead.

"Where's the Doc?"

"Sleepin'," Axl says, heading over to the Nissan.

"Don't you think you should get him?" Trey doesn't take his eyes off me.

"He'll be up soon. Got to get her somethin' for the fever."

I'm still shivering, and every shake hurts. My head, my bones, my throat. I close my eyes because Trey won't stop staring at me.

"Take these," Axl says.

I open my eyes. He's back in front of me like he never walked away. He has a bottle of water in one hand and some pills in the other.

"Open your mouth."

I do what he says, and he puts a couple pills on my tongue. His stormy eyes meet mine as he lifts the bottle to my lips and gently pours a little in my mouth. I wince when the pills go down. They feel like nails against my swollen throat.

"Do you need a blanket?" He's being so gentle. Not gruff like usual.

I nod. The movement makes my head pound even more. I can't believe how awful I feel; I felt fine when I laid down last night. A little more tired than usual, but not sick.

Axl lays the blanket over me. I'm so glad this camp chair reclines now. So thankful Axl and Angus robbed those convenience stores.

I try to sleep, but it doesn't work. I drift in and out, but it's more like delirium. Voices float around me, but nothing they say makes sense. Hands touch my face. Some boiling hot, some icy cold. Someone sings. It sounds like a little girl.

"Emily," I whisper.

"Vivian, put this under your tongue."

I don't know who's saying it or why, but I obey.

"How bad is it?"

"Not good."

I open my eyes. Everyone stands around, staring at me. Either the sun is coming up or the fire is really bright, because everything is orange. But dark at the same time.

I close my eyes and lay my head back down. I can't stop shaking.

The next time I wake up I'm in the car. I don't know how I got here, but the sun is up now, and it's insanely bright. Squinting, I put a trembling hand to my head. I'm drenched in sweat and my head still throbs. Every inch of my body is moist with perspiration, but I can't stop shivering. Every movement hurts. Every bounce of the car, every twitch of my muscles.

A hand touches my forehead, and I look up. Axl is next to me. My head is in his lap.

"How you feel?" He still has the same non-nonsense tone, but it's so much gentler than before.

That first night we spent together by the fire crosses my mind, and my insides constrict. We're so much alike. I hope he doesn't get the virus from me.

Shaking my head, I try to talk, but it comes out as a cough. I swallow—a difficult thing to do—and try again. "I'm sorry." The words scratch their way from my throat.

He frowns. "Why?"

"Because you may get sick from me." Talking hurts more than breathing.

He shakes his head. "Don't be dumb. If we were gonna get sick, it would've happened either way." He pauses and frowns again. "I'm sorry you won't get to see your daughter."

Tears fill my eyes. I try to keep them in, but I can't. They spill over, running down my cheeks. Leaving wet trails on my face.

Axl wipes them away. It's not a gentle gesture. It's brusque, just like he is. He leans forward just a bit, careful not to smother me. "Doc."

I turn my head, trying hard to ignore the pain, just as Joshua looks back from the second row. Trey is next to him, but I can't look his way. The look he gave me earlier is burned into my memory. It will probably be the last thing I see when I close my eyes to die.

"Vivian, how are you feeling?" Joshua asks.

"Awful," I croak.

"Specifically. Is your throat sore?" I nod and he frowns. "Do your bones ache?" More nods, more frowns. "Headache?" Same.

"How long?" I whisper. More tears come to my eyes. I shouldn't cry. I'm not leaving anything behind, not really. Just my daughter, and it's not like she knows me. She won't be affected by my death.

Joshua looks away. "Two days, maybe less." His voice is flat, emotionless.

I start to cry again and I turn away from him.

"We need to stay."

I open my eyes to an argument. The car isn't moving anymore and I'm alone in the third row. I'm in just as much pain as I was when I fell asleep. Not that I expected to feel better.

"We need to get movin'." It's Angus, he sounds pissed.

"She's in pain." Axl, that same straightforward way of speaking. "Every bump in the road hurts her. She's moanin' in her sleep."

"I can't listen to it anymore." Parvarti. Pleading. Her voice is high, kind of whiny. Angus is going to love that.

"Tell him, Doc." Axl again. His voice has more emotion this time, it's not as flat. Why is he so upset?

"When they're getting close to the end, every movement hurts them. The closer she gets to death the more pain she'll be in." Joshua, his voice tense. I guess he's seen too many people die the last few weeks. "If we keep driving, she'll be screaming in agony by the end of the day."

"Then she can stay here—alone. What's the point of takin' her with us anyhow? If she's just gonna die?" Angus. The bastard.

"We. Ain't. Leavin'. Her." Axl. The emotion is gone. His voice is firm. Final.

Somewhere, deep inside my aching body, there's a different kind of ache at his words. I've never had another person stick up for me like that. Never.

"Fine," Angus growls.

I'm in a hotel room. A Best Western. That's what the sign outside looked like, anyway. It's dirty, but I don't care. I'm shivering and my skin is sticky with perspiration. I'm in pain. Outside, the sun is setting. I'll be dead in a day.

They only had two rooms available. Angus didn't want to be

anywhere near me, so he's in the other one, along with Trey and Parvarti. Axl and Joshua stay with me. Although, it's just Axl and me at the moment.

"You should drink somethin'," he says for the millionth time.

My lips are cracked and painful. He's right, but my throat is so inflamed it's almost swollen shut.

"I'll try," I whisper. It hurts to breathe. I don't want to drink any water, but he won't stop saying it. This may be the only way to get him to shut up.

He helps me sit and tips the cup up to my lips. I sip the water and attempt to swallow it. It can't be more than a tablespoon of liquid, but it's difficult to get down. I cough and end up spitting some of it out. It dribbles down my chin and onto my shirt. I don't care.

Axl pats my back. "Easy." He helps me lay back down and sets the glass on the bedside table, staring down at me.

"You don't have to stay," I say. "I heard Angus. He's right. I'm dead."

A pained expression crosses his face. "We ain't leavin' you." His voice is thick.

I close my eyes. This must be awful for them. Waiting to find out if they're immune. One of them could be laying in this bed a couple of days from now. After I'm dead.

"Did Joshua say how long it would be before you and Angus knew?"

"Couple days." He's so blunt, unemotional.

How can he face his own death with so little fear? I can't. It makes my body shake and my heart pound. I'll be gone by the time they know for sure.

I look up into those stormy eyes of his. It doesn't make sense why they're so comforting.

I swallow and take a deep breath. It hurts to talk, but there are a few things I need to say. "If you make it to California, will you go see Emily for me?"

He frowns and his eyebrows pull together. "What would I say? She's four."

"I know. It's just…" He's right. It's a stupid request. "Just lie to me."

"'Kay then. We'll go see her."

"Thanks," I whisper, closing my eyes again. Just talking wears

Chapter Ten

I shiver through the night, drifting in and out of sleep. Axl sleeps next to me in the bed. I doubt he gets much rest. He tries to get me to drink something, and he carries me to the bathroom when I have to go. I could walk—I think—but he won't let me.

He's gentle. Where did that come from?

I stare at a large hole in the curtain, watching the light go from a soft glow to a blinding yellow that hurts my eyes. I'm still shivering. I'm still sweating. My throat is inflamed. I will die today.

My fever goes up and down. When the medicine kicks in, I can almost focus on the things around me. I can carry on a small conversation, take a few sips of water, and swallow the chicken broth Axl forces into my mouth. It all hurts, but I'm there. Present.

But when the fever comes back nothing makes sense. I have the same dream about Emily. She plays in a field, singing a silly song. She smiles at me. It's so real…

I have other dreams too. Dreams about dead bodies being picked apart in tents, birds feasting on their eyes. I moan and thrash in my sleep, and Axl's voice constantly breaks through the delirium. It's so much more soothing in my dreams than it is in real life.

And Roger is there. Sometimes it's his body in the tent, an eye missing, a bird sitting on his shoulder. But sometimes I'm back in that trailer while he stands over me. An empty bottle in one hand, a leather belt in the other. The leather on my bare skin stings when he hits me. I scream.

Axl always wakes me.

No one comes to the room but Joshua and Axl. Joshua checks my temperature and asks how I feel, but he doesn't stay. He probably can't stand to see me die. Maybe he's just seen too much lately, or maybe it's because he kind of knows me. Either way, he doesn't hang out for long.

Axl never leaves my side. He's always there. Always ready to get me some water or help me to the bathroom. He wipes my forehead with a cool washcloth. I've never had someone do that for me before.

The light through the hole in the curtains gets softer and I wait to die. But the sun sets and I hang on.

"I've never seen anyone make it this long." Joshua stands over me with his arms crossed. He bites his lip.

"Maybe it's somethin' else?" Axl suggests

Joshua's back straightens and his arms drop to his sides. "Do you have a flashlight?"

"In the car." Axl glances at me and frowns. "I'll be right back." His voice is soft, like he hates to leave me.

My eyes follow him out the door. Hope flickers inside me, like the tiny flame of a candle. Is it possible I caught something else? That in the middle of a killer virus sweeping the country, I somehow picked up a different bug?

Axl is back in no time, and Joshua takes the flashlight from him. "Open your mouth, Vivian. Stick out your tongue."

I do. My heart pounds and I squeeze my eyes shut, saying a silent prayer. I've never really been a religious person, but if there's ever a time to pray, this is it.

"Damn," Joshua says.

My eyes fly open. He frowns. Is that good or bad?

"What?" Axl snaps.

"I need the keys to the Nissan. I don't know for sure. I don't want you to get your hopes up, but it could be strep. I need to find a pharmacy and get you some antibiotics."

Axl grabs the keys off the dresser. "Do it."

Joshua runs out of the motel room without another word, and I'm left speechless.

I might not die.

Axl stands with his back to me. He crosses his arms over his chest. He stares at the door Joshua just disappeared through for a few seconds, then he turns around. There's a tense smile on his face. "You might be immune yet."

I nod, but I can't talk. I'm trying not to get my hopes up. This could still be the end.

Axl paces the room, and I lay in bed with my eyes closed. Waiting.

Joshua is back in what seems like seconds. He charges into the room with a white paper bag in his hand. He gasps, like he can't catch his breath. "They were closed, but the pharmacist was still inside, so I banged on the door until he let me in." He opens the bag and pulls out a rectangular box. "This is a Z-pack. It's strong stuff." He looks at me with an intense expression on his face. "If this is strep, we should see an improvement within forty-eight hours."

Two days. I'll either be dead or better. It seems like an eternity.

"Take two today and one for the next four days," Joshua says, popping the pills out of the pack.

Axl waits with a cup of water. Joshua gives him the pills. Axl puts the pills in my mouth and helps me sip. He doesn't talk, but his eyes hold mine as I swallow the liquid. It's like swallowing hot coals, and I wince.

"Sorry," he whispers.

"I'm sorry," Joshua says. He stands in the middle of the room and his eyes are dark. "I should have checked earlier. I should have considered it might be something else."

"How could you?" I whisper. My voice is so hoarse that it doesn't sound anything like me.

"I should have known," he repeats. His face crumples. He clears his throat, turns, and walks out of the motel room without another word.

"His mom and brother died yesterday. Dad's sick too." Axl shakes his head. "He ain't been able to reach him today."

My heart aches. He's been here, taking care of me while his family died. Maybe he could have gotten there to say goodbye. If it hadn't been for me.

Night is the same as the one before, only I get a little more sleep. When I wake, my body aches less. My throat is still raw, but my bones don't hurt with as much intensity as they did before.

I roll toward Axl. He's asleep next to me, and his face is relaxed. He looks younger. It's a comfort to have him here.

"Axl," I croak.

He bolts upright, startling me. Joshua jerks awake in the other bed.

"What?" Axl seems panicked, like he's expecting bad news.

I almost laugh, but it would hurt too much, so I try to choke it down. "I don't hurt as much."

Joshua is next to me in the blink of an eye, and they both touch my face. Their hands are on my cheeks, my forehead.

"She feels cooler," he says.

He runs to the other side of the room, but I can't take my eyes off Axl. My fever is down, I know it is, because for the first time I can truly appreciate everything he did for me the last two days. It makes me want to take back every negative thought I ever had about him.

"Thank you," I whisper. Talking tickles my throat. I turn my head away from him so I can cough.

He doesn't say anything, but when I look back his eyes shimmer with hope.

Joshua comes back with a thermometer. "Put this under your tongue."

I open my mouth and allow him to put the thermometer in. Axl doesn't say anything, but his hand rests on my shoulder. I don't want him to move it. It's more comforting than a warm blanket on a cold day. Better than a hug from your mother. I'm assuming. I don't really ever remember getting a hug from my mom, but there's no way it could have made my insides feel as warm and silky as they do now.

The thermometer beeps. Joshua removes it and lets out a sigh. "One hundred point eight." He smiles a little, but it's too sad to make me feel really, truly better.

I tear my eyes away from Axl and focus on Joshua. "What was it before?"

"One hundred and four point nine," he says. "Strep or not, the antibiotics are kicking in."

No wonder they thought I was dying.

"How do you feel?" Axl asks.

I try to sit up, and it's no surprise when he helps me. "The aches are almost gone and I'm not as cold." I have to whisper because my throat is still killing me. I swallow and cringe. "My throat is still just as swollen."

"A couple days and that will be better too," Joshua says.

He lets out a sigh and a genuine smile crosses his face. He looks— relieved. Maybe after all the death of the last few weeks, he needed this. A simple illness that didn't result in a horrible, painful end.

"You should eat," he says. "I'll run to the café and get you some soup." He grabs his pants and pulls them on.

Axl doesn't move from my side. His hand is still on my shoulder. "I should tell Angus."

"I'll stop by their room on my way to the café." Joshua is out the door before anyone can stop him.

My heart swells, and tears come to my eyes. I'm so thankful for this group of strangers. That they were willing to take care of me. To put their lives on hold while the world ended. Just for me. No one has ever done anything like that for me before. Not even my own parents.

"You need anythin'?" Axl asks. He finally moves his hand. He puts it on his leg and stares down at it, flexing his fingers for a moment like he doesn't recognize it.

I start to tell him I'm okay, but stop. "I need to go to bathroom."

My legs shake when I try to stand. I haven't had much to eat or drink in two days.

Axl is by my side before I can even take a step. "I'll help."

He puts his hand on my arm and supports me while I walk toward the bathroom. I think I could probably manage on my own, but it's comforting, so I don't protest. Thankfully, he doesn't try to follow me in. I vaguely remember a few times over the last couple days when I was feverish and not really with it where he might have. I try to push the thought from my mind. It doesn't matter now, because I am going to live.

You are not going to die. I let out a huge sigh of relief. I was so sure this was the end.

When I'm done, I head out to wash my hands. I catch a glimpse of myself in the mirror. It doesn't look anything like me. My skin is pale and moist with sweat. The make-up smeared under my eyes gives my face a hollow and terrifying appearance. My greasy, blonde hair clings to my head. I probably smell.

"I need a shower."

"Go 'head. There's probably a long line at the café," Axl says from behind me.

"Is my suitcase in here?"

"I'll get it. Go 'head and jump in."

"Thanks."

The shower isn't hot. More like lukewarm. But I can't complain. I can practically feel the layers of sweat and sick slide off me. I don't spend a lot of time, not because of the water, but because I'm weak. It wore me out just to strip off my clothes. Standing in the shower to wash my hair makes my legs shaky. I sit on the floor of the tub to rinse off.

When I turn the water off, I pull myself to my feet, holding onto the wall for support. I shiver. The air is cold and my fever still isn't completely gone. My body is covered with goosebumps. I find a towel hanging just outside the shower and grab it, hoping to get warm. But it's cheap. Scratchy and thin. It's soaked by the time I've wiped myself down. I wrap it around me anyway. It's barely big enough to go completely around my body.

I head back out into the bedroom, still wet, barely covered, and shivering. All I want at this point is find something warm and comfortable to wear.

Axl is laying on the bed when I walk out. My suitcase is on the floor by the sink. He sits up but doesn't move, and I lower myself next to him on the edge of the bed. I'm exhausted.

"Can you bring my suitcase over here?" I whisper, not looking at him.

He grabs the suitcase without saying anything. My stomach flutters when he walks back and I pull the towel tighter. The idea of getting dressed in front of him has me nervous. Why? I was a stripper. But this is different somehow. Like a first date or something.

He sets it next to me, but doesn't move. I keep my eyes down as I dig through it. I find a clean pair of underwear and a bra, black and lacy. I set them aside while I search for a shirt and some pants. When I look up his eyes are on my skimpy undergarments. I chew on my bottom lip. What's he thinking? I'm still too sick to really focus on this thing between us, but that doesn't stop my heart from beating faster.

Thankfully, he turns away without me having to ask. I bite back a smile while I get dressed, thinking about the rough guy I met a few days ago. Where did this guy come from?

I pull on my clothes as fast as I can, then wrap the towel around my wet hair. "I'm decent."

Axl turns back and stares at me. Totally silent.

I swallow and wait for him to say something.

"I'm glad you're okay," he finally says. I can't read his expression, but his eyes are soft.

"Me too," I whisper.

His eyes search mine, and I don't know what to say. He has me shaken. At least I think it's him. Maybe it's the near-death experience, or maybe I'm just weak. Everything feels jumbled right now.

Chapter Eleven

"Your brother started packing up the second he heard she was better," Joshua says between bites of his burger.

Axl pauses mid-bite. "Well, we ain't goin' yet. She's still sick."

I sip soup by the spoonful while they eat giant burgers that smell amazing. I had no idea how hungry I was until Joshua walked in with the food. It wouldn't work, though. Swallowing the soup hurts.

I clear my throat, which feels like someone scraping the inside of my esophagus. "We can go. I'm feeling a lot better."

Axl shakes his head, but he doesn't say anything. He isn't convinced.

"The café wasn't nearly as busy as it was a few days ago." Joshua takes another bite, but it looks forced. Like he's lost his appetite.

I clear my throat again. It feels like something is trying to claw its way out of my throat and a shudder runs down my spine. God that hurts. "What's been on the news?"

Axl shakes his head. "They're bein' more honest 'bout what's happen' now. That's somethin' at least."

I look back and forth between him and Joshua, waiting. Joshua lowers his head and his mouth tightens into a grimace. Axl keeps eating.

"What?" I croak.

"They've finally come out and admitted the virus isn't contained. They're saying some infected people snuck out of New York." Joshua doesn't look up. He pushes his burger aside.

Axl snorts. "President died. VP's in charge now. They're still sayin' most people are immune."

"All official news reports correspond to what the government is saying, but the Internet is full of crazy stories and rumors." Joshua pushes the fries around in his Styrofoam takeout box. Every word he mutters sounds more dejected than the last.

"What kind of crazy stuff?"

"Conspiracy theories. Chemical warfare, terrorist attacks, a plot to overthrow the government." Joshua stares at his half-eaten burger like he can't remember why he ever wanted it in the first place.

"They're sayin' that ninety percent of the population is gonna be dead by the end of the week. There's even crap 'bout bodies coming back from the dead. Stupid shit like that." Axl talks with his mouth full, and the words come out muffled. But I get the point. No one has any idea what's going on for real, so they're grasping at straws.

The door bursts open, and Angus saunters in. "You ain't dead." His lip bulges and he grips a soda can in his hand. "Good. Let's get the hell outta here."

Axl's burger falls to the floor when he jumps up. "She's still sick, Angus. We gotta hang out 'nother day."

Angus's face turns red and his jaw tightens.

He looks like he's about to explode, and I don't want to cause problems. "It's fine, Axl. I'm well enough to sit in a car."

Axl starts to protest, but Angus speaks up before he can say anything. "Well, good. Get your shit together so's we can get the hell outta this town." He turns toward Axl, his expression hard. "Got that, *brother*?" The challenge in his eyes is unmistakable.

Axl's jaw tightens. He nods.

Angus smiles and turns to the door. "Thirty minutes," he calls over his shoulder.

Joshua stands up and tosses the rest of his burger in the trash. "Guess we need to get packed."

Axl doesn't say anything. He starts packing up our stuff, not looking at me. I bite my lip and try to think of something to say. The brothers are close. I get the impression I've somehow screwed that up. I don't think this is the first time a woman has messed with the dynamic of their relationship, either.

I set my soup on the nightstand and climb off the bed on shaky legs. I have to rest for a minute because I'm dizzy, so I close my eyes and wait for the room to stop swaying. When I'm more stable I walk over to my suitcase, still sitting on the other bed, and start packing it up.

"Sit back down," Axl snaps. "I'll take care of that."

"I can do it, Axl." My hands shake, though. The little bit of soup I ate wasn't enough.

He walks over and puts his hand on top of mine. I look up into his stormy eyes, and my heart skips a beat. We're so close, and he's done so much for me…

"Let me do it," he says in a soft voice.

I sit down on the bed, right next to my suitcase. He stares at me for a few seconds more with his hand on top of mine. The contact makes my skin tingle. It's not right. Finding myself attracted to him when I'm so sick, when the world is falling apart around us.

He finally looks away and goes back to packing up the room. Joshua looks back and forth between Axl and me a few times, but he doesn't say anything.

"So where are we, anyway?" I ask.

"Vega, Texas," Axl says. "'Bout forty-five minutes from New Mexico."

We didn't make it very far before we stopped. I've really slowed them down.

"I'm sorry."

"Don't hafta be sorry. You didn't get sick on purpose."

"I know, but if we hadn't stopped…" I look at Joshua.

He watches me with a frown on his face. "I still wouldn't have made it in time." His voice sounds thick with emotion, and he has to turn away.

"I'm sorry."

He nods, but doesn't look up.

"What are you going to do now?"

"I'm not going home. Thought maybe Axl and Angus had the right idea. Get to the coast and find a good place to wait this out. I don't want to go back to Arizona."

Yeah, the brothers have a good plan. Maybe when I get Emily we'll tag along.

I sit on the bed and watch the men pack everything up. It's strange not to help. It makes me feel awkward and useless. I should help, but to be honest I don't know if I have the energy. It's amazing how much being sick can take out of you.

When everything's packed, we head out to the car. Joshua and Axl carry the bags. I trail behind them, trying to make my exhausted body cooperate. Thankfully, the Nissan is parked close.

"Let's get the hell outta this ghost town," Angus says, grabbing the bags from Joshua and loading them in the back.

There are cars everywhere, but few people. I peer in the window of a gray sedan parked next to us. The driver sits behind the wheel. His head leans back and his mouth hangs open. His eyes are closed, but I don't think he's sleeping.

Axl opens the back door for me. "Go lay down. You look like you're 'bout to fall over."

I climb in, taking one last look over my shoulder at the gray sedan. I have a bad feeling about what's coming.

I get stuck in the third row with Joshua while Axl sits up front with his brother. Angus insisted. He's pissed we lost so much time sitting around, waiting for me to die. Any leeway I may have made with him before is gone completely now. Plus, I get the feeling he's not thrilled with all the attention Axl gave me. I have no idea what he's thinking, but I can't deny the twinge of disappointment that surged through me when I found out Axl wouldn't be sitting in the back with me.

My head pounds when I wake up. In the front seat, Angus curses. I sit up too fast, and my head thumps harder. Squeezing my eyes shut, I wait for it to ease up. I open them when we start to slow. We're approaching another checkpoint, and it takes about two seconds to figure out why Angus is upset.

"We're in a shitload of trouble now," Axl says, looking out his window at the bodies of two soldiers.

Angus puts the car in park. I lean forward, trying to get a better look at what's going on. There are no military vehicles and no living soldiers in sight. From what I can tell, the two bodies, which are slumped over next to a makeshift shelter, are pretty fresh. They probably haven't been dead for more than a day.

"Was it the virus?" Trey asks.

"Only one way to find out," Angus says, opening his door.

Axl follows him. The rest of us watch silently from the car as they walk around the area. Once they've thoroughly checked the soldiers out, the brothers head to the shelter instead of back to the car. Probably looking for any supplies they can take. It's what I would do.

After a few minutes, exhaustion sets in and I have to sit back. I'll rest while I wait for the lowdown.

I don't get a chance though, because Parvarti turns to me with worried eyes. They always look worried. "How are you feeling?" she asks meekly.

I nod, which makes my head ache, and clear my throat to talk, which makes me wince. I'm a mess. "Like shit," I croak.

She bites her lip. "I'm glad you're okay. And, I'm sorry I didn't come check on you when you were sick. It's just…I saw so many people die in New York."

I start to shake my head but think better of it. "Don't sweat it. We barely know each other."

She relaxes, but doesn't say anything.

"Are you going home still?"

She shakes her head. "No, I'm going to Berkley with Trey."

Trey absentmindedly pats her shoulder. He's too preoccupied with watching the brothers to do anything else. They seem closer than they were just a few days ago. Maybe it was sharing a room with Angus that pushed them together even more. I can't imagine that was any fun.

Parvarti isn't going home, and neither is Joshua. We don't have any stops between here and California.

Angus climbs back in while Axl carries a few things to the rear of the car. "Looks like the virus, alright," he says. "No other injuries that we could see. I figure these two got sick, kicked the bucket, and the others took off."

"They just left the bodies?" Parvarti looks like she's about to cry.

"People do some crazy shit when they're scared."

Axl climbs in and slams the door. "Let's get the hell outta here."

We drive through New Mexico without stopping. Even Angus doesn't grumble about eating some of our provisions. We've passed too many cars pulled off to the side of the road. Too many discarded bodies. We're all anxious to get off Route 66.

We cross into Arizona low on gas, but every station we've gone by the last few hours has been out.

"We ain't gonna make it," Angus says from the driver's seat. "We got maybe fifteen miles to go till the next town, we'll be lucky if we make it 'nother five."

We make it six.

The sun is low on the horizon when the car drifts to a stop at the side of the road. Luckily, we're next to a relatively flat area, although a lot more sandy than any of the other places we've camped so far.

Before anyone even has a chance to get out of the car, Angus is giving orders. "Let's get camp set up first off. Make sure we got a fire goin' and some food. After that, either Axl or me will hike on down the road and get some gas."

"What if they're out, too?" Parvarti asks.

"Then we're shit outta luck, that's what. Got no control over that, so there's no reason to worry about it 'til the time comes."

He climbs out without another word. I don't like the idea of us being stuck here alone with Angus. Hopefully, he decides to go for gas.

It doesn't take long to get camp set up. Trey seems to be a fast learner and puts the tent up by himself without a problem, while Parvarti and Joshua collect wood for a fire. Axl refuses to let me help, something that causes Angus to roll his eyes and glare at me more than once. I hate just sitting back and watching, but it's probably better this way. I don't think I'd be of much use. My fever seems to be gone, but I still feel like crap.

Once the camp is set up, Angus heads for the car. "Better get a move on."

"You ain't goin' alone," Axl says, following his brother.

"Which one of these pansies you want me to take? The Doc? Or maybe the drama queen over there?" Angus tilts his head toward me.

"Shut up, Angus. I'm serious. You need backup." He turns and looks us over, pursing his lips like he does when he's thinking. "What 'bout Trey? He's a big guy. Probably be useful in a fight."

Angus grunts and frowns, clearly unhappy about the situation. "What'd you say, homeboy? You up for a walk?"

It's probably one of the least offensive things Angus could say to

Trey, considering the other things I've heard him mutter under his breath, but I immediately tense up. I'm not sure how Trey's going to react. Angus watches him with a steady gaze, waiting.

Trey just nods. "Whatever I can do to help."

Angus gives him a smug smile and turns to his brother. "Lookie there, the boy can take orders." He chuckles to himself as he goes back over to the Nissan.

Axl shakes his head, but doesn't say anything. Joshua grinds his teeth together.

I turn to Trey, who stands behind me with Parvarti clinging to him. "I'm sorry, Trey. That was rude."

He shakes his head and squeezes Parvarti's shoulder. "You think I'm going to let some redneck hillbilly get to me? I go to Cornell, my dad's a doctor, and my mom's an artist. He's an ignorant bastard who enjoys making others feel little. There's nothing little about me, and I won't give him the satisfaction of letting him get under my skin."

As much as I dislike Angus, a brawl isn't the best thing for our group right now. Not after everything we saw today. At least Trey can let Angus's comments roll off his back.

"Let's get a move on!" Angus shouts, coming back with the gas can and flinging it at Trey. "I got the gun, you carry the can."

"I can shoot a gun," Trey says. "If you need me too."

Angus smirks. "Bet you can. Hold up some liquor stores, have you?"

Does he even know how ironic he's being?

Trey turns away from him without a word and gives Parvarti a hug. "We'll be back before morning."

When he leans down to kiss her, I turn away. Not because I'm uncomfortable, but because she doesn't seem like the type who would enjoy PDA. I don't want to make her feel awkward. She doesn't seem like the type to date, if I'm being honest. She seems more like the study-all-weekend kind of girl.

"Come on," Angus says impatiently.

Trey pulls away from Parvarti and follows Angus into the dark night.

Chapter Twelve

We eat rabbit again. My throat is still sore, so I have a difficult time getting it down, but Axl frowns whenever I stop eating.

"What?" I ask.

"You gotta eat more."

"My throat is killing me."

He gives me a disapproving look, and I find myself smiling. He reminds me of a worried mother. It's cute on him.

"Whatever you say, Dr. Axl." I wink at him.

He gives me a half smile. "Doctor. That'll be the day. Like I could ever be somebody so important."

"Don't put yourself down, you have other skills."

Axl scoffs. "Like what? Hittin' a nail with a hammer?"

"You got us dinner. We're out in the middle of nowhere, and you found something for us to eat and cooked it. Not a lot of people can do that," Parvarti says. She actually sounds a little in awe.

Axl's mouth turns up a little more and he looks away, like he's embarrassed. Probably isn't used to compliments. "Not the same as stitchin' a person up. Not nearly as important."

"Depends on what happens tomorrow, or next week," Joshua says. His voice is sad. "Who knows what's ahead for us. If everything goes to hell, your skills could be just as handy as mine. Maybe more."

Axl sits back in his chair and purses his lips, studying all of us. He looks more relaxed with his brother gone. Is this what he would be like if Angus wasn't around so much? It's nice.

He opens his mouth to say something, but before he can the sound of footsteps cuts him off. Quick as lightning, he jumps to his feet and pulls out his gun. "Who's there?"

No one responds. I instinctively reach for my purse. My body goes rigid when the footsteps get closer.

Axl raises his gun and turns toward the sound. "Better make yourself known."

"We're just passing through," a deep voice calls from the darkness. "No need to shoot."

"I'll be the judge of that." Axl takes a step closer. "Step into the light, so we can see ya."

I don't move. My hand wraps around the gun inside my purse, but I don't pull it out. I don't want to give away the fact that I'm armed. Parvarti and Joshua both have that deer-caught-in-a-headlight look on their faces. They'd be useless in a fight.

"Relax," the voice says.

Axl takes a tiny step closer to the voice. His hand tightens on the gun when two figures emerge from the darkness. Two men, both in the early to mid-forties, walk toward us. They each wear a backpack and about four days' of growth on their faces. They look filthy, like they've been walking through the Arizona desert for weeks.

"We're just passing through. Saw your fire and wondered if we could sit for a while, that's all," the same man says.

So far his companion hasn't spoken. But he's observing. Checking each one of us over carefully, surveying our equipment, sizing Axl up. Warning bells go off in my head like crazy, and I squeeze the gun a little tighter.

"Where you comin' from?" Axl's voice is strained and he doesn't lower the gun. He has no intention of letting these guys near our stuff, but he's smarter than his brother. Angus would just tell them to go to hell. Axl knows how to be diplomatic.

"Small town, no place you ever heard of. We're heading to a bigger city," the same man says.

"Why's that?" I ask, drawing their attention my way.

Axl grinds his teeth together when they turn toward me.

"Everyone else in our town died." The silent man finally speaks. His voice isn't as deep and he sounds less threatening. But he doesn't look it.

"Everyone?" Joshua asks. I'm surprised he was able to find his voice. His eyes are so wide and terrified-looking I'm actually afraid he's about to pee his pants.

The men both nod, and the first one says, "Wasn't a big town."

Joshua looks like he's been punched in the gut. Not for the first time, I wonder if he's going to make it, assuming this is in fact the end of the world.

"Sorry 'bout your luck," Axl says. "But we can't help you out, so you should just keep on walkin'."

"Looks like you have plenty. Some nice camping gear, too," the first man says.

The second man just nods. He sticks his hand in the pocket of his jacket. He's trying to be subtle, but I can tell Axl notices by the way the muscles in his jaw tighten.

"We gotta think of ourselves first. I'm sure you can understand."

"Sure, sure," number two says. "But you need to think this through a little." His voice is calm and soothing, but his eyes are dark and ruthless. "You're out here, protecting two girls and a guy who, no offense, looks like he couldn't handle a whole lot. We could help."

He takes one menacing step toward Axl. Axl's eyes flit toward me and down to the purse in my lap. His mouth twitches just a bit. Not enough that the two newcomers would probably even notice. But I do.

"A shitstorm's coming, which you obviously realize or you wouldn't be out here with all this fancy gear. You're going to need some strong allies if you want to survive," the first man says.

"We're doin' good," Axl says.

The second man gives him a condescending smile. "Is that right? Doesn't look like it from where I'm standing. From over here it looks like you're about to get your asses kicked."

The man whips a gun out of his pocket and pulls the trigger without aiming. A gunshot echoes through the dark night, and Parvarti screams. My heart races. I take out my own gun as Axl drops to one knee and returns fire. I raise my gun with steady hands. It barely registers in my mind when the second man goes down, shot in the shoulder by Axl. The first man doesn't look my way. He stares at his friend. His face contorts with rage when he sees his companion hit the ground, and my stomach tightens. He draws his own gun, then aims at Axl. The first man struggles to his feet and does the same. My heart pounds harder. Two barrels point at Axl. He can't take them both.

I don't even pause long enough to think about it. Aiming at the first man's head, I take myself back to my days at the shooting range. I pretend his forehead is my target. I exhale through my nose and allow my body to relax, then squeeze the trigger. Another gunshot follows mine. They ring in my ears, hammering my temples. It makes my already throbbing head hurt even more. Both men fall to the ground with a thud that seems even louder than the actual gunshots. The second man hit by Axl, a bullet in his chest. The first by me. Right between the eyes.

"Damn girl." Axl gets to his feet. "You weren't kiddin'."

I'm frozen. The shock of killing a man hits me in the gut and knocks the wind out of me. My gun is still clutched in my hands, still raised like I'm ready to kill again. But I can't make myself move.

Axl walks over and tucks his gun into his belt. He checks the two men over, probably to make sure they're dead, then turns to me. A smile of approval lights up his face.

It melts away when his eyes meet mine. "Vivian?"

I look at him, but my eyes won't focus. I can't speak.

He walks over, hesitantly. "Vivian, put the gun down."

"I—I shot him."

He stands up a bit straighter and takes the gun out of my hand. "Hell yeah you did. And don't feel bad 'bout it. That son of a bitch woulda killed all of us."

The truth in his words snaps me out of it a little. I look around the campfire at Joshua and Parvarti. They both stare at me with wide eyes, mouths hanging open. I'm not sure if it's awe or shock or maybe even repulsion. I'm not even sure how I feel about it except I'm glad I'm not the one lying on the ground. Dead.

Axl studies me for a moment, and his face is as expressionless as usual. Then he hands the gun back. "Sit down an' rest. I'm gonna check out their packs."

I collapse into the chair. My legs shake.

"Are you all right?" Parvarti asks.

"Yeah," I whisper. "I just pulled the trigger without thinking."

Parvarti lets out a breath, and a puff of steam floats from her mouth up into the dark sky. "That was amazing. I could never do anything like that."

"Amazing?" Joshua says. "She killed a man!"

He sounds hysterical and his hands tremble uncontrollably. He gets to his feet and starts pacing the small area around the campfire, running his hands through his hair, muttering things under his breath about the end of the world.

Axl ignores him for a few minutes while he goes through the supplies left behind by the two men. His back is to me, but he shakes his head. He's annoyed by Joshua's outburst. How will he handle it? Angus would explode. Tell Joshua to stop being a pussy. But I don't know if that's how Axl will react.

Finally, he stands and walks over to Joshua. His mouth is tight. "You gotta pull yourself together, understand? Angus won't put up with this shit. Doctor or not, he'll leave your ass behind."

"What does it matter? If this is the end I just want it to be over."

"This is the end for them." Axl points to the two dead men. "It ain't for you. You're immune. You're one of the lucky ones. Get your shit together. People are gonna be dependin' on you. How many doctors you think are gonna make it through all this? You're necessary, so cut the bullshit." He doesn't raise his voice, but there's a harsh edge to his words.

Joshua swallows and nods, bobbing his head quickly. He's pale and still shaking, but he tightens his jaw in a determined way. "Okay. Okay, you're right."

"I'm always right," Axl says, turning away.

Trey and Angus stumble back into camp a little after seven in the morning, just as we're packing up the tent. They look dead tired, but they each carry a gas can.

Axl takes the can from his brother, who immediately collapses into a camp chair. Trey puts his can down next to the car and goes over to Parvarti, wrapping her in his expansive arms.

"You have any trouble?" Axl asks as he goes over to the Nissan to gas it up.

"Naw. Town was pretty much deserted. Lots of bodies, though."

Angus spits into the fire.

"What the hell?" Trey says.

He stares at the bodies with his mouth hanging open. Axl dragged them farther away from camp last night, but not far enough.

Angus glances toward the dead men, and his face hardens. "You have some trouble, little brother?"

"These two assholes came into camp thinkin' they was gonna steal our gear. Vivian and me took care of it."

Angus gets up and walks over to the bodies, looking them over. "Nice shot. Right between the eyes."

"Can't take the credit. Vivian took that shot. I got the other guy."

Angus looks over at me and raises an eyebrow. "You kill this guy, Blondie? I underestimated you. You're a little badass in a stripper's body, ain't ya?" He smiles. Looks like I'm back in his good graces. "I'm gonna have to be careful not to get you on my bad side. Be nice to get you on my good side though, know what I mean?" His eyes roam and he winks at me. A shudder to goes down my spine.

Axl gives his brother a hard look. He doesn't say anything. He gets to his feet and helps Joshua pack the gear into the back of the Nissan. Parvarti gives Trey and Angus bowls of oatmeal, then packs up the food. Once again, I feel useless in my camp chair. I'm stronger this morning, and my throat isn't nearly as sore as it was yesterday. But Axl still insists I sit down and rest.

"So what's the plan for the day?"

"Drive our asses off," Angus says with his mouth full.

"Thought you didn't like to sleep in the car."

"Don't, but I wanna get the hell off Route 66 and up into California. We got 'bout eleven hours to go to Sacramento. That's close to your place, ain't it?"

"Yeah, Fairfield's a little more than an hour from Sac," I say. My stomach tightens. We're getting close.

"We're just gonna drive. We'll drop Ice-T over there off when we get close, so he can get on up to his people. Then take you on up to Fairfield."

He gets to his feet and tosses his bowl and plastic spoon into the fire. Everything's pretty much packed, so I stand too and fold up my camp chair.

I glance at Trey. His jaw tightens and his hands are clenched. It must have sucked, walking with Angus all night long. Angus is no dummy, he's careful not to go too far with his racist comments. Trey's more than fifteen year younger than him and in much better shape. Angus has got to know he'll get his ass kicked if he takes it too far.

"Let's move out people!" Axl calls.

Chapter Thirteen

We stop only to get gas and eat, but we don't even see many other people at the gas stations. Everyone we pass looks like they're in shock. Some are still on the move, trying to make it to their final destination despite what they've most certainly lost. But others just sit, staring off into the distance with blank expressions on their faces.

There's very little conversation. Angus snores in the third row, with Joshua crammed up against the wall, while Trey sleeps in the second. His head rests peacefully in Parvarti's lap. Axl drives and I ride shotgun, but even we don't say much.

We hit California, and my spirits lift a little. Emily isn't far now.

"What 'bout Emily's dad?" Axl asks, breaking the silence that's been hanging over us for the past few hours.

I don't even hesitate to tell him. His presence is somehow calming. "Some guy from the trailer park. He was eighteen, still living with his mamma. She freaked out when she found out he got me pregnant. Told me to take care of it and stay away from her son. She didn't want me to ruin his life. Like he was going places." I shake my head. "Last I heard, he was in jail."

Axl snorts. "What'd he do?"

I look at him out of the corner of my eye and try not to smile. "Robbed a few convenience stores."

Axl frowns. "Seriously?"

I laugh and slap him lightly on the arm. "No! Drugs. That's how I met him. My dad used to buy pot from him."

Axl chuckles and looks back toward the road. "Bitch," he says. But there's a lightness to his voice I've never heard before.

"He was an ass," I say. "First in a long line of asses."

"Look!" Parvarti says from the backseat, interrupting our conversation. "There's a man out there."

I glance out the window and Axl slows the car a little. Southern California is dry and brown, with mountains and hills in the distance. The landscape around us is flat, though. There's nothing in sight but flat, rocky dirt. No cars, no buildings, no people. Except one man. He's about a hundred yards away, walking with his head down, his body slack. He walks without looking ahead. Aimless.

"Son of a bitch looks shell-shocked," Axl says.

"Should we stop? Try to help him?" Parvarti asks.

"Look at him," Axl says bitterly. "He don't want help. Looks like he just gave up."

My heart aches just a little. There's something so sad about watching him walk across the dust alone. His shoulders are slumped low, like the weight of the world is on them.

"Let's get out of here." I turn away. My throat tightens, and I try to fight back the tears, thinking about what he's lost. Probably everything. And he isn't alone in that.

We reach the area where we're going to drop Trey and Parvarti off around six in the evening. The sun is low on the horizon when we pull off the interstate.

"We'll find you a car. Looks like it's 'bout an hour and a half from here," Axl says.

"What are you going to do, steal it?" Parvarti asks.

Axl snorts. "Where you think we got this?"

Parvarti and Trey both look at him with their mouths hanging open and their eyes wide. I don't even bat an eye.

The streets are almost deserted. We pass the occasional car or see a random person dart down the street, but for the most part things are quiet. It reminds me too much of a post-apocalyptic movie, and it's terrifying.

"Have you spoken to your parents, Trey?" I ask, watching a woman dart from a small grocery store with busted out windows toward a car. She acts like she's being chased.

I've been too focused on how crappy I feel to ask him lately, but now I want to know what's going on. It's obvious the virus has hit California. Hard. I don't know what to attribute the empty streets to, though. Death or panic.

"People really started getting sick a couple of days ago," Trey says. "My parents haven't left the house, so last I heard they were good. But cell service has been sketchy the past two days. Haven't been able to get through since yesterday evening,"

I turn around so I'm facing him. "You mean your cell phone hasn't been working?" Trey shakes his head. I look at the others. "What about you guys? Joshua, have you been able to get ahold of your lab tech friend? Have you tried anyone, Parvarti?"

When they shake their heads fear sweeps over me. That's a strange turn of events.

Axl pulls into a car dealership and parks the car. "Trick is gonna be finding one that's gassed up."

"You're taking a car from here?" Trey's eyes dart around, surveying the lot, and he shakes his head. "This is a bad idea."

"Listen here, we ain't doin' nothin' different than anybody else. You saw the stores we passed. How many had their windows busted out?" Axl's voice is rougher than usual. He's getting impatient with Trey and Parvarti's squeamishness. "Look, the window's already broken! Somebody else had the same idea as us."

"What's all the yellin' 'bout!" Angus pulls himself up in the back. He's been asleep for most of the trip.

"We're gettin' a car for these two so they can be on their way." Axl opens the door and jumps out.

Angus grins, like it's the best news he's heard all year. "Well, let me help you."

Everyone climbs out, and even though I'm still a bit weak I decide to get out too. We've been cooped up in the car for hours, and we still have more than an hour until we get to Fairfield.

The guys take off, stepping through the giant hole in the window of the dealership in search of keys, while Parvarti and I stand next to the Nissan.

"How are you feeling?" Parvarti asks.

I lean against the car. "Tired, but a little better. What about you?"

She sighs. "Worried."

"What about?"

"Trey is so sure we're going to drive off to his house and find his family well, but I'm not. He really thinks things are going to be okay, that you guys are overreacting and all this will be sorted out in a couple of weeks." She chews on her lower lip. "I think he's being overly optimistic and I'm afraid we'll get there just to find everyone dead. Then we'll be alone."

My throat tightens. "I understand."

"At least with Axl and Angus we'd have two capable people. Trey can shoot a gun, but he can't hunt and he's never made a fire. What if this is the end?"

"But he has to try to find his family," I say. "He can't just assume they're gone without even checking it out."

"I know, I know. I just…" She shakes her head and looks toward the building.

"We'll work something out." I put my hand on her arm. "Maybe we can set up a place to meet, in case."

A sound echoes across the parking lot, and Parvarti and I both look in the direction. It was like an empty can or piece of metal being kicked across the asphalt, and it makes me think of Angus and his Coke can. I expect to see him sauntering toward us, but it isn't him.

"There's a man," I say. He walks through the line of cars, maybe searching for one himself. Doesn't look like he's spotted us. I look toward the building, hoping to see the guys. There's no one in sight.

Parvarti looks ready to bolt. "Should we hide?"

I turn toward the open car door and grab my purse. "No, he may need our help." I pull my gun out and make sure it's loaded.

Parvarti squares her shoulders, trying to look brave. She doesn't. She's shaking like a leaf and I can practically hear her heart pounding. Maybe that's mine.

I walk toward the man, and Parvarti falls in behind me. His back is to us. He wears a dark suit that's filthy and tattered. His feet drag against the ground when he walks, shuffling across the parking lot aimlessly.

I clear my throat. "Sir?"

He pauses, but doesn't turn. His head snaps up. I wait for him to say something or look at us, but he doesn't move.

Parvarti's eyes met mine and she shrugs. She's as clueless about what to do as I am. I study the man and take another step toward him. "Are you okay?"

This time he twists around so he faces us. His face is sunken and his skin is a strange shade of gray. His eyes are blank. They're empty and unfocused, and for a moment I'm not even sure if he can see us.

Parvarti takes a step back. "You think he's in shock?"

"He must be."

We both stand silently, looking at him. Waiting for him to speak. But he doesn't. He begins to stagger toward us. A soft moan comes from his mouth.

I swallow and take a step back, grabbing Parvarti's arm. "Are you hurt?"

He doesn't answer, he just keeps walking. If that's what you can call it.

"Vivian," Parvarti whispers.

I raise the gun. "You need to back off."

He doesn't stop.

My pulse races. Why the hell did I think it was a good idea to approach this guy? There's something strange about him. Unnatural.

"Run." I turn around and pull Parvarti toward the building.

Footsteps follow us, faster than a few minutes ago. The moans grow louder.

"He's chasing us!" Parvarti yells.

I don't say anything, I just move faster. Dragging her with me. My heart races, and my breaths come out in short gasps.

"Axl!" I scream as we get closer to the building.

The man is right behind me, he has to be. His footsteps are louder and the grunting more persistent, but I don't want to look over my shoulder.

Angus sticks his head out through the broken window in front of us. "What the hell's all the screamin' 'bout?"

I don't have to answer. His eyes go to the man behind us and his body stiffens. He steps from the building and yanks his gun out of his waistband. He aims it at the man.

"Better stop," he warns.

The man doesn't. I'm not positive because he's behind me, but I think he runs faster.

"I ain't jokin'," Angus growls.

We reach Angus and rush behind him. I spin around, trying to catch my breath, and watch the crazed man run toward us. He's fast, but he still drags his feet.

Now that I'm safely behind Angus, I can relax a little. The man isn't big and he doesn't have a weapon of any kind. I'm not even sure he's really much of a threat, because I'm pretty sure Angus could easily take him.

Anyone else may have tried to reason with the guy. Wrestled him to the ground and tried to talk some sense into him. But not Angus. He pulls the trigger without giving the guy another warning.

The bullet hits the guy in the head, directly above his right eye. His body goes limp and he drops to the pavement.

Angus lowers his gun and spits on the ground. "Dumb son of a bitch."

"What was wrong with him?" Parvarti asks.

"What the hell's goin' on out here?" Axl steps outside with a handful of keys.

Trey and Joshua follow him, and their eyes go to the dead man on the ground.

"This crazy bastard was chasin' the girls. Had to take him out," Angus says.

"Are you okay?" Trey wraps his arms around Parvarti.

She nods but doesn't say anything, and for a moment everyone just stares at the dead man.

"What happened?" Axl asks. "What'd he say?"

"Nothing." I sweep my hair off my face. It's moist and sticks to my forehead. "We saw him walking around and went to see if he needed help. He looked—lost. He didn't say anything to us. Just started running toward us like a crazy person." I look at the keys in Axl's hand. "What took you so long?"

"No electricity." Axl turns toward the parking lot. "Makes it hard to look for keys."

The men walk off without another word, headed toward the cars. I don't follow. I'm too exhausted to wander through the rows of cars, and the crazy man has me a little shaken, so I head back to the Nissan.

Parvarti follows me and stands awkwardly by the door as I climb up and sit in the passenger seat. "He just killed that guy."

I sigh and lay my head back against the seat. "I know. I don't really like it, but I don't think talking to him would have helped. You saw him. He was out of his mind."

"He could have tried to talk to him," she whispers.

I don't answer. I'm too tired to comfort her, and to be honest, I don't think I really care. Maybe the guy wanted to die. Maybe he saw Angus and that gun as his way out.

Parvarti eventually goes to the back of the Nissan and opens the door. She gets busy pulling bags out and I know I should help, but I don't. I just want to get to Fairfield and see if Emily is okay. To make sure she's taken care of. My worst fear is finding her dead, but the second very real possibility is that she's alone. That both her parents succumbed to the virus, and she's having to fend for herself. That would be awful.

A few minutes later a black Honda Pilot pulls up next to us, and the men all climb out.

"Got this mother gassed up and ready to go," Axl says.

He gets to work, helping Trey load the car while Angus climbs in the driver's seat of the Nissan. I climb out. No way I want to sit in a car with Angus. Plus, I need to talk to Trey before they take off.

I find him at the back of the Nissan, going through the car to make sure he has everything. "Hey, I wanted to talk to you before you guys headed out."

"What's up?"

I look over at Axl to make sure he can't hear us. "Parvarti's worried about you guys heading back to your place and finding things aren't good there. She doesn't want you to be alone."

He frowns and stares at the ground. "I know it's a possibility, but I can't just walk away if there's a chance my parents are still alive."

"I know. Nobody expects you to. I just think we should come up with a plan to meet up in a few days, just in case."

He glances toward the front of the car, and I follow his gaze. Angus isn't paying attention to us, thankfully. "What did you have in mind? Cells aren't working, it's not like I'm going to be able to call you."

"I was thinking we could pick a place, maybe in San Francisco or something, and set up a time to meet. We can go there and wait for a day or so to see if you show. If you don't, we can assume everything is good on your end."

"That's a good idea. It would be nice to be able to meet back up in case..." He swallows and blinks a few times, then clears his throat. "But will you be able to get them to come?"

I look over my shoulder. Axl is watching us. "I can get them there."

"Okay. So where do we meet?"

"I don't know. What do you think?"

"Someplace that would be good for you guys to hang out for a day or two. A hotel maybe?"

I perk up. "Yeah. That sounds like a good idea."

"My parents always stay at the Mark Hopkins when they go into San Francisco."

"I don't know where that is, but we'll figure it out. Will two days be long enough?"

"Yeah. That will give me time to get home and check on my family, and get some things together if I have to head out."

"Okay then," I say. "I'll get them to the city and to the hotel. Be there by Sunday at the latest."

"What're you two yappin' about?" Axl asks, walking over to us.

"Nothing," I say. "Just saying goodbye."

"Well let's get on with it. We still got a good hour to go ourselves."

I turn toward the Pilot where Parvarti stands, waiting for Trey. "Be careful," I say, giving her a hug. It's a bit awkward. We didn't really get a chance to know one another that well, but it seems like the right thing to do.

"We will," she says.

I put my mouth up to her ear and whisper, "Trey and I talked. We worked out a plan."

She smiles when I step back, her eyes full of relief.

"Thanks for the ride," Trey says to Axl.

Axl nods and walks back to the Nissan without saying anything. Angus doesn't get out to say goodbye. Not that any of us expected him to.

"Hope your parents are okay," Joshua says, shaking Trey's hand.

Trey gives me a quick smile, then he and Parvarti get in the car. I watch them drive off, and my stomach feels heavy, like it's full of rocks. I don't think he's going to arrive home to find his family untouched by all this, and I fully expect to see him in San Francisco in two days. As long as I can get the brothers to agree to go.

Chapter Fourteen

The drive to Fairfield is as quiet and uneventful as the rest of the day has been. We pass ghost town after ghost town. The world's population seems to have disappeared overnight. The closer we get, the heavier my stomach becomes. By the time we pull off the interstate, I'm pretty sure I'm going to throw up.

"Which way?" Angus asks.

I lean forward so I can get a better view. The sun has set and there are no streetlights. The electricity is out, just like it was at the dealership.

"Make a left at the next street."

"Pretty swanky neighborhood," Angus says. "Looks like you made the right choice, givin' her up."

I have the sudden urge to punch him in the throat. "Turn right at the next street," I say through clenched teeth. "And drive slow. I'm not positive which house it is. I haven't been here in over four years."

Angus slows while I try to make out the house numbers in the darkness. Most of the homes are completely dark, but a few have flickering or faint lights illuminating the windows. Like the inhabitants are using flashlights or candles. There are other survivors.

"What's the number?" Joshua asks.

"4513," I say. "It's a one-story."

"There." Axl points out the window.

Angus pulls over in front of the house. It's dark, just like most of the others, and my heart races.

"I'll go with you," Axl says.

I give him a smile even though there's no way he can see it in the darkness. We climb out and head up the driveway in silence. The entire neighborhood is so quiet it makes me jumpy. There should be noise in a neighborhood like this. Music or talking, kids laughing or even a car driving down the street. But there's nothing.

I knock on the front door and try to peer through the decorative glass. No one answers, and there's no visible movement. Axl shrugs and shuffles his feet. I knock again. He looks as jumpy as I feel. He has a gun in one hand and a flashlight in the other. He thought ahead.

When no one answers again, I exhale. My shoulders slump. She didn't make it. We were too late.

I'm about to turn away when a shadow darts across the room. My heart jumps to my throat. "Did you see that?"

He hands me the flashlight, then tries the doorknob. It doesn't turn. He steps back, studying the outside of the house.

"What are you thinking?" I ask.

"Gotta be a way to get in. The front door's got a deadbolt on it. Maybe we can get in through a window or side door."

"We could just break a window," I say. "If they're dead they won't care, and if she's alone we can't leave her."

Axl raises an eyebrow. "Don't wanna scare her."

That's a good point. "Okay. We'll try the other doors first, but if breaking a window is our only option…"

He heads to the side of the house and reaches over the gate to unlatch it. In the backyard, I can just make out the shape of a swing set in the darkness. Axl moves swiftly through the dark yard, but I stumble a couple of times before finally flipping the flashlight on. There's a sliding glass door. When Axl yanks on the handle, it actually opens.

"Lucky for us they forgot to lock it," he says.

I exhale, and a lightness I haven't felt since this whole thing started comes over me. Maybe not even for years, if I'm being honest. We're here and the door is open. I can't believe we made it.

We step in, and my eyes water. The air reeks of spoiled food and death. I cough and cover my nose. My feet are rooted to the ground. Do I want to keep walking? Do I want to go all this way just to see her dead and bloated?

"She could still be okay," Axl whispers.

I swallow and fight to keep calm.

Axl walks forward, and I force my feet to work. The beam of the flashlight shakes as I pan it around the room. We're in the living room with the kitchen right in front of us. Axl heads that way. I follow him on wobbly legs.

"Anybody here?" Axl calls.

I jump as his voice echoes through the empty house, like we're in a cavern from which there's no escape. I can't stop shaking. There's no answer. We find the kitchen floor covered in food and trash. Bags from cookies and crackers, empty boxes. It's weird to see such a nice house so messy.

"Why's there trash everywhere?"

Axl steps closer and snatches the flashlight out of my hand. "Looks like the work of a kid. Somebody tryin' to fend for themselves."

"She's here." My heart jumps. She's hiding somewhere. But where? There's a small table in the corner but she isn't under it, and the pantry door is wide open. It's empty.

"She's somewhere." Axl purses his lips. "Just think 'bout it for a sec. She's alone. Scared. Where would she feel safe?"

My heart pounds so hard that it's like a jackhammer thumping against my insides. The answer to that question is obvious, and just thinking about it makes the contents of my stomach churn. "With her mom."

Our eyes meet. "Follow that smell and we'll find her."

We head back through the house, past a playroom full of toys and a bathroom, and down a dark hall with open doors. The smell increases with each step.

"Emily," I call out, trying to sound as unthreatening as possible.

No one responds, but there's movement at the end of the hall. Coming from a sealed-off room.

Axl puts his gun away and turns the knob. My heart pounds faster. He pushes the door open. I suck in a deep breath through my nose and the putrid smell of death almost knocks me out. My stomach turns. I can't lose it now. Emily needs me.

Axl shines the flashlight on the bed, illuminating two bodies. They've probably only been dead a day or two at the most. They don't look too bad. A little swollen and much, much too pale, but otherwise they could almost be sleeping. A person might think they're taking a nap, if it wasn't for the smell.

I step forward and do my best not to focus on the bodies. Thankfully, Emily isn't on the bed with her parents, but she has to be in this room. I open a closed door. It's a walk-in closet that's bigger than my bedroom back in Kentucky. Axl comes up behind me and shines the light inside. It's empty.

"Under the bed," he whispers.

I take a deep breath, then bend down so I can look under. Axl does the same. When he shines the light underneath, Emily's frightened eyes stare back at me.

They are large and brown, just like mine. She's filthy, and she clings to a stuffed animal. Her eyes are red and swollen. Tears stream down her cheeks.

"Emily." I try my best to sound calm. "It's okay. My name is Vivian, and I'm here to help you."

She doesn't move. Her eyes dart past me to Axl.

"S'okay," he says gently. His voice is so much softer than I've ever heard it. "We ain't gonna hurt you."

Emily looks back and forth between us for a second, then crawls forward. I help her out, then check her over to make sure she's okay. I'm not even sure what I'm looking for. Her hair is in tangled knots and she's wearing pajamas that are as filthy as her face.

I brush the dirty hair aside and give her a tentative smile. "Are you okay?"

She looks over toward the bed. "Momma's sick."

Tears come to my eyes and I bite my lip. What do I say to that?

"Your momma's gone, sweetheart," Axl says. Emily and I both turn to look at him, and he reaches up, gently patting her on the shoulder. "So's your daddy. But it's okay, 'cause they called and asked us to come an' take care of you."

Emily looks at me with eyes wide. "Do I have to leave momma?"

I nod and try to ignore the tear that rolls down my cheek. "Yes, baby."

She looks over at her mom and dad, and I do the same. I can't stop myself. It's grotesque and horrifying, and I don't want her to have to stay in here a moment longer.

I scoop her up and turn toward the door. "Let's get out of here."

I'm just about to walk out when something catches my eye. I

freeze.

Axl almost runs into my back. "What?"

I stare at the bed. "I thought I saw something move."

"Nothin' movin' in here."

I nod but I can't take my eyes off the bodies. The flashlight isn't pointed in that direction. Long shadows stretch across the bed, playing tricks on my eyes. That's all it is. There's no way a finger actually moved just now. That would be impossible.

The hair on the back of my neck stands up.

I turn away, rushing down the hall to Emily's room. Axl is right behind me and my heart is still pounding when I set Emily on her bed. There are goose bumps all up and down my arms. We need to get out of this house as fast as possible.

"I'm gonna check out the rest of the house while you get her things together." Axl hands me the flashlight.

"How are you going to see what you're doing?"

"I'll be alright," he says. "Maybe I'll find a flashlight. We could use a few more anyways."

"Be careful," I call as he disappears out the bedroom door.

Emily sits on the bed. Her eyes are huge and she watches me silently as I move through the bedroom, opening drawers and pulling out clothes and shoes. I'd like to be able to clean her up, but even if the water is still on, it will be cold. There's no electricity. But there's also no guarantee that the water is running at all.

I find a small suitcase in Emily's closet and stuff it full of clothes before I get her changed. She's quiet the entire time, just watching me with her big, brown eyes. I don't talk either, mostly because I don't know what to say, and I work fast. I want to get out of this house. The smell is making me more and more nauseated by the minute, and I can't shake that uneasy feeling from the master bedroom. Something just isn't right here.

Once she's dressed in clean clothes, I take her to the bathroom and set her on the sink. I cross my fingers as I turn on the faucet. Water pours out, cool and clean, and I let out a sigh of relief. I have to rinse the washcloth three times while cleaning her face. She never says a word. She just stares at me. It's like looking in a mirror. And it's strangely unnerving.

"Are we going on a trip?" she asks in a quiet voice, finally breaking the silence.

I smile at her. "We're going to find a safe place to stay. Somewhere with food and lights."

"Can I take my doggy?"

I forgot about the small stuffed animal she had when I pulled her out from under the bed. It must be in her bedroom.

"Of course you can. In fact, why don't we go to your room and get some other toys and books to take. Okay?"

A grin stretches across her face and she jumps off the bathroom counter, then dashes out into the hall without me. I grab the flashlight and bag of toiletries and run after her. She shouldn't be alone. When I get to her room, she's filling a small backpack with toys and books.

Male voices float back to us from the other part of the house, and she looks up at me with wide, terrified eyes.

"It's okay," I say, kneeling down in front of her. "It's just my friends."

She picks up her stuffed dog and hugs it tightly. I zip her backpack and look around the room, making sure there's nothing else I might need before standing up.

"You ready?" Axl comes in the door behind me. "Angus is gettin' antsy."

Of course he is.

I turn to face Axl. "I wanted to talk to you before we got back out to the car."

He cocks his head to the side. "'Bout what?"

"I talked to Trey and Parvarti about meeting up in two days, just in case things aren't good for them. You know they won't make it on their own."

He sighs and shakes his head. "I knew you was cookin' up somethin'. Angus ain't gonna like it."

"We have to. You know we do."

"Dammit," he mutters. "Where?"

"San Francisco."

"I'll see what I can do, but I ain't promisin' nothin'. Angus is gonna be pissed." He grabs the suitcase off the floor and glances over toward Emily, who's still clutching her dog. "Come on. I got her booster seat outta the garage already."

A warm feeling rushes through me. That's something I hadn't even thought of. "Thank you, Axl."

He nods to me, but turns toward Emily and gives her a small smile. "You wanna go for a ride?"

She smiles shyly and nods, and my throat tightens when Axl holds his hand out to her.

Chapter Fifteen

When we get back to the Nissan, I buckle Emily securely into her booster in the second row. Joshua is on the other side of her and Angus is in the driver's seat, leaving the passenger seat for Axl.

Joshua stares at Emily out of the corner of his eye like he isn't sure what to do with her. "So what's the plan now?"

"Need to get some supplies," Angus says, doing a U-turn.

"There's a Walmart not too far from here," I say.

Angus grunts and concentrates on maneuvering the enormous car. He barely misses a truck parked on the side of the road. "Sounds like a plan."

"And then we can head to San Francisco," I say, biting my lip while I prepare myself for the argument that's sure to come.

Angus scoffs. "Hell no, we ain't goin' to the city. We gotta find an abandoned farmhouse and get us a generator and provisions. One with animals would be best."

I wait for Axl to pipe in, but he doesn't. His back is to me and his shoulders are as stiff as a board.

"We need to go to San Francisco," I say. "I set up a meeting place with Trey and Parvarti, just in case things aren't good for them at home. That way they can meet up with us."

I jolt forward when Angus slams on the brakes. He turns to face me and his face is bright red. "I ain't drivin' all the way to the city for some ni—"

"We can't abandon them!" I don't want to hear it. I heard it all my life, from my dad and his disgusting friends, and I don't want to listen to it anymore. It makes me sick. "Tell him, Axl!"

Axl turns and looks at me. His face is blank. "Angus is right. It'd be dumb to go to the city."

I jerk back, like I've been slapped. My lungs are empty. It's like the wind has been knocked out of me. Axl looks me right in the eye, calmly, totally unashamed of his betrayal.

It takes me a few seconds to find my voice, but when I do I say, "Fine. I'll go without you. I won't abandon them."

Angus laughs and raises and eyebrow. "You wanna drive there by yourself with a little girl? Be my guest."

"She won't be alone," Joshua says. "I'll go. She's right, we can't abandon them."

I give Joshua a grateful look. Putting himself on the line like this can't be easy, and getting on Angus's bad side is going to suck.

Axl slams his hand on the dashboard. "Dammit!"

"Let 'em go," Angus says, giving me a cold stare.

Axl looks at me and shakes his head, then curses again. "They ain't goin' alone."

Angus turns on his brother and his face gets redder than ever. That little vein on his forehead pulsates. "What the hell are you talkin' 'bout? We ain't goin' into the city. That's the last place we need to be."

"I ain't lettin' them wander off alone," Axl says. "You can come or not, but I'm goin'."

Angus lets out a string of profanities so colorful that I actually cover Emily's ears. She's going to learn all kinds of new vocabulary being around him. But I'm so thankful I'm not going alone that I'm not even pissed. I wouldn't have abandoned Trey and Parvarti, but going to San Francisco by myself wouldn't have been ideal.

Angus starts driving again. He grips the wheel like he's ready to rip it off. His eyes stay straight ahead. "Tell me how to get to Walmart."

I give him directions to the store. We don't pass a single car or person on the way, and I pray it's because it's so late at night. Not because the whole world is dead.

The store parking lot is empty except for a few stray cars, and the front door is wide open. The electricity is out, but emergency lights are on inside the building, giving off a soft bluish glow that illuminates the registers and racks through the window. Angus parks in front, and we sit in silence for a few minutes while we check things out.

"Joshua, will you stay in the car with Emily?" I don't want to take her in, but I need to grab some things.

"I was going to check out the pharmacy," he says. "Get some antibiotics and other things, just in case."

I bite my lip and look at the little girl I gave birth to. It's hard to think of her as my daughter, it's just so surreal. But there she is, staring up at me with my eyes, big and round. Frightened.

"We should all go in," Axl says.

I sigh and try to smile at Emily. It's shaky. "You want to do a little shopping?"

She doesn't respond. She hasn't said much since we found her. Maybe she's in shock.

"So what's the plan?" Joshua asks.

"Angus is gonna go back and check out the huntin' gear. They don't carry much, but it's worth a shot," Axl says. "I'm gonna get a cart and fill it up with food. The bread's gonna go bad soon, I wanna take advantage of it while we can."

"I'll go with Joshua," I say. "I wanted to get some things for Emily anyway."

"Sounds like a plan," Angus says.

"You two stay together, and keep your eyes open. Never know when you're gonna run into another crazy person like before." Axl opens the door and jumps out.

We follow suit and head into Walmart. I carry Emily. She clings tightly to me, laying her head on my shoulder and crushing me in her grip. She's heavy, though. There's no way I'll be able to carry her through the whole store, so I grab a cart and put her in it.

Joshua and I head over to the pharmacy area without saying anything to the brothers. As soon as we're away from them I say, "Thanks for agreeing to come with me. I knew Angus wouldn't be a fan of the idea."

"That's because it's stupid," Joshua says. I start to argue, but he holds his hand up to stop me. "I agree we shouldn't abandon them. I wouldn't want to be alone either. But going into the city is a bad idea. We should have chosen a different place to meet."

I bite back the urge to tell him to go screw himself and walk for a few seconds in silence. It doesn't take long for me to acknowledge he's right, though. Somewhere else would have been better.

"You're right," I finally say with a sigh. "I just didn't have time to really plan. I was trying to set it up before Dumb or Dumber got wind of what we were planning."

Joshua gives me a wry smile. "It would have been nice to have a discussion about it, but we all know how that would have turned out." He exhales and runs his hand through his hair. "Like these guys or not, I think being with them is our best bet of surviving until all this gets sorted out. *If* it gets sorted out, that is."

"You're telling me."

We get to the pharmacy and Joshua heads back to dig through the drugs. There's something I want to look for, plus I don't want to wander around the store alone, so I get Emily out and carry her behind the counter with me. It's dark back here. The emergency lights aren't quite enough to make it possible to read the labels on the bottles, so I dig a flashlight out of my purse and search the counters.

"What are you looking for?" I ask him.

"Ampicillin, Keflex, Zithromax. Any antibiotic, really. I also wanted to grab some painkillers in case we had an issue, although I think we should keep that between us. I have a strange feeling Angus would think they were for recreational use."

I snort. "Nothing would surprise me."

"Are you looking for something?"

I bite my lip and try to decide what to tell him. He is a doctor, and I guess he's *my* doctor now since I don't have any other options. "Nuvaring."

Joshua steps over to where I'm standing. He tilts his head to the side and his eyes narrow on my face. "You planning a romance?"

My cheeks get hot, but I roll my eyes and try to play it off. No way to do I want him to think Axl has anything to do with this, because he doesn't. Not even a little. "Yeah, right."

"I saw how cozy you and Axl were acting when you were sick."

Joshua may have been on to something yesterday, but I'm not feeling very cuddly after Axl's betrayal. "Yeah, let me know where that guy disappeared to."

"His moods are pretty much all over the place, aren't they?"

"No. I know exactly where his moods are. When Angus is around he's an ass, when Angus is gone he actually decides to be a decent person."

Joshua shakes his head. "Whatever. Nuvaring isn't going to work for you. It has to be refrigerated."

"Dammit." He's right. It's been a few years since I was on it and I'd forgotten that part. "I remembered you could use one after the other and not have a period. I thought it would be convenient. You know, no running water, being on the road, not knowing where we're going to end up."

"Okay." Joshua walks away and I grab Emily so I can follow him. "This one may work then. You can take it every day and have no periods at all, at least until you run out of pills. They only have five packs here."

"Thanks." That's one worry out of a thousand off my mind, at least.

"Remember, it's not effective as birth control for thirty days..." He raises his eyebrows and shrugs.

"Please." I shove them in my purse. He has to be joking. Sure, I can't deny I'm drawn to Axl when he's being sweet, but that doesn't happen very often. And Angus seems pretty determined to make sure Axl and I do not end up together.

We continue to raid the pharmacy. Joshua has our cart almost full, and he gets everything from antibiotics to Ace bandages and even some crutches. I keep joking that he's opening his own clinic, but he just says he wants to be prepared.

Axl and Angus show up before long, both with their own carts full to the top.

"What the hell are you two doin' over here?" Angus growls.

"Getting supplies," Joshua says without even glancing his way.

"What's takin' so long?" Axl's voice is just as tense and annoyed as his brother's.

I give him a cold look, but he just returns it. He doesn't even bat an eye. Jerk.

"It takes a bit longer sorting through drugs than it does grabbing some food off the shelves," Joshua says. "You want to do this?"

Neither one of the brothers says a thing, and Joshua goes back to the pharmacy. I'm actually impressed with how he's handling himself. He seems to have pulled his act together. I guess Axl's little lecture helped.

I lean against the counter. Emily is asleep in my arms and she's getting heavy.

Angus walks over to a shelf and grabs a couple boxes. He tosses them into his cart with a smug look on his face. I glance down and roll my eyes. Condoms.

"We might need to repopulate the Earth," he says, grinning like a chimpanzee.

"Yeah, and condoms are the way to go."

Axl actually cracks a smile, but Angus just glares.

"All done," Joshua announces, tossing a few more things into the cart. "Let's head out."

The drive to San Francisco is a quiet one. I sit in the passenger seat next to Axl, looking behind me every couple minutes to make sure Emily is okay. Angus snores his head off in the third row, and Joshua leans up against the wall next to the booster seat, not snoring but out cold.

"She seems to be takin' all this pretty well," Axl says.

"I don't think reality has hit her quite yet."

"Ain't sure it has for any of us," he mutters.

"True, but hopefully we're all better equipped to deal with it than a four-year-old. Although, I've had my doubts about Joshua a couple of times. Not sure if he's really up for this end-of-the-world shit."

"Yeah, the Doc is havin' a rough time." He looks at me and clears his throat. "You can stop being pissed. I didn't take Angus's side just for the fun. I think this idea is dumb as shit."

I shrug and look away. I have no interest in discussing this with him, I agree but I also don't agree. We should do whatever it takes to make sure Trey and Parvarti are okay; it's the right thing to do.

We only see one other car driving on the road, and it's headed in the opposite direction. Other than that we pass a few abandoned vehicles, but no people. When we reach the tollbooths just outside the city, they're deserted and the gates are down. Axl doesn't hesitate. He drives right through, breaking the wooden board in half and waking up everyone else in the car.

"What the hell?" Angus growls from the back.

Emily whimpers. Joshua starts to comfort her. I turn around and join in, whispering soothing words and telling her it's okay.

"Mommy." Her eyes are barely open. I'm not sure if she's dreaming, but her cries make my heart ache. I can't think of a single thing to say that will make her feel better.

I'm having a tough time really connecting in my mind that she belongs to me. In theory it sounded great, and driving across the country it was all I could think about. But I didn't get that warm fuzzy feeling that I expected to when I found her alive. I was relieved, but there was none of that motherly love I've heard so much about. Now I'm not sure what to do with myself, or her.

We drive over the bridge and I look out toward the bay. During the day, when it isn't foggy, you can see Alcatraz from here. It's pitch black now, and it gives me the chills.

"It's gonna be rough, driving through the city with no lights. We're gonna have to take it slow, make sure we don't run into anyone," Axl says as he follows the directions the GPS gives him.

The car is as deathly silent as the city as we make our way through the narrow streets. Axl curses and slows down repeatedly when we go up and over hills. It's difficult to see anything without streetlights, but the hilly and narrow streets of the city make it even more complicated. It doesn't take long to reach the hotel without the normal bustling traffic, though. I'm relieved when it comes into view, even if it's just as dark and silent as every other building in the city.

"Penthouse?" Angus leans close to the window and stares up at the top of the hotel.

"Hell, yeah," Axl replies, pulling to a stop in front of the hotel.

"We should get as much out of the car as possible," Joshua says. "We don't want anyone breaking in."

Axl shoves his door open. "Yeah. First let's get inside and find us a key."

I climb down and open the back door to get Emily. No electricity is going to make this rough. "Will those little cards they use still work with no power?"

"The locks run on batteries, so they still work if there's a power outage," Joshua says. "I worked at a hotel in college. But we're going to have to find a master key somehow. At the front desk or off a cleaning lady."

The hotel lobby is pitch black, but we all have flashlights so we can see a little. A slight smell of decay makes my nose wrinkle in disgust, but it's nothing too strong. Just enough to let us know someone died here. Hopefully, there's no one in the penthouse.

I sit on a couch in the lobby with a sleeping Emily, while the men head off to find a key. Even Joshua goes, though he would normally hang back, because he has a better idea of where to look for a master key.

They're only gone for about five minutes, and when they come back Axl holds a card up. "Found it on the cleanin' lady. She was dead in the employee break room."

I get to my feet and shift Emily a little on my hip. She's heavy. I take two steps before I stop. We're going to have to use the stairs. "How many floors are in this building?"

Axl glances my way, and by the expression on his face, I'd guess he's about to tell me to quit my whining. Then his eyes land on Emily and his expression softens.

"Give 'er here." He tosses the key to Angus and holds his arms out.

I smile gratefully and pass her over, taking the bags he was carrying instead.

The climb is going to be awful. We head up right away, but no one utters a word. My legs would ache even if I wasn't still getting over being sick. As it is, I'm shaky and weak. We're all huffing and puffing by the time we make it halfway. I power through though, using the railing to pull myself up. The stairs come to an abrupt end at the eighteenth floor. We're not at the top though, and when we walk out into the hall we don't find the penthouse. Just a door marked *California Suite*.

"Ain't the penthouse," says Angus as he sticks the key in the door. "But I ain't climbin' no more."

No one argues, and I start to feel really grateful that I don't have to go down and get supplies out of the car with the others. Not that I think I'd make it. I'm pretty sure I'd collapse after one floor.

The suite is twice the size of my apartment in Kentucky. It has a dining and living room, plus two huge bedrooms. Everything is elegant, like a palace or something. It's incredible.

"There're candles in that bag," Axl says, laying Emily on the couch.

Right, candles. I drop the bags to the floor and dig through them, then set the candles all over the room, lighting them as I go.

"You stay put and we'll head down, grab more shit," Axl says.

Angus grumbles but heads to the door. Joshua follows, dragging his feet. I don't blame him. None of us have gotten much sleep in the last twenty-four hours. I'm exhausted.

Chapter Sixteen

I wake up in a king size bed with Emily curled up next to me, clutching her dog. How did I get here? Axl probably. He must have had another mood swing.

The room is dark and the curtains are drawn, but small rays of sunshine peek through the cracks. It's light out. It's impossible to tell what time it is. I don't own a watch, and my phone died a few days ago. Charging it in the car seemed pointless.

Then it hits me. Does it even matter what time it is anymore? What difference does it make if it's two o'clock on a Saturday or five o'clock on a Monday? Everything's the same. I don't have anywhere I need to be, and chances are I may not again for a very long time.

The thought makes me feel both depressed and exhilarated at the same time. It sucks that the world has gone to shit, but it's nice not to have to worry about bills and work anymore. It's slightly freeing.

I crawl out of bed, careful not to wake Emily, and stumble across the dark room to the bathroom. Wouldn't it be wonderful if the faucet still worked? It's a long shot, but it's worth a try. I turn the knob and smile when water runs out. I should take this opportunity to get clean. Who knows when I'll have a chance again.

I flip the shower on and strip down. Before I step in, I take a deep breath. This is going to be cold, and it's going to suck big time.

But when the liquid runs over my body it's warm. Why? There's no logical answer and to be honest, I don't care. I turn the temperature up and let the near-scalding water pour over me. I wash my body and scrub my hair, even taking the opportunity to shave my legs, which I haven't done in a while. Being clean is something I've taken for granted. Never again.

When I'm dressed I head out to the main room. Angus and Axl sit at the dining room table talking. Axl is eating a bag of chips. Angus is holding a beer in one hand and his empty soda can in the other. Why doesn't he just spit on the floor? It seems like something he would do.

The lights are on. I have the sudden urge to jump up and down and squeal like a cheerleader at homecoming. "We have electricity?"

"Found a generator," Axl says.

I smile and grab a handful of chips out of the bag in front of him.

"Mini bar's stocked if you feel like getting trashed," Angus says.

Suddenly, I have the urge to get drunker than I ever have before. I grab a couple small bottles of wine and plop down in the seat next to Axl. Then I take a big swig without even bothering to get a glass. Maybe if I drink enough I can forget all the dead bodies lying around the city. Pretend I'm on vacation instead.

"So how long do we have to sit here?" Angus asks, spitting into his can.

I grab a bag of cookies and rip them open. "Until Sunday."

"It's Thursday!" Angus glares at me.

"So? You have somewhere to be? We're in a nice hotel with electricity. Enjoy yourself and shut up for a change."

Axl shakes his head and gets to his feet. "Where's that spray paint we took from Walmart?"

"In the green bag," Angus says, still giving me the evil eye.

I stop mid-chew. "What are you doing with the spray paint?"

"Gonna go down and leave Trey a note, so he knows where to find us. I don't wanna hang out in the lobby. Do you?"

Axl digs through the bag and pulls out a can of neon orange spray paint, then heads toward the door.

"I'll go with you," I jump to my feet, then pause and look around. I shouldn't leave Emily. "Emily's asleep."

"Angus is here," Axl says.

I frown and study Angus. He does not seem like a reasonable alternative. "Where's Joshua?"

"Sleepin'," Angus mutters. "Go on, I ain't gonna scare the girl. I can play nice." He flashes me a grin that is anything but nice.

I look at him doubtfully, but Axl grabs my arm and pulls me toward the door. "She'll be fine with Angus. Come on."

"Hey, check out that shop downstairs. See if they have any cards. And more booze!" Angus calls after us. "Shoulda got some at Wal-"

The door shuts, cutting him off.

Axl heads down the hall and I'm right on his heels. Was leaving Emily with Angus the mom thing to do?

I turn toward the stairs, but Axl takes my hand and leads me to the elevator "Electricity's on, remember?"

"Thank God." He doesn't let go, and something in me flutters. I pull my hand out of his grip and do my best to focus on the task at hand. We need to go downstairs and leave a note.

The door opens and we step in. "Are you sure Emily is going to be okay with Angus?"

"She's good. Believe it or not, Angus lived with a woman for a while that had two little girls. He was actually good with 'em. He can be a hard ass, but he likes kids."

"Seriously?" Angus likes kids? I don't buy it.

Axl shrugs. "Maybe he just likes girls. He was tough as shit on me, but he treated them girls like they was his own daughters."

Sure, he's been nothing but sweet to me. But I trust Axl, and he sure seems to like Emily. Maybe Angus has a soft side too?

The elevator opens in the lobby and we head toward the front. Axl pauses and looks through the glass, out into the parking lot, before opening the door. I flex my hands. They feel uncomfortably empty. Why didn't I bring my gun? The image of that man charging Parvarti and me at the car dealership goes through my mind. I shudder. At least Axl came prepared.

We walk out and I look around nervously. The metal ball inside the can rattles when Axl shakes it, making me jump. I shift from foot to foot while he sprays a message across the sidewalk. Right in front of the stairs. Vandalizing the hotel doesn't exactly make me feel warm and fuzzy inside, but I have to learn how to let stuff like that go. This is a different world and I need to get used to the way things are now.

"There," Axl says, stepping back.

Tray- 18th floor, California Suite.

I don't have the heart to tell him he spelled Trey wrong, so I just nod.

Movement catches my eye. My heart goes into double time when my head jerks up. There's a man across the street, walking slowly up the hill. He has his head bowed and he stares at the ground.

"A man," I say, pointing at him.

Axl looks over and we both stand quietly for a few seconds, just watching him. He's alone and unarmed, but my heart still pounds. We should just walk away. Leave him alone.

Axl cups his hands around his mouth and shouts, "Hey!"

The man stops and lifts his head, but he doesn't look around. He just stands there. I hold my breath while we wait for him to respond, to acknowledge us in some way. But he doesn't. He doesn't do anything. After a few seconds he starts walking again. The same sluggish pace as before: his head down, his arms slack and swinging at his sides. It's creepy.

"Guess he don't want company," Axl says.

I nod, but something inside me tightens. It makes me think of that man we saw in the field a few days ago. He was walking the same way. Aimless. Defeated. There's something unnerving about it.

My scalp tingles and the sensation of being watched sweeps over me. "Let's get back inside."

We walk into the lobby and both freeze in our tracks at the sight of a woman standing there. She's wearing a uniform—looks like housekeeping—and stands perfectly still, staring at the ground. She slowly raises her head and I suck in a deep breath. She's sick. Her face is pale and gray, her skin droops and her eyes are cloudy. She looks awful. Death can't be too far away.

"Son of a bitch," Axl mutters, pulling his gun out. His body goes rigid and his hands even shake a little.

"What's wrong?"

"That's the maid."

What does he mean? She's wearing a uniform; it's obvious she's a maid. "What?"

"The maid we took the key from," he says, stepping back. "She was dead."

I laugh a little, but it comes out strained and nervous. My heart pounds, but I can't process what he's saying. She's clearly alive. She's standing in front of us, staring at us.

"You're wrong," I say.

"I ain't wrong," he growls, grabbing my arm and trying to pull me back.

I shake him off and take a small step forward. "She's sick."

"Vivian, get back!"

I move forward again. "Are you okay? Can we help you?"

She doesn't talk, but she tilts her head to the side and studies me. A chill runs up my spine, but I ignore it. Axl is freaking me out, but he's crazy. There's nothing to worry about.

"We can help. We have a doctor with us." I try to sound reassuring even though a doctor can't really help her.

She starts walking toward me slowly, raising her arms. Her mouth opens, but at first no sound comes out. When it does it's a low moan that makes my blood run cold. My pulse quickens and I take a small step back. This is so unreal.

"Get back, Vivian," Axl growls again.

I start to take another step back, but before I can she lunges at me, knocking me to the ground. I scream, but it's cut short when my head bangs against the floor. Pain surges through my skull and stars burst behind my eyes, but I don't have time to react. The woman is on top of me, grabbing at my face, trying to pull me toward her open mouth. The stink of rot envelops me and I scream again, struggling to get her off me.

Axl grabs her by the hair and jerks her back. He flings her across the room. It doesn't stop her. In less than a second she charges him again. He lifts his gun and pulls the trigger. The bullet hits her in the chest. She jerks back, but doesn't stop. She has a gaping hole in the middle of her chest, but there's no blood. Instead a thick, black goo oozes out, filling the room with a pungent odor so strong it makes me gag.

"She ain't stoppin'," Axl yells, stepping back.

She claws and chomps at the air, and the sounds coming from her mouth are no longer moans. They're screams.

Axl pulls the trigger again. This time the bullet hits her in the forehead. Right between the eyes. Her body goes slack and she drops to the ground.

I'm still on the floor. I can't move and my heart beats so fast I'm afraid it's going to jump out of my chest. Axl is breathing heavily. He takes a slow step forward and kicks the woman with the toe of his boot.

"Goddamn it," he mutters. He turns and looks at me. "Was that a fuckin' zombie?"

I'm speechless. So shaken I can't respond. What he's suggesting is impossible, but I saw it with my own two eyes.

I stumble to my feet and he starts walking, nudging me as he goes by. I jump. I can't look away from the maid. What the hell does he want? He jerks his head toward the elevator. Right. We need to move. My feet move on their own. Like I'm a zombie....

We ride up in silence. I move automatically when the door opens, following Axl toward the suite without even thinking. His body is so stiff he looks like a walking statue, and he keeps cursing under his breath. Mumbling stuff about zombies and Hollywood. I'm not even sure what else because I can't really focus on it.

"You ain't gonna believe what just happened," Axl says as he bursts into the hotel room. He slams the door behind us and locks it.

Emily and Joshua are up, both sitting at the table with Angus. Eating Pop-Tarts.

"What?" Joshua's mouth is full, and crumbs spray all over the table.

Axl hurries to the window and looks out over the city. "Damn."

I know what's down there before I walk over, but I can't stop myself from going anyway.

Joshua and Angus get to the window just as I do. We're eighteen stories up, but that doesn't mean the people staggering around on the ground aren't visible. And they are everywhere.

Joshua leans closer, practically pressing his face against the glass. "Are those people?"

"Not exactly," Axl says.

My mouth won't work. I stumble away from the window and collapse into a chair. Emily's eyes are wide with fright. I should comfort her, but I just can't. Maybe I'm not cut out for this mom thing. She should come first, but at the moment all I want is for someone to comfort me. Taking care of another person is the last thing on my mind.

"Zombies," Axl says, making my whole body jerk.

The word is ridiculous, even after what I just witnessed. But it's true. I close my eyes and lay my head on the table.

Angus snorts. "Don't be an ass."

"I'm serious. That maid we took the key off of when we got here, she was standin' in the lobby. Tried to take a big ol' bite outta

Vivian."

"She must not have been dead then," Joshua says.

"I shot her in the heart and she kept on comin'. Had to shoot her in the head to get her to stop."

No one talks, and I have no idea what they're thinking because my head is still on the table. My eyes still closed. I don't want to deal with this.

Chapter Seventeen

"We need to go down there and check it out," Angus says.

Slowly, I lift my head. Angus walks across the room and pulls a gun out of his bag. He checks to make sure it's loaded. I blink and try to wrap my brain around what he's doing, but it's like I'm trapped in some kind of fog.

"Are you nuts?" I somehow manage to get out.

"Need to know what we're dealin' with," he says, shoving the gun in the waistband of his pants and pulling out a few knives.

"That maid attacked me! What more do you need to know?" My heart races and the sudden urge to scream is so overwhelming that I have to ball my hands into fists. There's no way this is happening. I take a deep breath and try to get my pulse to slow, to stop the pounding in my ears, but it doesn't work. The urge to or throw something or rip out my hair gets stronger. Maybe I'm hysterical.

"Angus is right," Axl says, copying his brother's movements. "You can stay here."

I jump to my feet and shake my head. "I don't want to be alone."

Emily starts to whimper and I jerk. I forgot she was here. What's wrong with me?

I kneel down next to her and rub her head gently. My hand shakes. "Shhh, it's okay. We're just going to go downstairs and check on something. I'll carry you, okay?"

"You takin' her down?" Angus asks doubtfully.

I stare at Emily for a few seconds, trying to focus through the fog.

Should I take her? Leaving her alone in the room seems irresponsible. It's eighteen floors up and she'd be terrified. Plus, what would she do if we never came back?

"We can't leave her alone," I whisper. "She's four."

I lift her up and scan the room. Where's my purse? I spot it on an end table. When I pull my gun out, Emily's eyes get even bigger. They are so brown.

"Give me a gun," Joshua says.

Angus purses his lips and his eyes narrow. "You know how to use one, Doc?"

Joshua keeps his hand out. "Point and pull the trigger, right? How hard can it be?"

Angus snorts, but hands it to him anyway. "Just make sure you're close so you don't miss."

No one says a word when we head to the elevator. Hell, I'm not even sure anyone is breathing. The tension is so thick that my skin tingles, and I cling tightly to Emily as if she's some kind of lifeline. Hopefully, everyone thinks I'm trying to comfort her, and not the other way around. I don't want them to know what a selfish bitch I'm being.

Axl's eye catches mine and he frowns. He shakes his head. He can read me like a book. I look away. I need to get it together.

The doors open on the first floor and my arms tighten around Emily. I hang back while Angus and Axl step out with their guns raised. Even Joshua goes before me. It's for Emily, she's the reason I'm being this way. I'm just trying to protect her.

Even I don't believe it.

"Clear," Axl says.

I follow the men to the door. The lobby reeks of death, and the stench is even stronger than before. I breathe out of my mouth as much as I can, but it doesn't help. The air is so thick I can taste it. It leaves a film in my mouth that turns my stomach.

We don't even need to step outside. A bald man shambles past the door and I have to bite down on my lip to keep from screaming. There are more dead in the distance. Dozens of them.

A shiver runs up my spine. I pull Emily closer.

"Shit," Axl says. "Where'd they all come from?"

"They weren't here before?" Joshua asks.

"We saw one guy, walkin' on the other side of the road. But that was it." Axl takes a step closer to the window and my heart pounds.

They're everywhere. Stumbling up and down the street, walking aimlessly. Some are even standing in the middle of the road. A woman with stringy, blonde hair walks across the parking lot toward the Nissan. She doesn't stop until she's inches from it, then she freezes. I hold my breath and wait for her to move, but she just stands there. A few other bodies head our way. Their heads are down, so they can't see us, but I still have the urge to run. The glass is too thin.

My stomach tightens and Emily squirms. She tries to turn so she can see out the window and I put her down. Her small hand slips into mine and we watch the walking corpses in silence.

"Look at it out there," Joshua says. "It's like *Night of the Living Dead.*"

My heart races and I shake my head. I push Emily behind me and she clings to my leg, her fingers digging painfully into my thigh.

"Shut up," I whisper.

But he's right. That's exactly what it's like. Dozens of dead bodies, walking around. Mindlessly roaming the streets. Their heads down, their bodies slack. Just like a horror movie.

Emily's parents. All the air leaves my lungs. I did see her mom's hand twitch. I convinced myself I was seeing things. That it was just the shadows playing tricks on me. Now I know better. I grab Emily and swing her up into my arms, holding her tightly to my chest. She lays her head on my shoulder and her little body shakes. Or maybe that's me.

What would have happened to her if we hadn't gotten there when we did? Would her parents have come back? Would they have attacked her?

"This happen in Baltimore?" Axl asks Joshua.

He shakes his head. "No, nothing like this. Nothing like this anywhere on the East Coast." He pauses and runs his hand through his hair, looking at the ground. "We burned all the bodies," he mumbles.

"What?" Angus asks.

Joshua looks up. "In the beginning, they cremated all the bodies to stop this thing from spreading. There were a few bodies they took to the CDC, but the brains would have been destroyed during the autopsy, so they wouldn't have known about this…" He looks out at the dead walking through the parking lot. "Every other body was burned."

"Shit," Axl says.

"How can this be possible?" I ask.

Joshua shakes his head again. "I'm not a neurologist, so I'm no expert. But as far as I know, it can't. I mean, medically speaking there's just no way to even hypothesize how a dead body would reanimate and walk around the place! I've always laughed at zombie movies."

He's right. This can't be real. I have to be dreaming because in real life the dead stay dead and I'm not a selfish bitch who only worries about herself.

"I can't be here." I take a step back. It's too overwhelming. "I'm going back to the room."

Axl's eyes meet mine and his expression hardens. "Never took you for a coward."

I glare at him, then turn on my heel and practically run to the elevator. Who cares what he thinks? Not me. All I care about is getting away from the bodies walking around on the street.

Back in the room, I set Emily at the table with some Crayons and a coloring book. I didn't get them when we were at Walmart, which means either Angus or Axl did. It pisses me off that one of the brothers thought of it and I didn't. It should have occurred to me to get Emily something to keep her occupied.

There's nothing else for me to do, so I start drinking the wine I got out earlier. I walk back and forth between the table and the window, looking out into the street before going back to take another drink. I don't really want to see the bodies walking around out there, but for some reason I can't stay away. It's like there's some kind of tractor beam pulling me toward the window.

When the men come back they're talking about going outside to check things out.

"Are you insane?" I say. "You can't go out there!"

"Why the hell not?" Angus says. "We got guns. We need to find out what's goin' on."

"Don't be a moron," I say, taking another drink.

Axl frowns and rips the bottle out of my hand before turning to Emily. "How you doin' sweetheart?" he asks. His voice is so soft and gentle that it takes me a second to realize he's the one who said it.

Emily smiles up at him. "I'm coloring a picture for mommy."

My heart aches, but I'm not sure if it's for Emily or me. She's lost more than I have, but she's young enough that she won't even miss it. I'll remember it all. Tears fill my eyes until Emily's face becomes blurry and distorted. Sick-looking, like those things walking around outside. I have to look away. My legs wobble. My body is heavy with exhaustion and my chest is tight. It's like nothing I've ever felt before. I'm so overwhelmed by everything that I don't know what to do with myself. Or Emily.

Axl sits down and starts talking to Emily, but I walk away. I can't breathe out here. That window is too big and there are too many bodies. The bedroom is just as bad, though. The tightness in my chest gets worse and it feels like the walls are moving, making the room bigger. Big enough to allow anything in. I pace the floor for a few minutes, but my legs start to shake until I can't stand. I can't stay in here. I'm too exposed.

I go into the bathroom and shut the door, then lock it. My heart pounds so hard it pulses through my body, and my legs almost give out. I sink to the floor and pull my knees up to my chest, hugging them as hard as I can while everything from the past few days falls down around me. All the death and desolation, the despair of thinking I was next. The realization that the hope for a real life I've been clinging to all these years was worthless. Life is over. For all of us. The sobs shake my body before the tears manage to break free. My throat is so tight that when they finally come out it hurts. Like my esophagus is being ripped to shreds. Tears stream down my face and I can't catch my breath. What's my problem? I never cry! And I am not a weak person. But this is all too much to take in and I can't cope.

My body shakes as the tears pour down my face, and I wait for Axl to pound on the door. To tell me to pull myself together or yell at me to take care of my kid, but no one does. So I stay where I am. Sitting in the darkness, pretending the world around me hasn't crumbled into a million pieces.

When I finally come out of the bathroom, the sun is just touching the horizon. The room is quiet. Deathly quiet. My heart pounds and a sudden panic squeezes my insides. What if everyone died? What if I'm alone now? Nothing but me and millions of bodies walking the Earth?

I walk faster. When I reach the living room, I almost collapse with relief. Angus is passed out on the couch and Emily is curled up with him, her head resting on his chest. Joshua is sitting in a chair reading a book. Axl stands at the window, staring out across the city.

Axl turns around. The judgment in his eyes makes me squirm.

"You done freakin' out?" His voice is softer than I expected.

I walk over, so I can look out the window. There are more of them now. "I'm not sure," I say. "You're not mad at me?" I feel stronger, like I managed to cry out most of the fear crushing my insides. But seeing those creatures still makes me tremble.

He frowns, but shakes his head. "Everybody deserves to freak out every now and then. Guess you weren't really prepared for a zombie apocalypse."

A jolt shoots through me, and I have to swallow before I can talk. "Was anyone?"

He laughs bitterly. It's not like him. Axl isn't really a bitter guy. "Guess not."

He's not as gruff as usual, but there's something in his voice I can't quite place. I study his expression. When his gray eyes meet mine I get it. Disappointment. I guess he expected more out of me. Truth is, I kind of expected more out of myself. With everything I've been through, I thought I could handle anything.

I lay my face against the cool glass and close my eyes. "What the hell are we going to do?" I ask. "Everything's so screwed up. So broken."

Axl scoffs and I open my eyes. I take a step back so I can see him better.

"Hell, the world's always been broken. You of all people should know that. It's just a different kinda broken now. We both adjusted to the old way, we'll just have to adjust to the new way too."

For some reason, his words help loosen some of the panic knotted in my stomach. He's right. Things have always been crappy for me, but I learned to deal with it. To survive. I can do it again.

We go back to watching the dead in the streets below. It's oddly mesmerizing, watching them slowly lumber up and down the street.

A sudden knock on the door makes me jump. My heart hammers against my ribcage. Axl and I stare at each other for a second without speaking, frozen in place.

"Maybe it's Trey," I whisper.

"Could be anybody. We left a note out on the damn road," Axl says, pulling out his gun.

Joshua stands next to his chair, and his book lies on the floor at his feet. His eyes are big and round. They take up his whole face.

Axl nudges his brother. "Angus, wake up."

Angus grunts and starts to sit up, but stops when his eyes land on Emily. I gently pick her up. She barely moves. I cradle her in my arms. Her face is so peaceful and innocent. God, I'm selfish.

"What the hell," Angus says, rolling off the couch.

Just as he opens his mouth—probably to bitch more—there's another knock at the door. He pulls his gun out so fast it reminds me of a gunslinger in an old western. Angus nods to Axl, and they walk toward the door. I lay Emily down on the couch, covering her with a blanket, then follow the brothers with my heart beating a million miles a minute. Joshua walks behind me, and he's shaking. He looks even more terrified than I feel.

"I'm sure it's just Trey and Parvarti," I say.

Joshua nods but doesn't say a word. His mouth is so tight I'm not sure he could. I bite my lip when Axl leans forward to look out the peephole.

"It ain't Trey."

"Who is it?" Angus's fingers flex around his gun.

"Some other people, looks like five of 'em." Axl takes a step back and glances back at us before calling out, "What do you want?"

"Just looking for survivors," a man with a deep, baritone voice answers.

"You lookin' for trouble?" Axl asks. "We're armed and we got no problem killin' if it comes down to it."

"No one's looking for trouble. We're armed, but we don't mean you any harm."

"What you think?" Axl asks.

Joshua shuffles awkwardly next to me and his hand shakes so hard there's no way he'd be able to hit anything if he had to fire that gun. Not that I'm doing any better. My legs are like Jell-O.

"We should hear 'em out. See if they know what's goin' on," Angus replies.

Axl nods and turns back to the door. "We'll let you in, but we want you to leave your weapons outside."

"Can't do that," the man answers. "We need to protect ourselves. We've got women and children."

Axl purses his lips. "Then you can send in one person. After we talk we'll decide if the rest of you can come in."

There's silence for a second and I hold my breath. The man says, "Sounds reasonable."

Axl and Angus step back and raise their guns, aiming at the door.

"Open it, Doc," Axl says through clenched teeth.

Joshua stumbles forward and jerks the door open. A black man in his mid-forties steps in with his hands in the air, and Joshua slams the door behind him. The man has broad shoulders and a thick beard. His eyes are dark and intelligent, and they sweep across the room the second he's inside. Taking us all in. His body is as stiff as a board and he doesn't relax for a second.

"That's far enough," Axl says.

The man nods, but doesn't speak.

"Who are you?" Angus barks.

"Name's Winston. I'm just a survivor, like you, trying to get some place safe. I have a small group of people with me and we're trying to make it out of the city. That's all," Winston says.

Joshua and I don't move, and Winston's eye catches mine. He nods and gives me a small smile before looking back toward the brothers.

"Who you got with you? Relatives?" Axl asks.

Winston shakes his head. "My daughter is with me. Everyone else we've met along the way."

"Why'd you come up here?" Angus asks.

"Saw your note outside on the street, thought we'd see who was up here."

Axl lowers his gun and looks over at Angus. "This guy ain't tryin' to hurt us."

Angus grunts and drops the hand holding his gun, scratching his head with the other. "Let your people in."

Winston puts his hands down and walks over to the door, keeping his eyes on the brothers as he goes. Angus heads to the dining room table and grabs his dip while Axl puts his gun in his waistband. Winston's shoulders relax the second the gun is put away.

He opens to door, and his group files in. They range from a little girl around the age of five to a man who's probably in his sixties. They're all dirty and exhausted. I can't imagine what they've been going through the last few days. Why haven't they been able to get out of the city?

"You folks never told me who you are," Winston says.

"I'm Axl James and that there's my brother, Angus. This here's Vivian and her daughter, Emily is asleep on the couch. Over there we got the Doc, Joshua."

"Who's Trey?" Winston asks.

"A guy who was traveling with us. He and his girlfriend went off to Berkley to see if his parents were alive. We said we'd meet him here, in case things weren't good for them at home," I say.

Winston raises an eyebrow. "So you're not from the city and you actually came here voluntarily?"

"We didn't know 'bout the dead," Axl says.

"Was a stupid idea even then," Angus grumbles.

Winston turns toward his group, who are huddled together in the doorway. "Well, let me introduce you to everyone." He walks toward a tall, thin black girl in her early twenties. She has his eyes. "This is my daughter, Jessica. Here we have Arthur," Winston says, pointing to a thin, gaunt-looking white man in his sixties with silver wisps of hair. "And that there is Mike." The man he points to is big and burly, with a black leather biker jacket and a thick, gray beard. He reminds me of someone you'd see holding up a liquor store. "Over there is Sophia and her daughter, Ava." Sophia and Ava stand back away from everyone else. They're Hispanic, and the mother looks to be around thirty with a short, boyish haircut. Her daughter is probably a year or so older than Emily, and she has long, black hair and big, brown eyes.

No one moves. These men have no idea what to do.

I clear my throat and take a step forward. "Well, everyone must be hungry and dirty. Why don't you take turns showering? The men were smart enough to get the generator going, so we have hot water."

"Hot water?" Jessica's eyes get big and a smile spreads across her face.

She's not the only one who perks up. The others smile and shuffle around, mumbling stuff to each other about how nice it will be to get clean. They seem like a good group.

"There are two bathrooms in the suite, but we have a master key, so we can get into any of the rooms."

"I think it would be best to stay together," Winston says. "We can take turns."

The hair on the back of my neck stands up. I'd almost forgotten about the dead. "Good point."

Chapter Eighteen

Wintson's group is nice, but silent. They move wordlessly through the hotel room. They eat and take turns using the shower. Their presence makes my insides feel weighed down by everything going on. We're about to get a big dose of reality and it isn't going to be good.

Emily woke from her nap thrilled to find she had a new playmate, and Sophia was kind enough to offer to give both the girls a bath in the giant Jacuzzi tub. Why didn't I think of that? Who knows how long it's been since the girl had a bath, and the fact that I took a shower myself but didn't even think about Emily was a real blow.

This mom thing is so much more difficult than I expected it to be.

Winston and Mike let the others in their group get the showers first, so they can fill us in on what's happening. I sit on the couch between Angus and Axl listening to Winston talk, and that weight inside me gets heavier by the second.

"The virus really hit us about five days ago. We were naive, I think," Winston says quietly. "We really believed the government had contained it and the West Coast was going to make it through this unscathed. It was just a few cases here and there at first, and since the schools and most businesses had already been shut down we thought we could keep it that way. Then it just swept across the city like a plague."

"My wife got sick first. Four days ago she came down with a fever.

Shortly after that my seventeen-year-old son got it. My wife only lasted forty-eight hours and my son even less. We didn't leave the house, didn't take them to the hospital because we knew there was no point. So they died in our home. Jessica and I didn't know what to do with the bodies. By that point the phone lines were down. I moved them both to the guest room and planned on burying them as soon as I could." He pauses and wipes the tears from his eyes. "It was two days after she died that she came back."

His hoarse voice sends a shudder down my spine. I swallow. I don't want to hear the details, but at the same time I need to know. "What happened?"

"Jessica heard some movement in the guestroom and came to get me. I thought maybe someone had broken in. That was the only explanation I could come up with. So I got my gun, loaded it and opened the door. She was standing there in the middle of the room with her back to me. At first I thought she must have gotten better. It was the only thing that made sense. But then she turned around and as soon as I saw her face I knew." He shakes his head and closes his eyes. "It was worse than any horror movie you can imagine. Nothing can prepare you for how it feels to see your loved one come back from the dead. To have them charge at you. Try to bite you. The horror of having to put a bullet in their skull…" He breaks off and begins to cry. The sobs shake his body and he puts his face in his hands. My own throat tightens.

"He shot his son in the head before he could come back," Mike says.

"What about you?" Joshua asks.

Mike looks away. "Lost my girl. We'd ridden across the country to escape the virus. Had some wild idea that we'd go out to Alcatraz and live there after the end of the world. It was stupid and mostly a joke. She got sick five days ago and went real fast. I was still in the hotel room we'd gotten when she turned. I didn't have a weapon, so I just ran. That was yesterday." He clears his throat and downs the small bottle of booze he got out of the mini bar.

"So what's the story?" Axl says. "They turn and they attack, just like the movies? Do their bites change us?"

Winston scratches at his beard. "No idea. This is just as new to us as it is to you. Jessica and I packed our stuff up yesterday and headed out to find a car. We met Mike, who had Sophia and Ava with him.

Slept in the mall last night and ran into Arthur this morning. We don't know much more than you do, just that the city is suddenly crawling with them and we have to get out of here. None of us had a car, though. Trying to find one with keys in it hasn't worked."

"We have to wait until Sunday to leave," I say.

"Shit." Angus jumps up and starts pacing. He reminds me of a caged animal. "This is bullshit! We don't even know if they're comin'!"

"We can't leave without them," I say. "Anyway, they could be here earlier."

Winston gets to his feet and puts his hands in the air. "Let's settle down. Do you folks even know where you're headed?"

"We planned on findin' a farm somewhere, but that's before all this zombie nonsense. Now…" Axl shakes his head like he doesn't have a clue.

"Well, I think there's safety in numbers," Winston says. "How do you feel about traveling together?"

Angus grunts, but Axl ignores him. "Sounds like a good idea to me. We're gonna need another car, but we can get a group together and find one tomorrow."

Arthur comes out of the bedroom and heads over to join us. His hair is wet and he has a big smile on his face. "Looks like everyone is showered and dressed, except Winston and Mike. There's a restaurant on the top floor with a bar and a grand piano. Who wants to go on up and see if we can find any food that hasn't spoiled yet? The power has been out for less than two days, the stuff in the freezer probably didn't even have time to defrost completely before you folks turned on the generator."

Axl gets to his feet. He rubs his forehead like it hurts. "The booze won't be bad."

"We'll meet you up there after we shower," Winston says, tilting his head toward Mike.

I stand to go find Emily, following the giggles coming from the bedroom. Sophia sits on the bed with a smile on her lips. The girls are clean and dressed. Emily's hair is even more blonde now that it's been washed. The girls play with dolls and laugh like the world hasn't gone to shit. The bath and the company really helped Emily come around, I'm thankful Sophia did it. It will be nice to have a real mom around. Maybe I can learn something from her.

"We're going to head upstairs to the restaurant, see if anything is still good."

Sophia smiles and stands up. "Sounds good. Come on girls."

They giggle and follow her out. Emily doesn't even look at me, and my heart twists with pain. I need to find a way to connect with her.

Everyone in the living room is ready to go, except Angus who sits on the couch with his arms crossed.

I stop in front of him and nudge his leg with my foot. "Aren't you coming?"

"Gotta stay and make sure these guys don't steal our stuff," he says.

Talk about the pot calling the kettle black. I shake my head and follow the others out. "Suit yourself."

Arthur was right. The stuff in the freezer hasn't gone bad. On top of that, there are plenty of rolls, and even some fruit still good. Sophia and Jessica get to work in the kitchen. I try to help, but they're tripping all over me. Domestic stuff isn't really my thing.

"Why don't you go out and check on the girls?" Sophia finally says.

"Sorry," I say. "I don't cook."

"It's okay," Jessica says. "You can help in other ways."

The women give me fake smiles that make my shoulders go rigid. They're humoring me. They think I'm worthless white trash. I swallow and hurry out of the kitchen before they can see the hurt on my face. You'd think I'd be used to it after twenty years.

The girls are running around, playing a loud game of tag while Axl sits at a table, drinking and watching them with a smile on his face. I stand in the doorway for a moment, watching him and trying for the millionth time to understand him. And figure out what it is about this moody redneck that makes my insides unstable.

The soft sound of classical music fills the room and I look around.

Where's that coming from? A speaker? Nope. Arthur sits at a beautiful grand piano in the corner of the room. Playing.

He looks up and gives me a huge grin when I walk over. "I was a music teacher for over thirty years."

"It's beautiful," I say. "You're very talented."

He smiles and winks at me. "You want to hear something funny? I've been waiting to die for three years."

My eyes get so big they're in danger of popping out of my head. I have no idea what he means or why it would be funny.

He laughs and stops playing, patting the seat next to him. "Cancer. I was diagnosed three years ago. The doctors said I wouldn't make it through the year but I did, and I kept defying the odds. When this virus hit I thought, 'This is it! This is finally what's going to kill me!' But I beat that too. I guess God has a bigger plan for me."

"I'm sorry," I say, because I'm not sure what else to say.

"Don't be. I had a good life. Taught at the same school for three decades, had a wonderful husband and a fantastic life. I can't complain."

He's gay. Heaven help us if Angus finds out. "Don't tell Angus you're gay," I whisper, glancing toward Axl.

Arthur laughs and shakes his head. "Don't worry. I can spot his kind from a mile away."

"So your husband, did he die from the virus?"

He shakes his head and goes back to playing. A soft melancholy tune that brings tears to my eyes. "No. Car accident six years ago. It was unexpected and I didn't know if I would survive it. But I did." He smiles again. He's such a happy person. How? "What about you? Have you ever been married?"

I shake my head.

His smile stays, but he manages to make it look sympathetic. That will be a nice addition to our group. Maybe even balance out the moodiness of the redneck brothers.

"What about Emily's dad?"

"Well, that was a long time ago."

I tell him how I gave her up, how I came back to find her. It isn't easy. The guilt squeezes my heart. I really expected to love her.

"You're a good person," he says when I'm done.

"I don't know. I expected things to be different. I thought I would feel some kind of love toward her. When she was born the love I felt was overwhelming, but I gave her up anyway. Now I have her and I just don't feel the same." I stare at my hands, so I don't have to look him in the eye. Will he judge me?

"You'll learn," he says. "You made sure she had a family when you couldn't take care of her yourself, and came back to get her when you knew they might not be able to. If that's not love, I don't know what is."

"But I've been so selfish. I keep thinking of myself first, forgetting I even have her."

He stops playing and puts his hand on my back. "You'll figure it out. Don't be so hard on yourself."

Some of the guilt melts away. Maybe he's right. Maybe I just need time. "Thank you, Arthur."

Angus shows up with Mike and Winston in tow.

"Anything come up missing?" I yell. He gives me the finger. I laugh and stand up when Arthur starts to play again. "I'll talk to you later."

I head over to the bar to get myself a drink and Axl follows. "You ready for another drink?" I ask.

"Naw. I ain't a big drinker."

"Really?" I say, pouring a glass for myself.

He walks behind the bar with me and digs around until he finds a can of mixed nuts. "Mom was a drinker. Not somethin' I really want to relive."

"Understandable," I say. "Doesn't stop me, though. Of course, I guess it's not such a great idea to get wasted when I have a daughter now."

"You earned a night to relax. I'll keep an eye on 'er."

Smiling, I raise my glass. "Thanks."

He nods and walks away, taking the can of nuts with him. He joins Winston and Mike, and a scowling Angus. I take a few sips while I watch them talk. They're probably discussing our plan of action, so I head over too.

"We can go out in the mornin'," Axl says. "We're gonna need one more big vehicle like the Armada, or two smaller ones."

"No electricity," Winston says. "How are we going to get gas?"

"We'll have to siphon it out of some other cars," Axl replies.

Winston raises an eyebrow. "You know how to do that?"

The corner of Axl's mouth turns up and his eyes twinkle. "Used to siphon gas outta my boss' car when I was short on cash."

I laugh and he when his eyes meet mine his smile gets bigger. "You mean the Nissan that you are now driving?"

"Same one," he says, winking at me.

"Well that's a handy skill to have in a zombie apocalypse," Mike says. "Can't say I've ever done that."

"I'll teach ya."

Everyone laughs and Angus pats his brother on the shoulder. "We got lots of skills that didn't mean shit before all this. Ain't that right, little brother?"

Axl nods, but before he can say anything Winston interrupts. "We're going to have to hit up the parking garages to find a car. No other place in the city."

"That shit's gonna be rough," Angus says. "No electricity. Gonna be dark as hell in there."

"We'll need to take a pretty big group," I say.

The men turn and look at me like they just noticed that I was standing there, and I suddenly sprouted wings.

Angus looks like he wants to spit, but he doesn't have his can. "You ain't goin', Blondie."

I straighten my shoulders and meet his gaze head on. "And why not? I'm a good shot and I sure as hell can't chip in by cooking or anything. This is the kind of stuff I'm good at."

"It's not safe out there," Winston says.

"But it's safe for you guys?" I snort and take a drink. Sexist assholes. I'm not usually much of a feminist, but I suddenly have the urge to punch Winston in the balls. "You're going to need a big group and I'm going." I take another drink and turn away before anyone can argue with me.

Chapter Nineteen

"You ain't so bad, you know that Blondie?" Angus puts his arm around me while we walk to the elevator. He's drunk off his ass.

"I did know that," I say, trying to wiggle away from him. He's persistent though, and we end up walking all the way to the elevator with his arm draped over my shoulder.

I may be a little drunk—okay, really drunk—but that doesn't mean I want to be alone in a small space with Angus. I glance over my shoulder, hoping to see Joshua or Jessica, or anyone else who was playing cards with us in the restaurant. But no one else seems to be coming.

"Too bad you got the hots for my little brother. I could show ya what real man is like in the sack," he says, leaning closer to me than necessary. His hot breath reeks of alcohol and dip. Not a good combination.

I roll my eyes and maneuver out from under his arm when the elevator door opens. "I don't have the hots for Axl," I say, stepping into the elevator. "We're just friends. When he's not being an ass."

Angus starts laughing, but it's cut off by a raspy cough that makes me shudder. He gives me a big smile and steps toward me just as the elevator door closes. "In that case…"

I dodge out of the way just as he tries to kiss me. "I don't think so. Just because I'm not into him doesn't mean I'm into you."

He turns and gives me a big grin. "The pickin's are slim, girl. You can't be too choosy these days."

Ugh. He has a point, but that doesn't mean I'm ready to jump in the sack with him. "I can still have standards."

Luckily, it's a short trip to the eighteenth floor.

"Here we are!" I take off down the hall to our room the second the elevator door opens.

Angus grunts and tries to keep up, but I make it before him. And I have the key. The suite is dark when I step in and people are curled up on the floor of the dining room and sitting area. The soft sounds of their breathing fills the room.

Angus stumbles in behind me. I put my finger to my lips. "Sleep it off, Angus," I whisper.

I head toward the bedroom on the right and he goes to the left. When I open the door, I try to make it as soundless as possible. Axl and Emily are already in bed, and the guilt that squeezes my insides nearly takes my breath away. I should have come back earlier.

Axl sits up. "She's sleepin'," he whispers.

I put my finger to my lips again, then strip down to a camisole and my underwear. The bathroom light is on, probably so Emily doesn't get scared, illuminating the bed. Emily is asleep on the right side. Axl lifts the covers and motions for me to lay down on the left. Good thing it's a king size bed.

"You drunk?" he whispers when I crawl in.

I nod and close my eyes. "Just a little."

"Angus drunk?"

"He tried to kiss me in the elevator."

Axl swears. "Moron."

I smile and open my eyes. Despite my best effort, I can't stop my gaze from going over his bare chest. It's the first time I've see him without his shirt on. He has a lily tattooed on his right bicep, and I sit up a little so I can get a closer look. It's all black but very intricate. It's actually really pretty.

"Got that for Lily, my high school girlfriend. It was my first tat." He laughs quietly. "Angus hated her."

"Why?" I whisper.

"Probably 'cause he didn't get much say in my life when she was 'round. Angus likes to be in control, if you haven't noticed."

I snort and quickly cover my mouth, looking over toward Emily. She doesn't move. I turn back toward Axl. "What else?"

He sits up and turns, pointing to his left shoulder blade where there's a confederate flag. "Got that with Angus. He's got the same one."

I roll my eyes. "That's so cliché. You know that, right?"

He shrugs, but I'm not sure if it's because he doesn't know or he doesn't care. He points to the guitar on his other bicep. It has a rose twisted around it. "Got that for my mom. Ain't sure why. I was a 'lil drunk and feelin' bad for her, I guess."

"Why a guitar?" I ask, looking closer at it.

He smiles and it's hard to tell because it's so dark, but I'm pretty sure his cheeks turn red. "She was a pretty big Guns N' Roses fan."

I clamp my hand over my mouth and laugh. "Is that why your name is Axl?"

"Could be worse," he says. "She was into AC/DC when Angus was born."

I laugh harder and turn my face into the pillow, so I don't wake Emily.

"What 'bout you? You gotta have some tats."

I roll over and lift my shirt so he can see my lower back where I have a large purple butterfly tattooed.

"Tramp stamp?"

I roll back over and smile, not bothering to pull my shirt down. Maybe it's the alcohol or the fact that we're both half-dressed, but I'm feeling a little frisky. His eyes roam a little. They stop on my stomach. He reaches out and flicks the silver ring in my belly button, and his smile gets bigger. My heart pounds and my throat goes dry.

"Figures," he says.

"That's not my only piercing."

I raise my eyebrows suggestively. When he smiles and licks his lips, heat rushes through me.

"That right?"

I bite my lip. "My nipples."

He laughs quietly. "You should get some sleep."

"What if I don't want to sleep?" I whisper.

He stops smiling and his stormy eyes search mine. I chew on my bottom lip and my eyes move over his muscled chest to his firm biceps and his broad shoulders. When did I start thinking Axl was hot? I have no idea, but at this moment I can't focus on anything else.

He moves closer and I suck in a deep breath. My heart rate picks up. Then his warm lips touch mine and I come alive. Every nerve ending in my body tingles. I kiss him back and wrap my arms around him, running one hand up the back of his head and through his hair. He moves his hand down my back, over my butt and to my thigh, pulling my leg up around him. He parts my lips with his and dips his tongue into my mouth. It's hot and sensual, and I moan, whispering his name. His hips move against mine and I can feel how much he wants me. The blood shoots through my veins, rising in temperature until it reaches boiling point and my body threatens to overheat. His hand moves up my body. He cups my breast and rubs my nipple with his thumb.

My heart races and I gasp. I had no idea how much I wanted this until now. And I do want him, so much. His mouth moves faster against mine and I have a hard time catching my breath. All I want to do is strip off our clothes. But we aren't alone.

Emily starts to cry, and it's like a bucket of cold water has been poured over us.

"Shit." Axl lets me go and rolls over to comfort her.

I lay still and try to catch my breath. Axl's voice is so soft and soothing as he tries to calm her down. Her sobs puncture the waves of desire rolling over me. But it doesn't go away completely. I want Axl, more than I've ever wanted another man, and I don't want to wait another day. So I lay there, waiting. Eventually her whimpers stop and Emily's breathing becomes heavy. But he never rolls back over to me.

I sit up to look at him. Did he fall asleep? No. He's just lying there, staring off into the darkness. But he doesn't look at me and he doesn't say anything. I lie back down and roll over on my side of the bed so I can go to sleep.

When I wake up Axl is already gone, but Emily isn't. She's awake and lying next to me, and she studies me with her big brown eyes. They are so sweet and innocent.

I smile and brush the hair off her forehead. "Did you sleep okay?"
She shakes her head. "Bad dreams," she says in a tiny voice.

Her frightened expression squeezes my chest. If only I could do
something to comfort her. I'm so useless in times like this. Without
thinking, I pull her close and kiss the top of her head.

"I'm sorry," I whisper. "I wish I could make them go away."

She wraps her little arms around me and buries her face in the
crook of my neck. Her warm breath tickles my skin and my heart
swells with a sensation I haven't felt in a long, long time. Suddenly,
I'm thrust back in time and I remember how it felt to have her inside
me. Lying awake at night with my hand resting on my large belly,
feeling a hard bulge and trying to guess if it was a foot or an elbow.
How much I loved her before I even saw her. I remember vividly
what it felt like when she was born. Holding her and looking into her
blue eyes, her little hand wrapped around my finger. The devastating
sadness that almost crushed me when I had to hand her over to the
nurse. Had to say goodbye.

Tears come to my eyes and I squeeze her tighter. I have to figure
out a way to keep her safe. I have to go out today with the men and
help find a vehicle so we can get away from here, so she can survive.
I have to be there for her now, because she doesn't have anyone else.

"You ready for breakfast?" I ask, wiping the tears away and
reluctantly letting her go.

She nods and we climb out of bed. I throw on a pair of shorts and
hold her hand as we head out into the other room. The smell of
coffee greets me the second we step out, and I almost jump for joy.

"There's coffee?" I ask when I walk into the dining room.

"Pot's over there." Axl is at the table eating a bowl of dry cereal.
He doesn't even glance my way.

My heart jumps while my stomach clenches, but he still doesn't
turn my way. He's so confusing. Does he want me or not?

I help Emily into a chair and hand her a Pop-Tart before going to
get myself some coffee. My throat is so tight I'm not sure if I'll be
able to drink, but I'm salivating at the thought of it. I'll figure out the
Axl thing later. After we get somewhere safe.

Everyone is up, and a few people sit around in the living area
while others are at the dining room table eating a breakfast of Pop-
Tarts and packaged muffins. I grab a blueberry muffin and unwrap it,
taking a big bite as I plop into the seat next to Emily.

"Is that Pop-Tart good?"

She looks up at me with her innocent eyes and nods. I smile and give her a little hug. The coffee and muffins and all the new friends I've made help soften the blow that Axl's moodiness brought.

"Now you're interested 'n her," Axl mutters, shaking his head.

My eyes sting, but he still won't meet my gaze. His judgment hurts more than my own did. I have to fight the urge to cry.

I turn away and smile at Emily. I'm trying. That's what matters.

"We're gonna head out here in 'bout thirty minutes," Angus says, sauntering over to the table.

He looks me over, raising an eyebrow. I roll my eyes. He must remember last night differently than I do, because his chest is all puffed out and he looks awfully proud of himself.

"Who's going?" I get to my feet. I need to get to the bedroom and get dressed, so I'm ready to go.

"Winston and Mike, you, me and 'lil brother over there."

"Okay. I'm going to change real fast."

I run back to the bedroom, wolfing down the rest of my muffin and pushing thoughts of Axl out of my mind. I'm not going to let him distract me. Going out to find a car could be dangerous and I can't afford to focus on anything else.

I brush my teeth and pull my hair out of my face, then grab a clean set of clothes. My jeans are still around my knees when the door opens and Axl walks in.

"Don't you knock?" I say, yanking my jeans up the rest of the way.

"Didn't think it mattered."

He strips down to his boxers and I try hard not to watch. Dammit. Why do I still find him so attractive?

"So, are we going to talk about last night?"

"Nothin' to talk 'bout," he says. "We kissed."

I turn with my hands on my hips. "Seriously? That's all you have to say to me? We kissed and then you just disappeared!"

He gives me a hard look, and his gray eyes are stormier than ever. "Emily needed me and the last thing I want is some chick usin' me to get her through. I've had that. Lots of times. I ain't interested in havin' it again."

A sharp pain shoots through my chest, and I want to scream at him or throw something. "Fine. As long as I know. I was just feeling

a little lonely and thought you might be too. Sorry I was mistaken."
It's a flat-out lie. I like Axl. Most of the time.

"Try Angus," he mutters. He zips his pants and pulls a shirt over his head as he walks out the door.

I follow him out, but do my best to stay as far away from him as possible. My gun is tucked firmly in the waistband of my pants. The men are all gathered around the bag of weapons, arguing over who gets what. I stand off to the side with my arms crossed over my chest while I wait for them to get ready.

"Take a knife, Blondie." Angus hands me a six-inch hunting knife in a sheath.

"Thanks." I remove my belt and loop it through the holes in the sheath, so I don't have to carry it. "So what's the plan?"

"Goin' down the street to a parkin' garage Winston knows of. We'll locate us a vehicle, break in, siphon some gas, and get the hell outta there."

"How are we going to drive it with no keys?"

"Don't worry your sweet 'lil ass. I know how to hotwire me a car. Did some time in juvie back in the day for stealin' cars," Angus says.

"Are you serious?"

He gives me that monkey grin of his and raises his chin. "Hell yeah I'm serious. My friends and me used to go for joyrides in their parent's cars on the weekends."

Of course. I'm not sure why that would surprise me, because it seems like something Angus would have done. "Are we breaking a window to get in?"

"Yeah, only way. We'll break the window and then tape it back up, so's the zombies can't get in."

I give him a smile of admiration. I was right to stick with these guys. Angus isn't stupid. "Damn, Angus."

"Everybody ready?" Axl calls out.

"Ready," I say.

The others nod or call out that they're ready too, and Axl opens the hotel door. "Keep the deadbolt on and don't let nobody in. Doc, if somebody fishy comes up you shoot first, ask questions later. Got it?"

Joshua gives him a tense nod, then looks at me. "Be careful."

I take a deep breath and look around. My gaze stops on Emily and that protective feeling from the bedroom comes back, full-force. "I'll be careful." I give her a quick smile that doesn't feel the least bit real, then head out the door.

Chapter Twenty

The reality of the situation hits me when we reach the lobby. The stench of death is so strong I have pull my shirt up over my nose. The maid's rotting corpse lays in the middle of the room. The stink is only going to get worse. The sooner we get away from this hotel, the better.

I look toward the front door and freeze. Bodies stumble around outside. Dozens of them. Some so close I could reach out and touch them if I opened the door. Men, women, children. It's unnerving.

"Shit," Angus says. "There's more of 'em than yesterday."

"How are we getting to the parking garage?" My voice is muffled from the fabric of my shirt. "We can't go through all these...things." I still can't bring myself to say the word, like saying it will make it more real somehow.

"We're going out the back." Winston turns away from the front door and leads us through the hotel. "Axl and I checked it out this morning. The parking garage is just a block over and there weren't as many dead out this way."

We go past a banquet hall and through an employee area to get to the exit. My heart beats faster with each step. Are the others as freaked out as I am? Everyone looks pretty anxious: weapons held tight, bodies stiff and jaws tense. No one is taking this lightly.

We pause at the exit and Winston looks us all over. "Try not to fire your guns. We don't want to draw unnecessary attention to ourselves."

"What the hell are we supposed to use?" I ask. "Harsh language?"

"That's why I gave ya the knife, Blondie," Angus says, elbowing me.

I curse and stick the gun back in my waistband, then pull out the knife. This means I'm going to have to get close to these things. Someone should have mentioned that upstairs.

"Ready?" Winston asks.

I'm not, but I nod anyway. My neck is so tight that my head barely moves. Winston slowly opens the door and steps out into the alley, and I take a deep breath.

"You okay?" Axl asks.

"I'm fine," I snap. I refuse to look at him. Don't focus on Axl, stay alert. Easier said than done.

I step out behind Angus with Axl and Mike, who carries the empty gas can, taking the rear. It's chilly, which is pretty common for San Francisco, and the sky is overcast and gray. I glance nervously up and down the alley as I follow the others. No bodies are in sight at the moment, but I stay alert. I don't want to let my guard down.

Winston stops at the end of the alley and puts his hand up, signaling for us to halt. He peers around the corner, then steps back. "They're spread out, all over the street. Yesterday when we were out they didn't charge unless we made a noise to draw their attention, so if we stay quiet we should be able to make it to the parking garage without much trouble. Everyone good?"

I nod and the others must too, because Winston dashes into the street. Angus follows him and I stay right on his heels, holding the knife so tight my hand throbs. My eyes don't rest for a second as we move down the street. I glance from the road in front of me to the bodies we run past, constantly on the lookout for trouble.

My throat convulses and the scent of decay threatens to choke me. The dead are everywhere. Their gray skin hangs loose, and they walk around aimlessly, staring at the ground. They don't look up when we run by. Even our heavy breathing and pounding footsteps don't draw their attention. It's eerie and it makes me more jumpy than it would if they were racing us, because I have no idea what to expect.

We go over a hill and the parking garages comes into view. My heart races. Almost there. It's only about twenty feet away now, and so far the bodies have barely been an issue. We're going to make it.

Winston dodges a woman on the sidewalk and jumps out into the street so he can step around her. Angus does the same, but he steps off the sidewalk wrong and twists his ankle in the process.

"Shit," he mutters.

It isn't loud, but it's loud enough for the body of the woman they dodged to hear him. Her head snaps up just as I'm passing her, and her milky eyes look right at me. Before I even have a chance to react, she reaches out and grabs my arm. She moans. I bite down on my lip to keep from screaming as I swing my knife at her. She yanks my arm. It pulls me off balance and I stumble. The blade misses her head and my knife slices through her throat instead.

Black goo oozes from the gash and slides down the blade of my knife as I rip it from her throat. The stink makes my eyes water. She moans louder, but I'm not sure if it's because she's in pain or if she's hungry for my blood. Whatever it is, it's loud enough to get the attention of a few of the other bodies around us. Two heads snap up, then three more. It's like a domino effect, and before I know it more of the dead have turned my way. Too many to count while struggling for my life.

My pulse kicks up a few notches and I scream as I struggle with the woman. The bodies are everywhere and we need to get moving. But her grip is strong and her fingers dig into my skin. She desperately tries to pull my arm toward her mouth. I'm trying to free myself from her grasp when Axl runs up and jams his knife right into her eye socket. Her hands go slack and she drops to the ground.

"You 'kay?" Axl asks, grabbing my arm.

His eyes dart around, surveying the area, and I do the same. Angus is limping, but he stabs an elderly man wearing a hospital gown in the head. Winston has a similar battle going on, only his is with a woman who had to weigh over three hundred pounds when she was alive. He has to slam her in the head with a club several times before she goes down.

I nod at Axl and glance over my shoulder. Mike is behind us. He stabs another body in the head, then runs forward.

"Let's get to the garage," he says.

I run between Axl and Mike, with Angus limping down the sidewalk in front of us. More bodies have noticed the commotion and are coming to life around us. Moaning, walking or running toward us with arms extended. Winston is in the lead. He bludgeons body after body in the head with his club. He's not holding back.

"Stairs!" he calls, charging into the dark parking garage.

I pull my flashlight out of my back pocket and flip it on as we run, following Angus and Winston up the stairs. Angus hobbles as fast as he can, but he starts to fall behind.

"Help your brother." I shove Axl away from me and toward Angus, then turn to Mike. "Can they climb up stairs?"

"Yup, but we're faster," he says. "We'll get up a few floors and block the stairs."

I nod and pick up the pace. I pass Axl, who is now helping Angus, and charge ahead.

"Here!" Winston yells when we reach the fourth floor.

Rounding the corner, I find him struggling with a Coke machine. I jam my knife back in the sheath and help Winston push the machine toward the stairs. The muscles in my arms ache as I struggle to push it forward. I grit my teeth and shove as hard as I can, screaming in exertion. I'm not sure how much help I'm being, but it slowly begins to move. Then Mike comes over to help and it really gets going. We're almost to the top of the stairs when Angus and Axl make it up.

"The other one!" Winston calls.

I let the other two men struggle with the machine that's almost to the stairs and turn toward the other. Angus leans against the wall to rest, while Axl rushes to help. We reach the second machine at the same time. Axl's face is red and sweaty before we start pushing. We work together, but it's slow moving. We're only halfway there when Winston and Mike come to help. Footsteps echo through the stairwell, getting closer by the second.

"Got one!" Angus calls from behind.

I'm not sure if he's talking about a car or a body, but I don't look. I focus on getting the machine to the stairs. It only takes a few seconds once all four of us are pushing it, and before the dead even get close we have the stairwell blocked.

"Little help," Angus calls.

I'm out of breath and exhausted, but I spin around anyway. Two bodies lurch toward him. Before I can even move, Winston steps forward and slams them in the head with his club, one right after the other. Black ooze sprays everywhere and the foul smell fills the parking garage.

"Damn they stink." Angus waves his hand in front of his face. He nudges the nearest one with the toe of his boot. "Why no blood?"

"Because their hearts aren't beating anymore." Winston wipes his club on the dead man's shirt. "You stop bleeding when your heart stops pumping blood through your body."

"Damn, Hollywood sure got it wrong," Axl says, shaking his head.

"Big surprise," Mike mutters.

I step over the bodies and head toward the cars, pulling my flashlight back out. "Let's get on with this."

It only takes us a couple minutes to locate a few vehicles big enough. The parking garage is full.

"We got us a couple minivans and an Explorer. What'd you think?" Angus asks Winston.

"Think we should take two, just in case?" Winston looks through the window of the Explorer.

"Not a bad idea," Axl says. "Be nice to already have the space if there's car trouble."

"Okay then. We'll take that there minivan and this here Explorer." Angus takes the club out of Winston's hand and slams it against the window of the van. It shatters with one blow. "Take care of the Explorer while I get this one started," he says, tossing the club back to Winston.

Winston looks over toward Mike and me. "Keep your eyes open, we're making a lot of noise."

I nod and pull out my knife, scanning the garage. Moans come from the stairwell where the dead pound against the vending machines. They're shaking and rattling so hard that I start to really worry they'll get pushed over.

The glass shatters on the Explorer and I let out a little yelp of surprise. Angus rolls his eyes, but I ignore it and go back to scanning the garage. My heart pounds so hard in my ears that I can hardly hear anything else.

Angus works fast. Within minutes the engine roars to life. "This one's almost full," he says, hopping down. He winces when he puts weight on the ankle and limps over to the Explorer.

"We got company," Mike says to me.

Moans of the dead, much closer than the ones coming from the stairs, make me spin around. Two bodies lumber toward us. I inhale sharply, but the stink of death hits me so hard I regret it immediately.

My hand tightens on my knife and I follow Mike toward them. He takes the bigger one, a man in a suit, and I take what used to be a teenage boy. The boy charges more aggressively than most of the others we've come across, and I swing my knife, catching him in the side of the head. The blade cuts through the bone with a crack and slides deep into his brain. His body collapses, taking my knife with him. When I yank it out I hold my breath so I don't have to breathe in the stink floating off the body.

"Nice shot." Mike gives me a big grin. "You're pretty tough. What'd you do for a living before all this?"

"I was a stripper."

He throws back his head and laughs. "I would've guessed Pilates instructor or something. Them chicks always seemed tough and fit."

I smile just as the second car roars to life behind us. "Let's get the hell out of here."

Mike nods and we turn back to the cars.

"Explorer needs some gas," Angus says.

Axl swears and runs his hand through his hair. "Can it wait until we're out of the city?"

"Doubt it. Got less than a quarter of a tank."

"Shit," Axl mutters. "Well, let's break open a few more cars and see what we can siphon." He turns to me and Mike. "You okay taking watch?"

We nod and he takes off with Angus and Winston to break into a few more cars. Mike and I follow the others, constantly scanning the garage. Every sound makes me jump, and I have to wipe my palms on my pants. They're moist with sweat. The dead pound on the vending machines. Their banging and moans echo through the garage. Otherwise, we don't see a thing.

"Doubt too many people died in a parking garage," Mike says.

"Probably not." We keep our eyes open, anyway. I'm on edge. Everything is still so surreal. My brain is having a difficult time registering what's happening. Bodies trying to eat us. It's nuts.

I need a distraction. Mike scratches his beard. He's a burly guy with an arm full of tattoos, a Harley Davidson shirt and a leather jacket. "What about you? What'd you do before this virus hit?"

"Physical therapist."

"For real?"

He grins and nods.

"I was going to guess tattoo artist or truck driver."

"Don't judge a book by its cover, girlie," he says with a wink.

"This one's full!" Axl yells from a small, black two-door car. Angus has the gas can. He limps over to his brother.

The vending machines rattle and the moans get even louder. Are the bodies getting anxious, or are there more of them? I just pray we can get back to the safety of our hotel. Soon.

The screeching of metal fills the air. I spin around just as the vending machines come crashing down.

"Shit!" Mike backs away with his gun raised.

I'm frozen. Dozens of dead spill out of the stairway, tripping over one another, climbing over the vending machines. Clawing their way toward us. Moaning. Screaming. Desperate to get through.

Mike yells, "They're coming! Let's get out of here. Now!"

I snap out of it and take off after Mike. The moans follow us as we charge toward the minivan. Fear twists inside me, like something alive, coiling around my intestines. I don't stop running, but I glance over my shoulder to make sure everyone else is okay. Looking for Axl. He's with Angus, helping him walk. Angus must have really hurt his ankle.

"Get in the driver's seat!" I shout to Mike, spinning around to face the horde of undead charging us.

I switch weapons. The dead stumble toward me, their mouths hanging open and their arms raised. Unearthly moans come from their bodies that grow louder with each step they take. The stink of decay floats through the air, and the hair on the back of my neck stands up. I take a deep breath and aim my gun at the head of the closest one. I squeeze the trigger and barely register the loud boom that echoes through the vacant parking garage, briefly cutting off the moans of the dead. The body drops to the ground and I turn toward the next one, hitting him in the skull. I do the same with another and another, but they keep coming.

Axl is beside me, pulling my arm toward the van. "Let's go!"

I walk backward, firing as I go. Two more go down, but there are five left. They move faster, like the sound of our gunfire is driving them forward. Their moans have morphed into angry screams, and their outstretched arms flail around as if they're trying to grab me from five feet away. It's like nothing I've ever seen before.

I throw myself into the van, right behind Axl. Mike doesn't wait for the door to shut. He hits the gas, peeling out as I pull the door shut.

I'm out of breath and my heart pounds. "Are we all here?"

"Angus and Winston are in the Explorer," Axl says.

"Did we get enough gas?" Mike calls back.

"May have 'nough to get us out of the city, but I doubt it."

My hair is sticky with sweat. I rake my fingers through it. My hands shake. "We can always siphon from the other cars and split it up evenly between the three if we have to."

Axl cocks his head to the side and the corner of his mouth turns up. "Damn girl. How'd you get so smart?"

I shrug. "Necessity."

Chapter Twenty-One

When the cars pull into the parking lot of the Mark Hopkins, it draws the attention of every body on the street. Before we even have a chance to turn the cars off the dead are stumbling across the parking lot toward us.

Luckily, we aren't far from the front door. I hop out of the van and charge toward the entrance of the hotel with the others. I make it just as one of the dead grabs Winston from behind. He easily shakes the man off and slams his club against the side of his head. None of the other bodies even come close to us.

We stumble inside and I lean against the wall, trying to catch my breath. Winston locks the door, and I will myself to relax. We made it. Too bad my heart hasn't figured that out yet. It's pounding faster than a dozen charging horses.

Axl stops next to me. How does he still look so laid back? "You notice the other car in front of the hotel?"

I shake my head, still gasping.

"Big red Cadillac SUV. Somebody's here."

"Maybe it's Trey and Parvarti," I say hopefully.

He purses his lips. "Could be. Then we could get the hell outta this city."

"Well, let's be prepared," Winston says. "Keep an eye open for others, just in case. Especially when the elevator comes out on the eighteenth floor. I don't want to be taken by surprise in case it's someone hostile."

"Good thinkin'," Angus says grudgingly.

Guess he still isn't thrilled to be in such a mixed group. Seems like an idiotic concern with everything else that's going on in the world. He should just be thankful none of us are trying to eat his face off.

"Maybe we should stop on one of the lower floors and sneak up the stairs, just in case?" Mike suggests.

Makes sense. The others nod their assent and we hop on the elevator, riding it to the fifteenth floor. From there we take the stairs, walking as quietly as possible. I'm tense and my heart is racing yet again. I'm probably going to have to get used to it. Seems like things are going to be tense from now on. At least until we find somewhere safe to live. If there is such a place.

When we reach the door to the eighteenth floor, Winston pauses. Luckily there's a small window so we can get a better idea of what we're dealing with.

"It's clear," he whispers.

No one says anything, and the muscles in my hand clench automatically as I follow him down the hall, flexing around my gun. He slowly swipes the key, turns the doorknob as silently as possible, and pushes the door open. But the deadbolt is on, just like it's supposed to be.

"Coming!" Jessica yells from inside. Her voice is level and calm, so I immediately relax.

The door swings open. Winston looks past her, into the room. "Everything good?"

"Yeah." She turns to Angus, Axl, and me. "Those friends of yours showed up."

I let out a sigh of relief and tuck the gun back in my waistband. "Thank God."

I hurry inside, smiling when I spot Trey and Parvarti in the sitting room with the others. Good thing Joshua stayed behind since he was the only one here who would have recognized them.

"Thank God you're okay!" Parvarti says, running over to hug me. "I was so worried when we got here and Joshua was the only person we knew. I thought for sure something had happened to you!"

Trey's eyes meet mine and he smiles, but it's strained. His demeanor is different. He seems older and not as soft.

"What happened?"

"They were gone. My parents, my grandparents, my brother and his family. All dead before we even got there." He turns and tilts his head toward a teenage boy across the room. He's tall and thin, and Asian. Clearly not related to Trey. He looks like he's around seventeen. "Found my neighbor's son, though."

The kid waves and smiles. It looks genuine. Guess he's happy to be with other survivors. "I'm Al. Nice to meet everyone!"

"Great," Angus mutters. "More diversity."

My jaw clenches. So does my fist. I want to punch him, but Trey catches my eye and shakes his head. He handles Angus's bigotry better than I do, and it isn't even directed toward me.

I put my back to Angus. "I'm sorry, Trey." I pause and bite my lip. I'm hesitant to ask the next question. "Had they turned yet?"

"No, thank God. Although I wish I had known before we left so I could have put them out of their misery. I hate the idea of them walking around like that..." He clears his throat and looks away. "We didn't know about the zombies until we got to the city. We saw a few people walking around and stopped to see if we could help them. Al told us not to, that they could be zombies. We thought he was nuts of course."

Axl raises an eyebrow at Al, who just shrugs. "I was a huge fan of The Walking Dead graphic novels. Living it isn't quite as exciting."

There are a few nervous and strained chuckles throughout the room. His face turns red, but he smiles.

"I'm just glad Vivian suggested meeting. I don't know what we'd do if Parv and I were on our own." Trey puts his arm around Parvarti, who leans into him. "Although, meeting in the city may not have been the best idea I ever had."

"No shit, Sherlock," Angus grunts.

"We didn't know there were going to be zombies," I say, rolling my eyes. "How the hell could we have guessed that?"

Axl throws himself on the couch and closes his eyes. He looks exhausted. "If it weren't for the dead walkin' around, this place would be ideal to hang out in for a while."

I move closer to him without thinking, then stop when I remember our argument. He doesn't want me around. "You should get some sleep, Axl."

He snorts and shakes his head. "I'll sleep when I'm dead. Long as one of them bastards don't get me."

"Is it just like the movies, then?" Al asks. "Do you turn if you get bitten?"

"We don't know anything really," Winston says. "We're just guessing at this point."

"I ain't takin' no risks." Angus spits into his can. I'm not the only one in the room who cringes. "One of them bastards gets near me and I'll bash his brains in."

He spits into the can again and I look away. My eyes land on Ava, who sits on her mom's lap. Where's Emily?

My insides constrict. I'm not sure why. A gut feeling maybe, but something just doesn't feel right. "Emily?"

Sophia looks up. "I haven't seen her for a while, but she's around here somewhere. The girls were playing but Ava looked tired, so I made her sit down. Emily was coloring just a little bit ago."

I head back toward the master bedroom. "Maybe she got tired too."

She isn't in bed, and the room is empty. The bathroom door is shut and I knock lightly, but there's no response. I push the door open. Empty too.

"She back here?" Axl comes in the room behind me.

"No. Maybe she's in the other bedroom."

"She ain't," he says, turning around.

"What do you mean she isn't?" I call, running after him.

"I mean, 'she ain't.'"

My heart pounds and my stomach twists into knots. Where could she be? How could she have disappeared?

"Where's Emily?" Axl yells at Sophia when we get in the other room.

Sophia's eyebrows shoot up and her eyes get huge. "She's not back there?"

"If she was back there would I be askin'?" Axl snaps. "When'd you see her last?"

"I—I don't know. She was coloring at the table—"

"She couldn't have gone anywhere," Joshua says. "The deadbolt was on the whole time you were gone."

"Except when we went down to the car," Trey says.

The room spins. I grab onto the back of a chair, trying to steady myself. "What do you mean?"

Trey clears his throat and looks down. He won't meet my eyes.

Why won't he meet my eyes? "Joshua and I went out to the car to get an atlas. We left the deadbolt off while we were gone."

"You went out and just left the door open?" Axl yells. "What the hell was you thinkin'?" Axl gets in Trey's face.

Trey chews on his lip. Parvarti steps to his side and rubs his arm. She tries to comfort him. *Him.* Emily is the one missing and Parvarti is checking to see if Trey's okay.

I want to throw up. She could be out there. Alone.

Joshua's face is white, but he steps forward. "We weren't thinking." His body shakes, like he's afraid Axl may deck him. Maybe he will.

The severity of the situation hits hard and the room roars to life. Everyone talks at once, Sophia's crying. I'm frozen, squeezing the back of the chair like it's her neck. No. This isn't her fault. It's mine. I should have been here. I should have been watching Emily. But I was out running around, trying to prove I'm some kind of hero.

Jessica pats the sobbing Sophia on the back, whispering that it's okay. That we'll find her. Then reality slams into me like a baseball bat to the head and I start to shake. Emily's gone and she's alone. And there are zombies.

Tears come to my eyes and the knot in my stomach twists even tighter. Crying isn't like me. I guess this world has changed me into a blubbering fool. "Where could she have gone?"

"Maybe she went lookin' for her parents," Axl says.

Jessica's head snaps up and her eyes narrow on me. "I thought you were her mom."

My face gets warm. "I am. I mean, I'm not but—It's complicated."

"You done yappin'?" Axl snaps. "'Cause we got a little girl to find."

Arthur gets to his feet slowly, like the movement hurts. But his face is determined. "What's the plan?"

Axl grabs a few more guns out of a bag, not even looking up. "You comin'?"

He nods and Axl thrusts a gun at him. Arthur puts his hands up. "Never shot one before, doubt I'd be able to hit anything. Give me a knife."

Axl practically throws a knife his way. He straightens up and surveys the room. "We'll split into groups of three. Winston takes the old man here and Trey. Hit the middle floors. Angus, take Mike and the Chinese kid down to the lobby."

"I'm Korean," Al says, taking the gun Axl holds out to him.

"Whatever. Vivian, the Doc, and me'll go on up to the restaurant and work our way down. Chances are she's there. Probably got hungry or somethin'." He looks everyone over. "Let's go! Time's a wastin'!"

We head out, and I try to keep it together. She couldn't have gotten far. There's no way she would have left the hotel. She'll be fine. She has to be. But I'm still trembling. I put my gun away and pull out the knife instead. With the way my hands are shaking, there's no way I'd be able to hit a thing.

Joshua and I follow Axl up the stairs, calling Emily's name as we go. Axl's back is to me, but I can tell he's pissed by how stiff his shoulders are. I'm not sure if it's at me or the situation, but it doesn't matter. I'm plenty pissed at myself.

When we get to the restaurant, Axl says, "Check out the eatin' area. The Doc and me'll check out the kitchen."

I nod and head toward the dining room. It's big and has a raised area in the center where the grand piano sits at the back. The bar's off to the right. Other than tables, there isn't much around. I can tell right away she isn't here, but I walk through the room anyway, checking under tables and behind the bar. Nothing.

Axl and Joshua come out of the kitchen after only a few minutes. Axl's face is hard and his eyes are even stormier than usual.

"She ain't up here," he says. "Let's head to the next floor, check that out."

Joshua and I follow him once again. He pats me on the back as we head down the stairs and gives me a tense smile. "We'll find her. This is isn't your fault."

"Damn right," Axl mumbles. "It's your fault, you moron."

Joshua stiffens and glares at Axl, but doesn't say anything.

"It's not," I say. But Joshua doesn't look at me.

We sweep the next two floors, calling her name and checking every unlocked door we find. There aren't many. But there isn't a sign of her anywhere, so we head down to the next floor. The second we leave the stairwell I hear movement.

"You hear that?" Axl asks.

Joshua and I nod, but stay quiet. I strain my ears, hoping to hear something to indicate it's Emily and not a body wandering the halls. It's quiet, though.

"Emily?" I call hesitantly. My voice shakes down the empty hall and my heart beats even faster than before. We wait, but there's no response, so I call out again, "Emily?"

This time there's definite movement down the hall. I start to take off, but Axl grabs my arm and pulls me back.

"Easy," he whispers.

He inches forward with his gun raised. Joshua and I fall in behind him. More movement greets us, this time footsteps. My heart leaps in my chest. It has to be her.

We turn the corner and almost bump into the well-dressed body of a woman staggering toward us. Her face is gray and gaunt, and the stench of decay floats around her. I cover my nose and step back automatically.

"Shit," Axl says.

He's too close to get a good shot and before he can move the woman grabs him by the arm. Her mouth opens and she moans as she pulls him toward her. Thick, milky saliva drips off her teeth and her tongue juts out. It's dark purple, almost black, and swollen. Axl jerks out of her grasp and stumbles back. She reaches out to him again, but I step in front of him. I jam my knife into the side of her head. The thick black ooze that runs through her body leaks out as she falls to the floor, covering my knife and getting on my hand.

I quickly wipe it on her clothes, terrified it will somehow seep through my skin and get in my bloodstream. That it will turn me into one of these walking nightmares.

"Nice work," Axl says.

My heart pounds and I'm breathing so hard I can't catch my breath.

"Holy crap," Joshua says, waving his hand in front of his face. "They stink!"

"Yeah, it's whatever that black liquid is."

"Well there ain't nothin' else on this floor," Axl says. "Let's go down one more."

We're heading down the stairs when a child's scream pierces the air.

Chapter Twenty-Two

My feet move automatically. Axl's right in front of me, taking the steps so fast I'm sure he's going to fall. He jumps down, pausing at each landing for a split second to look through the windows. It isn't until he reaches the tenth floor that he pushes the door open and rushes in.

I follow him with Joshua right behind me. The first thing my mind registers is Winston. He's busy pounding in the skull of one of the dead. Emily crouches on the floor at his feet, crying. Arthur and Trey are at her side. Arthur whispers in her ear and Trey pats her back like he doesn't know what else to do. She's shaking and hysterical, and tears stream down her little face as she clutches her arm to her chest. There's blood everywhere.

My feet stick to the floor. I gasp, desperately trying to fill my lungs. All I can focus on is the blood. There's so much blood.

Emily's whimper moves me forward. I suck in a deep breath, thankful for air even though it's thick with rot and death. Axl rushes to Winston's aid and I throw myself on the ground next to my daughter. "What happened?"

"We heard her screaming and came running," Arthur says. "That thing had her…"

His eyes meet mine. They shimmer. He shakes his head and I almost choke on the lump in my throat. She's been bitten.

"Let me see," I say with a shaky voice.

Joshua kneels next to me and we pry Emily's arm away from her chest.

"Mommy." Her tiny voice is like a knife through my heart. She isn't asking for me.

Tears fill my eyes and I can hardly focus on the injury. There's so much blood, and the gash in her arm is huge. I had no idea human teeth could do something like this.

"Get the elevator." Axl pushes his way through and sweeps Emily into his arms.

We jump to our feet and scramble toward the elevator. Trey reaches it first and pushes the button. Emily's sobs dig the knife deeper into my heart. All I want to do is hold her. Comfort her. But Axl is doing it. And doing a damn good job. Her face is buried in his chest as he whispers soft words in her ear.

He runs inside the second the door slides open, but there's no way we can all fit. It's an old building and the elevator is small.

"Come on, Doc," Axl says. "She needs you."

He doesn't ask for me. Doesn't look my way. Why would he? The guilt threatens to crush me. I step in, anyway. All I want to do is touch Emily. Comfort her. I can't get close enough to her, not with her in Axl's arms. I have to satisfy myself by clinging to her hand as the elevator goes up.

"Tell me you can do something," I mumble without looking at Joshua. I can't look at anything but Emily. At this moment, she's the only thing that exists.

"I don't know." He doesn't say anything else, but he doesn't have to. I can hear it in his voice. There's a pretty good chance this is the end for Emily.

The doors open on the eighteenth floor and Axl starts yelling as he runs for the room, "Open the damn door!"

Jessica flings it open. Her face pales when her eyes land on Emily. "Is she bit?"

"Yeah," Axl snaps.

He runs into the room and lays her on the couch, then steps out of the way so Joshua can look her over.

"Get that bag with the medical supplies," Joshua says.

I grab the bag and drop it on the floor at his feet, then kneel down next to him. "What do you need?"

"Alcohol and gauze. We need to get it cleaned off and get the bleeding to stop."

I dig through the bag. Thank God we stopped at Walmart. Thank God we have a doctor.

Joshua cleans the wound and I sit next to Emily on the floor, rubbing her head and whispering soothing words. She's still crying, but only faintly. What if she's turning already? We have no idea how long it might take. If it happens at all.

When he's done, Joshua sits back and just stares at her. Everyone is frozen. No talking. The room is as silent as the outside world. This has to be a dream. It's all too surreal to actually be happening.

"What now?" I ask.

Joshua shakes his head and runs his hand through his hair. "I don't know. Give her some acetaminophen for the pain. Maybe some antibiotics to help fight off infection. Otherwise, all we can do is wait. I'm totally ill-equipped for this."

"You did a good job," I say. "Thank you."

The door opens and the others walk in. Winston, Arthur, and Trey must have gone down to get Angus and the others, because they're with them. Every single one of them looks shaken and pale, but still no one talks.

I turn back to Emily and continue rubbing her face.

"Looks like we're gonna find out 'bout that bite soon 'nough," Angus says.

I sit up straight, ready to tell him to shut his stupid mouth, but his expression is twisted and miserable. He's just as upset as the rest of us.

"Least we know we got two days before she turns, if she don't make it. Damn." Angus shakes his head and walks away.

"We got to git outta this city." Axl jumps up and grabs his bag. "Everybody start packin', I want to be on the road as soon as we can load them cars!"

I ignore the bustle in the room while everyone gets their things together. I can't take my eyes off Emily's pale face. She's drifted off to sleep. The possibility of what might happen to her is almost too much for me. My hands shake. I have to think about something else.

Arthur sits next to me, groaning as he lowers himself to the floor. "Are you doing okay?"

I try not to let the tears in my eyes spill over, but it's hopeless. They run down my cheeks, burning me with their intensity.

"This isn't your fault. You know that, right?" Arthur says calmly.

"I should have been with her," I whisper.

"You were out trying to get a car so we could be safe. That's just as important." He sighs and looks around. "No, this isn't your fault. It's everyone's. Mine included. We all should have been paying closer attention." I start to argue with him, but he shakes his head. "Things are different now. We can't just keep looking out for ourselves and hoping for the best if we're going to survive this thing. We're going to have to adjust our selfish, American way of thinking and include others in our concerns. That goes for me, too. We're going to have to learn how to work together."

Some of the guilt slips away. I'm still to blame, but Arthur's right too. We need to adjust, to think of the group as a whole and not just ourselves. It's the only way we'll survive this catastrophe.

"Thank you, Arthur." I put my hand on his.

He smiles and climbs to his feet. "Sixty-six is too old to be sitting on the floor. I'm going to go help pack."

"Crap," Joshua says from across the room. He's digging through the bag of medical supplies, shaking his head.

"What's wrong?"

"There's a bag missing. Looks like I must have left the antibiotics in the car."

I jump to my feet. "I'll go get them."

"Wait a minute there, Blondie," Angus says. "You ain't goin' alone. Give us two minutes to pack up some of this shit. Axl an' me'll walk out with ya."

I cross my arms over my chest and stare at Emily's face while I wait. Her expression looks pained, even in her sleep. It only takes a few minutes for the men to be ready, but it feels like forever. When they're finally set, Angus hands me a bag and we head out.

The ride down is silent and tense. Axl and Angus have the same expression on their faces and they look more like brothers than ever. Their eyes are hard and their eyebrows drawn together, their lips are pursed and their jaws clenched. It makes my skin crawl.

When we reach the lobby we head over to the front door, stopping so we can look out into the parking lot. It's empty.

I blink several times. My eyes have to be playing tricks on me. "Where did they all go?"

Angus spits on the floor. Right on the carpet. "Don't care, long as they ain't botherin' us."

"There's some 'cross the street," Axl says. "But they're walkin' down the hill."

"Whatever," Angus mutters, pushing the door open.

We head out to the Nissan and I keep my eyes open as we go. But the handful of bodies in sight are doing exactly what Axl said. Walking down the hill.

Whatever. Like Angus said, as long as they aren't bothering us.

I toss the bag I'm carrying on the ground behind the Nissan while Angus opens the door. The back is empty. The bag of medicine Joshua is talking about must be in the backseat. I run up and throw the door open, digging under the seats until I locate it. I yank it out and slam the door at the same time as Axl and Angus. We're just heading back to the hotel when a man screams for help.

I spin around and scan the area. "Did you hear that?"

The others stop. It takes a few seconds, but eventually the man screams again.

I throw the bag on the steps right by the front door and pull out my gun as I charge through the parking lot. The brother's footsteps pound on the pavement behind me. A steady stream of profanity flows out of Angus's mouth. Of course *he'd* be pissed about helping someone.

When I get to the street, I check out the area. There's a horde of bodies, at least twenty of them, at the bottom of the hill, and a man dashes down the street in front of them.

"We have to help him!"

"Leave him," Angus growls. "He's a goner. Look at all of 'em!"

I ignore Angus and turn my glare toward Axl. He has to be reasonable. "We can't just leave him!"

"Shit," Axl mutters. "Come on, let's get the car."

We run back to the Nissan with Angus cursing the entire way. Axl jumps in the driver's seat.

"You're gonna have to shoot," he says, backing out of the parking lot.

I roll the window down and climb up, so I'm sitting on the door with my upper body hanging out. Just like in the movies. Angus tries to do the same thing in the back, only the window won't go all the way down. He won't stop swearing.

Axl speeds down the road. The man is barely visible through the mass of dead. He still has a lead, but not much of one. He's carrying a leather briefcase and a black and white umbrella. He stops every now and then to jam the umbrella into the face of one of the dead. Sometimes it works, sometimes it doesn't. Either way, he's running out of time.

When we get close enough, I start firing. I miss with the first two shots. I've never had to fire out the window of a moving car before, and it's harder than I ever imagined. I take a few more shots and adjust my aim. On the fifth try, I hit my target and a body goes down. After that they fall one after the other. Angus does the same from the other side. I take six down before my gun clicks. Axl comes to a screeching halt next to the horde and he begins firing too.

The man looks up. His face is red and streaked with dirt, and his eyes get huge. Hopeful.

"Run!" I yell. I release my clip and slam a full one in, then take out a body stumbling toward him.

The man dodges a few and heads toward the car. Just as he's about to break away, one grabs him and they both fall to the ground.

"Shit!" I turn around and throw my legs out the window, jumping to the pavement. My feet slam into the ground and I stumble forward a few steps before I regain my footing. Then I take off running.

"Dammit, Vivian!" Axl calls behind me.

I ignore him and keep moving, raising my gun as I go. The man screams and fights under the body and I take aim. He's not making any progress. The head is in my sights. I take a deep breath and squeeze the trigger. The bullet pierces the dead man's temple. It falls on top of the man and I have to kick it off.

"Come on!" I yell, grabbing his arm and jerking him to his feet.

He's right behind me as we run for the car. Axl kicks the passenger door open when I get there, and Angus does the same with the back door. We're barely inside when Axl hits the gas and speeds away from the hotel.

"Gonna lead them away," he says, looking over at me. "You're dumb as shit, you know that?"

"I'm not going to just sit back and let someone die when I can do something."

Axl looks over his shoulder at the man. "You're welcome."

The man is panting. "Th-thanks," he manages to get out.

"So who are you?" I ask, turning around in my seat. He's in his mid-thirties and has dark hair and dark eyes. He's good-looking. Like movie star good-looking, and wearing top-of-the-line designer clothes that barely look wrinkled despite his near-death experience

"Mitchell Harrington," he says. "I've been hiding in my condo for a week. I was supposed to have a ride out of the city, but they never showed. I decided to get out myself, but those things attacked me." He shakes his head. "What's going on?"

"You're smack dab in the middle of a zombie apocalypse," Angus says.

Mitchell shakes his head again, like he can't focus or doesn't believe us. All the color drains from his face and his eyes get huge. "You have to be kidding."

I push a mass of blonde hair out of my eyes and point back the way we just came. "Wasn't that horde of dead bodies attacking you proof enough?"

He turns even paler and sits back in his seat, clutching his briefcase tightly to his chest.

Axl does a quick drive around the block before taking us back to the hotel. We pull into the parking lot and jump out. There aren't many bodies around; most seem to have run off after Axl when he drove away the first time, but there are still a few.

Mitchell drags his feet, so I grab his arm and pull him forward. "You're going to have to move faster than that if you don't want to get eaten."

I scoop up the bag of medicine as I walk by. Once we're inside, the three of us walk to the elevator with Mitchell trailing slowly behind us.

"The Mark Hopkins?"

I slam my finger against the button. "We're on the eighteenth floor."

"The California suite? That's over $7,000 a night."

"Not anymore it ain't," Angus says.

Mitchell must be in shock. He won't stop clutching that stupid briefcase to his chest like it's some kind of life preserver. This guy is going to be a major pain in the ass. Not only that, but I'm not sure he's going to be able to adjust to the fact that he's no longer rich and important.

"So what did you do, before the virus hit?" I ask as the elevator goes up.

"I started my own Internet dating service," he says. "Soul mate dot com."

Angus and Axl both laugh, but I don't. It may sound lame, but that service was huge. This guy was loaded. Not that it's going to do him any good now.

"How'd that treat you?" Angus asks with a smirk.

Mitchell doesn't seem to understand that Angus is making fun of him. "I made fifteen million dollars last year."

Angus's mouth drops open just as the elevator door does the same.

Chapter Twenty-Three

"So where are you guys headed?" Mitchell asks.

He sits on a chair in the living area still clutching the briefcase while he watches everyone else pack. He hasn't moved from that spot since he got here, and I'm beginning to wonder if he's ever going to snap out of it.

I'm on the couch across from him with Emily's head is in my lap. She's out cold. "I think we're going to try and head into the country somewhere. Find a farm or vineyard that's been abandoned and try to survive."

Mitchell looks down at the briefcase like it holds the answers to all of life's problems. I wish it did. Maybe there's a genie in there, and if we rub it he'll pop out and make all this horror disappear. Or at least find us a safe place to live out the rest of our sad lives.

"You could come with me to Vegas," Mitchell says so quietly that I wonder if I heard him wrong. I search his face, but he doesn't even blink. Yup, I heard him right. He must be insane.

Before I can say anything Angus, who just happened to be walking by when Mitchell said it, cuts me off. "Hell no, boy. We ain't goin' to Vegas."

"Well, it's not Vegas exactly," Mitchell says. "It's um…in the Mojave Desert." He pauses and licks his lips nervously. His grip on the briefcase tightens. "It's about an hour outside of Vegas. In the middle of nowhere, really."

I shake my head. He's nuts alright. "Why would we want to go to the middle of nowhere?"

"Shit. We gotta find someplace green where we can grow us some food. Not the desert. That's the dumbest idea I ever heard," Angus barks.

"Well, it's not like there's nothing there." Mitchell clears his throat like he's working up to something big. "There's a, um—a shelter there."

My heart races. What's he talking about? Why doesn't he just come out with it? "What kind of shelter?"

A few other people have stopped packing and are now standing around, staring at Mitchell. No one talks.

"It's an old missile silo that was built by the government back during the Cold War. There was this company that bought a bunch of them and renovated them. They sold them off to wealthy clients as a place to go in the event of a catastrophe."

"Wait a minute!" Al steps forward. He's practically bouncing up and down. "Are you talking about the Atlas missile silos?" Mitchell nods and Al's smile stretches across his face. He looks around the room like an eager kid. He acts like we should all know what Mitchell's talking about. "I read all about these places online." He turns back to Mitchell and his eyes are so big and full of excitement that my heart starts pounding faster. "Did you buy into one of these things?"

"Yes," Mitchell says flatly.

"So it's kinda like a fallout shelter?" Axl asks. His gaze moves to Emily's face, slack from sleep. His eyes flash with hope.

Mitchell nods, but Al shakes his head. "It's more like underground luxury condos. These places are amazing. They have all the amenities of the most expensive apartment buildings in any city. And more. Complete with a gym, a pool, a movie theater, and library." Al puts up his fingers as he names things, like he's checking items off a list. "They even had small hospitals. But most importantly, they were stocked with enough provisions to sustain a group of people underground for five years."

My heart leaps. A small spark of hope lights up inside me. Five years? That's better than anything we could do at a farm.

No one speaks for a second, and then all at once the room

explodes. Mitchell just sits in his chair, still clutching his briefcase while everyone shouts questions at him. He doesn't answer any.

"Okay, everyone!" Winston calls. "Let's quiet down so we can get some answers." He looks at Mitchell. "You're saying there's a shelter out there you can take us to and there will be room for everyone?"

Mitchell nods, but then shrugs. "There should be."

"What do you mean, 'should be?'" Axl asks. "We ain't drivin' you all the way to the middle of nowhere for that."

Mitchell clears his throat again. Why does he seem so nervous and unsure? Is it us or him? "Well, the shelter was made to sustain fifty people for five years, and the condos sold out."

"So you're saying it was full?" Jessica asks.

Al shakes his head. "That's insane. Wasn't it like three million dollars to buy one of those things?"

"Something like that," Mitchell says with a shrug. There's something about his attitude that bugs me.

"So there isn't room." All the hope that had been there a few seconds ago melts off Sophia's face. She hugs onto Ava so tightly the little girl winces.

"That's just it," Mitchell says. "Most of the population has died. What are the odds that everyone who bought one of these condos is still around?"

"Not good," Winston mumbles. He looks at Mike and rubs the back of his neck.

Mike scratches his beard. "So what's this place like? Where is it?"

"It's literally in the middle of the desert. I have coordinates to get there." Mitchell finally pulls the briefcase away from his body and opens it. "And it's pretty much what the kid said it is. Underground condos with all the amenities. A generator, food and supplies to last five years, as well as a state of the art security system."

Emily shifts a little in her sleep and I brush the hair out of her face. We need this. I need to get her somewhere safe. I try to remain calm, try not to get my hopes up. It isn't easy. "So what's on the surface?"

Mitchell pulls out a couple papers and hands them out. I take one, and my eyes grow wide as I study it. It's a cutaway picture of the shelter and it literally looks like an underground apartment building, except it's rounded like a silo. There are eighteen floors underground, with living areas on most of them. But on other levels there's a pool and a clinic, a movie theater and a gym. Everything a rich person could need at the end of the world.

"On the surface it's just a small building made of steel and concrete. It's bullet and blast proof, and there's a keypad for entrance, so the owners can get access." Mitchell bites his lip and sits quietly while everyone passes the pictures around the room.

"So, you're just gonna let us in if we take you there?" Axl's voice is hard. His lips purse and his eyes narrow on Mitchell. He doesn't trust this man. It puts me on edge. Axl is a good judge of character.

"I was waiting for the company helicopter to pick me up. They were supposed to come a week ago, but obviously that didn't happen. They must have all died. I didn't know anything about these zombies, so I decided to just make it there on my own somehow. You saw how well that went." Mitchell shakes his head. "I'm obviously not equipped to handle this on my own, and you people seem to know what you're doing. If you could get me there I'd be more than happy to plead your cases with whoever is inside. I'm sure they'd let you in. There has to be room. You have a doctor with you, that's helpful, and I'm sure there are other skills you people possess that would make having you around useful."

He sits back when he's done talking and stares at us. Waiting. The way he keeps saying *you people* irritates me. It's condescending and arrogant. Axl may be right about this guy.

"So we drive you all the way out there and you're just gonna let us in?" Axl asks him.

"Of course. Why wouldn't I?"

Axl shakes his head. "He ain't gonna let us in. He just needs a ride and then he's gonna leave us out in the desert!"

"No, I wouldn't do that!"

"Why would someone do something like that?" Sophia asks.

Angus spits into his coke can and adjusts the gun at his waist, like he's trying to intimidate Mitchell. "'Cause he's rich and he thinks he's better than us."

"No one is rich anymore," Arthur says, watching Mitchell carefully.

I am too, so I notice the look of contempt that flashes through his eyes. But it's gone so fast I doubt anyone else caught it.

Mitchell meets Arthur's gaze. "I swear I will let you in."

Axl shakes his head, but doesn't argue. Emily moans in her sleep and he's by her side in the blink of an eye. His expression softens and he brushes the hair out of her face. Arthur glances toward Emily too, like he's checking to make sure she's okay. We're all on edge. Like it or not, this guy may be our only hope of survival.

The room is silent while everyone considers Mitchell's offer. Their expressions range from worry to excitement and everything in between. And I'm right there with them. I want to believe this guy. To think there's a place out there with our names on it where we'll be safe and taken care of, but a voice in my head tells me to be cautious. Something about Mitchell worries me. The calm way he just sits in the chair waiting for us to decide, like he thinks we owe it to him just because he's someone special. Someone important.

Winston clears his throat and steps forward, so he's standing right in front of Mitchell. "Look, I don't know if what Axl is saying is true, but he's right. If we go out of our way to take you across the desert, we're going to need some kind of reassurance."

Mitchell's face is blank as he meets Winston's gaze. "What did you have in mind?"

"The code. You said we can't get in without it, so share it with us."

He clutches the briefcase tighter. "How do I know you won't just kill me or leave me behind?"

"You'll have to trust us," Arthur says.

"Like you're trusting me?" Mitchell shakes his head again. "I can't."

Everyone's silent for a moment and Mitchell goes back to biting his lip. He seems to do it whenever he's thinking something through. "I'll make a deal with you. It's about ten hours from here to the shelter. I'll tell you the code when we're halfway there. If I feel like I can trust you. If you get me halfway and I don't think I can, we'll just part ways. How's that sound?"

Winston looks around at everyone else. No one argues, and a few people even nod. Axl's eyes are still hard.

"Looks like we have a deal," Winston says.

Mitchell smiles and relaxes for the first time since we picked him up. "When do we leave?"

"Soon as we're packed," Winston says. "Let's get a move on."

Everyone gets back to packing. Emily opens her eyes just as Axl stands. He stops and brushes his hand against her cheek so gently it makes my heart twist. Emily barely reacts. She turns her face toward Axl, but she doesn't blink or smile or talk. He swallows and gets up without saying anything.

I move Emily so she's lying on the couch with her head on a pillow. I need to help pack. She doesn't make a sound. Sophia darts a worried look her way, but I ignore it.

Winston pauses on his way through the room. "How is she?"

I stare down at my daughter. "She's awake, but seems to be in shock. She still hasn't said a word." I have to stop when my throat constricts. Reality has never been my friend, but this is almost too much to bear. Emily has to be okay. She doesn't have a fever, but I don't like how pale her face is or the lethargic way she stares at the ceiling.

Winston pats my arm, but there isn't an ounce of hope in his eyes. "She'll pull through."

"We're headed down," Angus calls.

Winston shifts the box he's holding and pats my arm again, then heads to the door. He, Axl, Angus, and Mike start making trips to the car while the rest of us get the room packed. I help, but I stay close to Emily. Just in case she needs me. Or in case she gets worse.

Mitchell doesn't move from the chair. Doesn't offer to help get things ready or take things down to the car. He even has the nerve to ask Sophia to get him a drink like she's his maid.

He watches Emily. Every time I look up he's staring at her with narrowed eyes, chewing on his lip. My body is tense. I know what's going through his head.

"Is she sick?"

I give him a cold stare. "She was bitten."

"She's not coming," he snaps. "She could be infected and it's too big of a risk. You have to leave her."

Emily looks at him with wide eyes. She turns to look at me. It's the most responsive she's been since she was bitten. I give her a reassuring smile. "Don't worry, honey. We're not leaving you."

"Yes, we are." Mitchell stands up. He's still hugging that briefcase.

"You got a problem?" Axl says from behind me. I'm not sure how much of the conversation he's heard, but I do know this is not going to end well for Mitchell.

"She's been infected." Mitchell points a shaky finger at Emily. "She's not coming with us."

"We don't know nothin' yet," Axl says. "It might not even work that way."

Mitchell squeezes the briefcase tighter. "We're not risking it."

Axl takes two quick steps forward, getting right in Mitchell's face. "You listen here. You ain't in charge and you ain't callin' the shots. We ain't leavin' that little girl behind, so you can just get over it."

Mitchell doesn't even blink, and he doesn't back down. "I won't be going if she does."

"What's going on?" Winston comes in from the other room.

Everyone has stopped what they're doing. They watch us. Silently. Whose side will they be on?

"He wants to leave Emily behind because she's been bitten," I say. Emily's eyes are still wide, so I hold her hand.

Winston turns toward Mitchell. "That's not happening. We're taking her and if you insist on making it an issue, the deal's off. You can find your own way to the shelter and we'll go somewhere else."

"You'd give up a chance at shelter for her?" Mitchell sneers. He clearly thinks Winston is a moron for making the decision.

Winston stands up straighter. "It can't be the only safe place in this country, so we'll just find another."

Mitchell chews on this bottom lip while he studies Emily. She looks terrified, so I sit down next to her and pull her into my lap. She snuggles her face up against me and my heart aches. If only I had been able to keep her safe.

"What if she turns? What will you do then?"

"We'll take care of it," Axl says. "But till then, she's with us."

"Can you live with that?" Winston gives Mitchell a challenging look.

Mitchell swears under his breath and throws himself back in the chair. "Guess I have to be. But I won't ride in the same car with her." He turns and looks at me. "And you keep her away from me. Understand?"

"Fine," I say, hugging Emily tighter. Her little fingers curl around a chunk of my hair.

Winston turns toward the door. "Good. Now that we've got that settled, let's head out."

Chapter Twenty-Four

I sit in the back of the Nissan with Emily cradled in my lap. She'd be safer in a booster, but there aren't any other cars on the road, so the chances of us getting into an accident are slim. Having her against me like this makes me feel better. She's getting more responsive by the minute. Her face isn't as pale and she twists a few strands of hair around her fingers. Maybe things will turn out okay.

Axl drives and Angus sits in the passenger seat, spitting into his can while he reads the atlas. Trey's behind us, driving the Cadillac with Parvarti, Al, and Joshua, so we now have plenty of space. Everyone else is spread out between the minivan and the Explorer.

"It'll be 'bout five in the mornin' when we get there if we drive straight through," Angus says. "Should probably stop somewhere to sleep. Probably ain't safe to drive with no streetlights."

"Yeah," Axl says. "I was thinkin' the same thing. Gonna be hard to convince moneybags, though."

"Don't matter 'cause he ain't in charge." Angus spits again and stares out the window.

"We're out of the city," I say. "He can't complain about that, can he?"

Axl scoffs. "I got a feelin' he can complain 'bout pretty much anything."

I roll my eyes and look down at Emily. Her brown eyes meet

mine, but she doesn't smile. A dark, red spot about the size of a quarter shows through her white bandage. We need to change it soon. It shouldn't still be bleeding, should it?

Getting out of the city wasn't hard, not with the cars. Only a few bodies were lumbering around in the parking lot of the hotel when we came out, and getting by them was simple. The roads out of the city were clear of cars, and we only had to maneuver around a few bodies. It really didn't take us long at all.

We've been driving for a little over two hours now, and it's getting close to seven o'clock. I'm tired and hungry, and Emily has to be, too. She didn't have lunch and she refused any snacks. I'd like to stop soon. The problem will be finding a good place.

"Holy shit!" Angus suddenly yells. "You see that? Turn the damn car 'round!"

My heart races and I squeeze Emily tighter, like I'm trying to protect her. Too little too late. By the way Angus is yelling, I expect to see a fire or an accident or a horde of bodies walking across the road. But there's nothing.

"What?" Axl asks, slowing the car but not turning around.

"That store! I shit you not. It was called Gun World!"

Axl slows even more and does a U-turn right in the middle of the interstate. He's in the lead and all the other cars follow him. I lean forward, craning my neck in search of the sign that has Angus so excited. Sure enough, right in front of us is a huge store with a red sign that says *Gun World: Hunting, Fishing, and Camping Gear.* There's even an indoor shooting range.

"Good. This'll give us a chance to load up." Axl maneuvers the car onto the exit ramp from the awkward angle. "Need to teach some people to shoot, too. Get in some practice and make sure everybody's prepared. Especially with a bow. Bullets ain't gonna last forever."

"Good thinkin'," Angus says.

We pull into the parking lot and I can't believe it. The front windows are intact and the doors are shut.

"I can't believe no one has broken in."

Axl pulls to a stop in front of the store. "Yeah, you'd think somebody woulda busted in by now."

The sun's shining when we climb out, and the parking lot is empty. An overwhelming silence looms over us. The clear sky and sunny day are at odds with the desolation that lurks around every corner. There's been too much death and tragedy for things to look this cheerful. It should be overcast and raining.

"Seems quiet," Axl says.

"Most people probably died in their homes," I say, but a shudder runs through me. "Not going to be a lot of bodies on the streets if they're locked in."

Angus spits into his can, something that I'm starting to get used to. "Yeah. Maybe a smaller town like this ain't so bad. If they can't get out, then there's no problem."

The other cars pull in and everyone climbs out. No one even has to ask why we're here. Sophia and Jessica start pulling boxes of food out of the car to take inside. Everyone looks pretty tired.

With Emily clutched in my arms, I follow the brothers toward the store. When they smash the window, the sound of shattering glass breaks through the silence and my heart speeds up. I can't stop myself from looking around. I expect bodies to appear and rush toward us. But there's nothing.

The store is pitch black. I stay with the other women at the front while all the men except Mike and Mitchell head toward the camping gear in search of lanterns. Mike pushes a shelving unit in front of the window to block the hole. Mitchell stands off to the side by himself, glaring at me occasionally.

A soft glow starts at the back of the store, growing brighter as more and more flashlights and lanterns are turned on. In no time that section shines with artificial light. They must have turned on every lantern in the place.

"Come on back!" Axl's voice echoes through the building.

I head back with the other women and find camp chairs and tables already set up. We eat a quick lunch and I try my best to coax some food into Emily, but she won't take a bite. She lies on a small cot Axl set up for her, curled up in a sleeping bag and clinging to her stuffed dog. I'm getting more and more worried about her as the day goes on.

"Does she have a fever yet?" Joshua kneels next to her.

"No, she's cool and I cleaned the bite not that long ago. It finally stopped bleeding, and it's not red or swollen. It doesn't look that bad."

Joshua's eyes are full of worry as he listens to her heartbeat. "I don't know. Maybe she's just in shock."

"Maybe," I say. But I'm not convinced.

Axl comes out from the shooting range where he's been busy setting up lanterns and lighting the room so he can teach people to shoot. It's a good idea. I'd like to get some time in with a bow. I've never shot one, and Axl's right. We're eventually going to run out of bullets.

"Everybody's gonna learn to shoot," he says firmly, looking around the room.

His authoritative attitude makes me smile. It's kind of hot.

People head back to the shooting range, some excited like Al, and some a little reluctant like Jessica. Angus and Axl giving shooting lessons? This should be interesting.

Before long, I'm alone with Sophia and Ava. I haven't spoken to Sophia since Emily disappeared, and I don't know quite what to say. I don't blame her really, but I'm still angry and I need to direct it at someone other than myself or I'll go insane. She's a convenient target.

"I'm sorry," she says suddenly.

I squirm in my camp chair while gunshots echo through the store, and I say the first thing that comes to mind, "It's not your fault. It's mine." Saying it out loud actually makes me feel lighter. Blaming her was wrong.

"At first I thought so. But Arthur told me what he said to you and I realized he was right. We need to look out for each other." Her eyes shimmer in the soft glow of the lanterns. "I thought you were a bad mom, running off like that. I shouldn't have judged you. I didn't realize you had just been reunited. What you did was brave."

I stare down at Emily. Her eyes are closed and she's so tiny. Helpless. "I should have done more. Obviously."

"Don't be so hard on yourself. You're still learning. I had six years to figure out how to be a mom, and there have been plenty of times when I had no idea what I was doing. I can't imagine jumping into it in the middle of a zombie apocalypse. As if it isn't hard enough." Sophia stops talking. She puts her hand to her mouth and looks away.

This is about more than just Emily. "What's wrong?"

She glances over her shoulder. When she looks back and her eyes meet mine, she exhales. "I haven't told anyone yet. I'd just found out, right before the virus hit. Only my husband knew."

My throat tightens. Deep down I know what she's going to say, but I don't want to acknowledge it because it's just too scary and awful.

"I'm pregnant," she whispers, and I can barely hear it over the sound of gunfire.

"Oh my God," I say before I can stop myself. Shit. That probably wasn't the best reaction. I put my hand on top of hers. "I'm sorry. I shouldn't have said that. I should have said congratulations."

"No, you were right the first time," she replies. "I just don't know what to do."

I have no idea what to say. No matter what I say I'm going to make it worse, so I just stay silent and let her talk.

"I didn't get to see my husband before he died. He worked at the hospital and got sick in the first wave to hit the West Coast. He refused to come home because he didn't want to expose Ava and me. We still thought they were going to be able to control it then." She shakes her head, and a tear slides down her cheek. "I was so mad at him for not coming home, and when I couldn't get in touch with him two days later, I knew. It was devastating, knowing we weren't going to be able to see him. But after I found out about the bodies coming back I was so grateful. What if he had died in our apartment? What if he had attacked me or Ava?"

"That would have been awful," I say. "He was a good man to protect you like that."

"The best." She lets out a heavy sigh. "What if the baby isn't immune?"

My vision blurs and I blink away the tears. I hadn't thought of that.

"At least we're with a doctor," Sophia whispers.

The birth control pills I got the other day at Walmart come to mind. I haven't started taking them yet. Sex hasn't exactly been on my list of priorities, except that brief moment with Axl, but Sophia's story scares me. I need to start taking them.

People wander out of the shooting range and Sophia leans toward me. "Don't tell anyone about the baby, okay?"

I squeeze her hand. "It's between you and me. But I do think you should tell Joshua soon."

She looks away. "I know. I will in a day or two. When I've been able to process everything a little bit better."

Emily moans and I turn toward her. She's still cool. Almost unnaturally cool. She keeps whimpering in her sleep. Hopefully, she's just dreaming and she's not in any pain.

"She's going to turn," Mitchell says.

My head snaps up. He stands over me, and a dark shadow looms across his face. He has a new toy in his hand, and he flexes his fingers around it. A big shiny handgun that he no doubt learned how to use.

"Stay away from her," I warn him.

He shrugs. "I will, as long as you can assure me you'll be willing to do the right thing when it happens."

"I won't let her suffer and I don't want her walking around like that."

"Good." He walks away.

I look at Sophia, and she frowns at Mitchell. "That man is trouble."

I'm becoming more and more worried about him as the day goes on. Maybe Angus was right. Maybe we should have let the dead eat him.

It's getting late. People begin laying out air mattresses and sleeping bags. There isn't any more gunfire coming from the shooting range, but Axl is still back there with Angus, Trey, and Winston, so I can only assume they're shooting bows.

"Arthur, would you mind watching Emily while I go back to the shooting range?"

"Of course," he says, smiling at me.

"You can come get me if she wakes up."

He pats my arm. "It will be fine. I'll stay with her."

I smile and get up, then head back to the shooting range. I almost bump into Angus and Winston as they come out.

"You gonna learn how to shoot, Blondie?"

"I wanted some time with the bow."

"Axl's a good shot," Winston says.

"He had a good teacher," Angus grumbles as he walks off.

I roll my eyes.

Winston just laughs. "He's not used to such mixed company."

"Well, he's going to have to get used to it."

Winston nods and walks off, and I head back to the range.

Trey's shooting the bow and Axl stands off to the side. "Nice shot." He looks over at me. "You wanna learn?"

"Yeah, I thought it would be useful."

"I'm about done here," Trey says. "Thanks, Axl."

Axl nods and Trey walks out, patting me on the back as he goes by.

"He's good with the gun." Axl puts the bow down and picks a different one up. "Guess his brother was a cop, taught him how to shoot. Picked up on the bow pretty fast too. He's tougher than I thought." He motions for me to come over. "Let's do it."

A thrill goes through me. Bad choice of words on his part. It makes me think of last night. His mouth on mine, his hands on my body. I try not to focus on it, but we're alone and it seems to be all I can think about. He moves closer and his arm brushes against mine. I shiver, but he doesn't react.

"Try this." He holds out a compound bow and our hands brush when I take it. His touch is like fire. "How's it? Not too hard?"

I shake my head while I do my best not to focus on the desire coursing through me.

Axl hands me an arrow. "Go ahead and try to shoot it, let me see what you can do."

I've never shot a bow, but I've seen it done, so I try to mimic what I've seen other people do. It's awkward. I have to be doing something wrong. I wait for Axl to correct me, but he doesn't. He stands silently off to the side and watches.

When I release the arrow, it goes about a foot and a half and way off to the right before falling to the ground. I look at Axl with my eyebrow raised, waiting for him to step in and instruct or something.

He walks forward. "You gotta follow through."

"I have no idea what that means."

He picks up the poorly-shot arrow and gives it back to me. "Try again."

I sigh and put the arrow on the bow, then pull the string back as far as I can.

"No, stand like this."

He grabs my hips and moves me a little, then pushes my left leg back a tad. Then steps back to study me. He purses his lips and his eyes go up and down my body. He's not checking me out, but it still makes the hair on my scalp tingle. I can't help picturing his muscled chest while I remember how it felt to have his hot mouth on mine. My cheeks warm. They have to be bright red.

"Good." He nods. "Now stand up straighter."

He puts his left hand in the middle of my back and the other on my shoulder, shifting my body until I'm standing straight. When that's done, he moves up next to me. His chest presses against my back. My heart races when he reaches around me to show me the right way to hold the bow. His warm breath tickles my neck. It's distracting, but I try to focus on what he's showing me. I don't want to make a fool of myself.

"Relax," he says. "Pull the back string till the feathers are touchin' your cheek. Focus. Let out a deep breath, look down the shaft and make sure the arrow's lined up with the target."

I let out a nervous giggle when he says *shaft*.

"Focus," he says firmly.

I exhale and push all thoughts of Axl and his body out of my mind. My eyes focus on the target, and when I think I'm good, I release the arrow. It flies through the air and sticks in the target. Not in the center, but not too far off either.

"Good." Axl steps back.

A triumphant smile spreads across my face. Axl grabs another arrow and hands it to me, nodding in approval. He even has a little smile on his lips. It's small, but it's there. He's so serious when he's teaching.

I repeat the process, getting the arrow ready and pulling back on the string. Trying to relax. Axl steps forward and once again presses his body against mine, adjusting my stance. A bulge presses against my hip that wasn't there the first time. A thrill shoots through me. It doesn't take a genius to know what it is.

"You enjoying yourself?" I ask. I can't help myself.

"Why?"

I lower the bow and turn to face him, moving my gaze to his crotch.

He shrugs, totally unembarrassed. "You know I got no control over these things, right? What'd you expect? I'm all pressed up against you. It ain't like I've gotten laid recently or anything."

I laugh. "You have a hand, don't you?"

His lips twitch. "It ain't the same."

"Fine," I say. "Whatever."

I turn around and resume my stance, raising the bow and pulling the string back. Axl presses up against me again. The bulge is even bigger than before. I try hard to ignore it, but I can't. Suddenly it's all I can think about. Him throwing me on the ground and screwing me right here in the middle of the shooting range. My pulse quickens and I bite my lip, trying to focus on the target. But it's impossible. All I can think about is the hardness pressed against my hip.

When I release the arrow it flies through the air, misses the target completely, and bounces off the back wall.

"What the hell was that?" Axl steps away from me.

I turn and smile at him, my face warm and my body hot. "I couldn't concentrate." I look at his crotch again.

His expression hardens. "Shit, are you kiddin' me? You're gonna let something as insignificant as my dick distract you? What're you gonna do when you got some dead guy chargin' you? You gonna freeze up?"

I didn't expect his anger. For a second I can't speak, but then annoyance builds up inside me. I glare at him. "What's your problem?"

His jaw tightens. "You gotta get your act together, lady! You got that little girl dependin' on you now. You can't mess around with this bullshit or you'll be dead and she'll be screwed!"

His words sting because they're true and he's right and it hurts that he's yelling at me. "Screw you, Axl!" I say, slamming the bow into his chest. I turn and storm out of the room. My entire body shakes. I nearly bump into Angus when I step out of the shooting range.

"What's all the hollerin' 'bout?"

"Your brother's an ass!"

He chuckles and puffs his chest out. He actually looks proud. "Taught him everythin' he knows."

I glare at him and head back to Emily. My face is on fire and I'm sure everyone who sees me will know immediately what happened. That Axl rejected me and I failed Emily. Again. It pisses me off that Axl can be so focused. What's wrong with me? Am I really this weak?

Not anymore. From here on out I will be the person I'm supposed to be. That I've always been. Strong and resilient. A survivor.

Chapter Twenty-Five

"Everything okay?" Arthur asks when he sees me.
I press my lips together as I lower myself to the floor next to Emily. Her forehead is still cool when I touch it, and a shiver runs down my spine. She doesn't have a fever. That should be a good thing, right?

I caress her cheek and her eyes open. She smiles.

I smile back and whisper, "How you feeling, Sweetheart?"

"I'm hungry."

My smile spreads, becomes more genuine. When I exhale some of the tension rolls off me. She hasn't eaten a thing since she was bitten. This is progress. "I'll get you some food. You want to sit up?" She nods, and my smile widens until my cheeks ache.

Ava's face lights up when she sees that Emily is awake. "Emily! You want to play?"

Emily climbs out of bed, and the girls run over to a tent that's set up for display. They duck inside. Giggles and whispers float through the thin walls. My body relaxes even more. I had no idea how tense I was until now.

"Sounds like she's doing better," Jessica says as I dig through the boxes.

I pull out a loaf of bread and a jar of peanut butter. "I know. I was starting to get really worried. She must have been in shock."

"Can any of us blame her?"

"Not really."

Giggles break through the room and the mood lightens drastically. Everyone seems to let out a collective sigh of relief. Conversations get louder, people move around more. We were all worried.

I make Emily a sandwich, then take it and a juice box to her. I slip my head through the door of the tent and smile at the two girls. "You need to eat, Emily, and then you can play. Okay?"

She nods and takes the food from me. I watch her for a second longer before heading back to the group.

"What a wonderful sound that is!" Arthur says with a smile.

I squeeze his hand, way too overwhelmed to say anything. Axl comes out of the shooting range and my eye catches his. His face is still hard, but the corner of his mouth turns up. He really does love that kid.

I plop down next to Jessica where I have a good view of the tent and let out a deep breath. "I never thought something as small as a laugh could make you feel so good."

She looks toward the tent and smiles, but it looks almost painful. "I was a teacher. There were bad days, but those good days made it worthwhile."

"What grade did you teach?"

"First. It was my first year, but I loved it. I could have done it for the rest of my life." She sighs and shakes her head.

"Well, it looks like you'll have two students," Sophia says.

Jessica's eyes light up. "I hadn't even thought of that. That's something at least."

She's quiet for a second, then her mouth turns down and her eyes fill with tears. "I can't believe everything that was here just a month ago is gone. It still feels like a dream." She plays with a ring on her left hand. A large diamond sparkles back at me.

"Oh Jessica, I'm so sorry."

She stares at the ring like she doesn't know what to do with it. "He proposed on the fourth of July. We were going to get married next summer. I'd just bought my dress..." Tears stream down her cheeks. She wipes them away with the back of her hand. "I can't believe I'll never see him again."

I bite my lip and search desperately for something to say. I can't think of anything. All these people have lost so much, and I just can't relate. I guess there's something to be said for not having any friends or family. The world ended and it barely affected me. In fact, I have more now with this group than I've ever had in my entire life.

"We all know how you feel," Sophia says.

I nod, because I don't want them to know it isn't true. There's something pathetic about admitting you've always been alone.

Emily giggles and it pierces my heart. I'm not alone anymore. I have Emily. And Axl...

I search the room until I find Axl. He's by the gun counter, putting ammo into a cardboard box, and the second my eyes land on him my heart pounds faster. Like it's trying to jump out of my chest so it can be near him.

"I'll be right back," I say as I get to my feet. I walk over to him, and my heart thumps faster with each step.

Axl purses his lips. "Sorry for bein' an ass."

An apology isn't what I expected, and it takes me a second to find my voice. I touch his arm. The contact takes my breath away. "No, you were right. I'm just not used to having someone else to look out for and I need to be reminded. I've always been on my own, so this is new for me."

He his eyes flit down to my hand. "Was still an ass."

"Yes, you were, but I'm used to it."

His face relaxes and the corner of his mouth turns up. "She's a good kid."

"She's amazing."

His eyes search mine, and that thing inside me stirs. He glances toward my mouth more than once and I bite my lip. The desire to kiss him is so overwhelming I have to hold myself back. We can't do that. Not in front of everyone. We need to talk about what's going on between us.

Mitchell appears out of nowhere and the intimacy of the moment melts away. Axl tenses and my stomach jolts. I'd love to kick that asshole in the balls.

"Looks like you were right about the girl," Mitchell says.

Axl's eyes harden. "Knew I was."

Mitchell holds his gaze. He tilts his head to the side and bites his lower lip. "What exactly did you do before the virus hit? You seem to have a very eclectic knowledge base."

Axl's jaw tightens. He shakes his head and turns away from

Mitchell. "Don't matter now. All that matters is I'm prepared to survive this thing and you ain't. How's all that money workin' for you?"

Mitchell frowns. "You need to think carefully about who you're making enemies with."

Axl spins around and gets right in Mitchell's face. "Is that a threat? I ain't scared of you, and you ain't nothin' special no more. You need to get that through your head. We're equals now."

Mitchell smiles and there's something sinister about it. "No, we're not."

He walks away, and my stomach clenches. "He's not going to let us into that shelter."

"Never thought he would," Axl says.

"Then why are we going?"

"Gotta try. It's our best chance at survivin' this thing."

I sigh and all the earlier tension returns to my body. My shoulders are tight and sore. I've always carried my stress there. "I'm going to check on Emily, it's getting late."

Everyone seems to be settling in and the store has grown quiet. Even the girls aren't giggling anymore, and I'm not surprised to find them laying down in the tent. After all the sleeping Emily did today, I can't believe she's tired already, but she seems to be.

Her sandwich and juice are sitting on the floor of the tent. Only one tiny bite has been taken out of the sandwich and the juice box is still full.

"I thought you were hungry?"

"It tasted yucky," she says, making a face that suddenly reminds me of her father. That's a pleasant thought.

I wish she would eat, but I don't have enough experience to know what to do about it. "Are you feeling okay still?"

She nods and I crawl inside, so I can feel her forehead. It's still cool.

"Okay. Are you ready for bed?"

"We want to sleep in here," she says.

I smile and kiss her forehead. "I'll make sure Ava's mommy says it's okay."

Both girls squeal with delight and I laugh. Hopefully, Mitchell turns out to be a better person than I think he is and he comes through for us.

"I'll be right back."

Sophia offers to sleep in the tent with the girls. I help her get sleeping bags set up before tucking Emily in and kissing her on the head. I'm so relieved she's okay that I hug her longer than I should. My heart aches with joy when her tiny arms squeeze me back. She's going to have times when she'll miss her parents, but right now it feels like it's always been just the two of us. And everything is going to be fine.

"Goodnight," I whisper, then crawl out.

I end up on a king size air mattress, and I'm not the least bit surprised when Axl lies down next to me. I scoot closer and my body relaxes even more. Within seconds I drift off to sleep.

When I open my eyes the store is pitch black, and the only sound is the heavy breathing of my companions. Axl's arm is draped across me. The pressure in my bladder is intense, but I'm comfortable and cozy with Axl's warm body next to mine. Getting up is the last thing I want to do.

I do my best to ignore it, but Axl shifts in his sleep and when his arm presses against my bladder I almost lose it. There's no way I'll be able to make it until morning.

Gently, I lift Axl's arm and roll off the mattress. It creaks under my weight and Axl's eye twitches, but he doesn't wake up. I grab a flashlight and head to the back. The chilly air tickles my skin. I shiver and wrap my arms around myself, rubbing them while I quickly make my way to the bathroom.

It's so dark. I should have brought a lantern. The flashlight doesn't do me a lot of good when I have to set it on the floor. The beam shines straight up, casting eerie shadows across the inside of the stall. The hair stands up on the back of my neck. I want to get back to the group. Being in this bathroom alone is freaking me out.

When I'm done, I grab the flashlight and practically run through the store. My heart pounds and all I want is to curl back up on the mattress with Axl. Where it's warm and safe.

My feet stop moving when I pass the tent. Maybe I should check on Emily before I go back to bed. Just to reassure myself that she still hasn't developed a fever.

When I push the canvas door aside, I cover the beam with my hand to mute the light. I don't want to blind them. I pan it around and inhale sharply. I have to be seeing things. I close my eyes and take a deep breath, but when I open them nothing has changed. Emily isn't in the tent. I move my hand away, so I can use the full beam, then feel the sleeping bag to be sure. But it's empty.

My heart pounds. This is stupid. I need to calm down. She probably got on the air mattress with Axl. I climb out and move the flashlight across the room, searching the sleeping faces for Emily. She isn't on the floor anywhere, and she isn't on the air mattress with Axl. I even check with Angus, but he's asleep by himself on a cot.

Emily is nowhere in sight.

My heart almost explodes.

"Shit," I whisper.

She must have had to pee or something, that's the only explanation. I tiptoe through the sleeping group of people and head to the bathroom. Once I'm a safe distance from the group, I start to whisper her name, shining the flashlight up and down the aisles.

I don't find her before I reach the bathroom. She has to be inside. It's the only explanation. But when I step in and call her name there's no response. I check the stalls, but they're empty, and my heart pounds so hard I can barely focus. Maybe she went into the men's room by accident? But when I check, it's empty too and my stomach twists so tight that for a second I'm pretty sure I'm going to throw up.

I swallow and do my best to hold the panic in as I step out of the bathroom. My shaky voice echoes through the store when I call Emily's name. Just like before, I'm greeted by silence. Where could she be?

The quiet sound of footsteps makes me jump.

"Emily?" I say again, shining the flashlight toward the sound.

The footsteps get louder and my pulse races. I take a few steps down the aisle and my hands shake. Why? There's nothing scary inside this store.

The footsteps move faster. Closer. They aren't Emily's. They're too heavy, too loud to belong to a four-year-old. I bite my lip and try hard to ignore the pounding of my heart as I walk forward.

"Who's there?" My voice is so shaky it scares even me.

I turn the corner and slam into something hard and solid. And warm. The flashlight slips from my hand and the beam of light spins as it rolls across the floor. Hands grab my shoulders. I jerk away and let out a little yelp that sounds more like a wounded animal than a terrified person. But my heart pounds so hard it makes it impossible for me to focus or react in a rational way.

"Vivian, you scared the shit outta me."

Axl. Shit. My heart races and his hands slip off my shoulders. I'm still trembling when I grab for the flashlight. I need to calm down.

When I stand up, Axl shakes his head. "What're you doin'?"

"Emily wasn't in the tent. I was looking for her."

He purses his lips and his eyes go past me, toward the bathrooms. "Did you check the bathrooms?"

"Empty."

"Probably got lost," he says. "We'll find her."

He takes the flashlight out of my hand and heads toward the back. I follow him, more relaxed now that he's with me. He's so capable. There's nothing to be scared of when he's here.

We search a few aisles with no luck, and the ache in my stomach comes back, growing more intense with each passing second. Where could she be? The store is so quiet. If she made even the smallest noise we'd hear it. But there's only silence.

We head to the left side of the store, completely opposite from where the bathrooms are. There's nothing this way, but we've checked everywhere else.

The walls of the store are lined with the heads of dead animals. Deer, bear, wild cats and even a few exotic animals. The small beam from our flashlight makes their shadows long and creepy, and their blank eyes stare down at us. Watching our progress. A chill runs down my spine. I shiver.

We turn the last corner and I grab Axl's arm on reflex. Emily is there. She's standing in the corner with her back to us, facing the wall. Not moving.

Every hair on my body tingles. "Emily," I say, taking a tiny step forward.

Her head jerks up and she slowly turns. Axl is still holding the flashlight and it catches her in the beam, lighting up her face in a spooky way. In this light, her skin is a strange shade of gray. Her eyes look blank and milky. She doesn't blink or shy away from the light. She just stands there. Staring at us. I take another step forward, but something about the way she's carrying herself makes me stop. Her arms are slack and she doesn't seem to register that we're standing here.

"Emily?" It comes out strangled and barely sounds like a word.

Axl grabs my arm and pulls me back, but I jerk away from him. "No." A half hiccup, half cry escapes my lips. I cover my mouth with my hand, shaking my head and refusing to acknowledge what's in front of me.

"Get back," Axl says.

"No, no, no…" I can't say anything else. My insides twist so tight it feels like all my organs are balled together into one giant knot.

Emily opens her mouth, and I pray for words to come out. It's only a soft moan. The sound rips my heart in two, shattering me from the inside out.

"No!" I scream as I run toward her.

Axl wraps his arms me, pulling me away from her. I can't stop screaming, and tears stream down my cheeks. Emily slowly moves toward us and the sound of voices fills the store. They echo off the quiet walls and bounce around in my head, mixing with the sound of Emily's moans and my own sobbing.

Out of nowhere people are next to us. Angus and Mike, Trey, and Winston. Maybe more. I'm not sure because I can't focus on anything but the milky eyes and gray skin of my little girl.

My legs wobble and finally give out. I fall to the ground. Axl is still here. His arms still wrapped around me. Maybe he's telling me everything is going to be okay, but I'm not sure if his words are real or imagined, because none of this feels real.

Emily keeps coming toward us, slowly. Her arms are raised and her moans are more deafening. I can't stop crying. My body shakes and all I want is to pull her close to me, to feel her little hands wrapped around me again.

Angus steps forward. He swears and raises his a gun. Aiming it at my baby. When he pulls the trigger my entire body jerks. Emily drops to the ground.

Chapter Twenty-Six

Axl pulls me up and tries to get me to walk. My feet drag. I try to focus on walking. Right foot, left foot, right…they won't cooperate. Axl sweeps me up into his arms and carries me. I'm dead inside. Empty.

He sets me down in one of the camp chairs. It reminds me so much of the morning I woke up sick that it brings fresh tears to my eyes. He can be so gentle when he wants to be.

Axl kneels in front of me. He brushes my hair away from my face and his eyes search mine. "You okay?"

I shake my head. Will I ever be okay again?

"I told you," Mitchell says. "You should have left her behind."

I blink and look up. Mitch stands behind Axl and his eyes are so cold. So emotionless.

Like a flash Axl is up. His knuckles make impact with Mitchell's jaw, knocking him to the ground. Mitchell grunts and lands on his stomach. He rolls over, but doesn't get up. He rubs his jaw and stares at Axl, whose hands are still clenched at his sides. Axl's shoulders heave. Mitchell doesn't move. I hold my breath and wait. Is Axl going to hit him again? I want him to. I want him to beat the shit out of Mitchell. But Axl doesn't move. He clenches and unclenches his right hand a few times, then walks away.

Mitchell doesn't look at anyone. His jaw is red and he won't stop rubbing it. I can't look away from him. I can't do anything.

A gunshot breaks the silence and I jump. Another follows, and then another, and another in quick succession. My body shakes and I squeeze my eyes shut, digging my nails into the palms of my hands while I wait for Axl to get it out of his system. By the time the gunshots stop, my nails have drawn blood. I open my hands and flex my fingers. Three little red half-moons stare up at me from my right palm. Four on my left.

"You're a real asshole, you know that?" Angus says as he heads back toward the shooting range. He spits on the floor at Mitchell's feet as he goes by.

Even Angus—the racist, redneck prick—has more of a heart than Mitchell.

People start packing things up, but I can't seem to make my body work. I failed her.

Sophia walks over and drags me to my feet. She pulls me in for a hug, but I can't seem to get my arms to move. They lay lifeless at my sides.

Just like Emily.

"It will be okay," Sophia whispers.

She's wrong.

Then it hits me. She and Ava were both asleep in the tent with Emily. I pull back and my hand flies to my mouth. Tears stream down my face and I can barely get enough air to fill my lungs. I'm suffocating.

"Oh, my God. What if she had turned in the tent?"

"Shhh," Sophia whispers. "Nothing happened. We're okay."

Axl storms out of the shooting range. "Let's get the fuck outta here."

He starts throws things in boxes and stomps around the room, giving orders. Normally, I don't think people would take it well, but no one argues.

I gather my things. When I get to Emily's stuff, I don't know what to do. My chest aches where my heart used to be. The emptiness takes my breath away. How do people do this? How do they recover from the loss of a child? I've only had her for a short time and the pain is so overwhelming that all I want to do is curl up on the floor and cry.

Sophia walks over with Emily's stuffed dog in her hand. She holds it out to me and I start to take it, but then stop. "I can't. Give it to

Ava. Let her enjoy it."

She gives me a sad smile and shakes her head. "I'll just hold onto it for you. You'll want it one day, but until then I'll keep it safe."

My eyes sting and I stare down at my palms. The little half-moons frown back at me. Maybe she's right. She knows more about being a mom than I do. I'm not even sure if my short time with Emily qualifies as motherhood.

I go back to packing, ignoring Emily's things. Everyone is busy except Mitchell, who sits off to the side, watching us as usual. His jaw is red and swollen, probably sore. I hope it is.

People glare at him as they walk by. If he wasn't our ticket to safety we'd be leaving his ass behind. But he's our only chance for salvation. It's ironic, like Satan ushering us through the pearly gates of heaven. But he's an outcast. Not even Arthur, who always has something good to say, wants to be around him.

The sun is just coming up. We have about eight hours of driving left, so that puts us at the shelter by late afternoon. Then we can relax. All I want to do is take a shower and crawl into bed. Maybe I'll sleep for a few days.

The early morning air is chilly, and I shiver. Almost everyone has a gun or a knife in their hands, but I don't. I'm not even sure where my gun is at this point.

When I climb into the passenger seat of the Nissan, I do my best to avoid looking in the back. I don't want to see Emily's booster seat. I wish Axl had thought to get rid of it.

Axl and Angus load the rest of our stuff, and I stare blindly out the front window. My eyes won't focus on anything. I have enough clarity to know that I need to snap out of it, if I get attacked like this I'm a goner. How do I do it?

Axl climbs in next to me and Angus gets in the back. He grabs the booster and tosses it behind him, and I dig my nails deeper into those half-moons. I want to scream at him to just get rid of it. To leave it behind. Like we did with her.

"What did you do with her?" I whisper. The idea of her being all alone in that store makes me want to throw up.

Axl exhales and his hands wring the steering wheel. Maybe he's pretending it's Mitchell's neck. "Put her in the break room on the couch. Wanted to bury her, but there weren't no shovels."

Bile rises in my throat and I swallow. She's covered. Comfortable.

Not cold and scared. "Thank you."

He grunts and I glance at him out of the corner of my eye. Are those tears?

"We ready?" Angus snaps from the back.

Axl blinks a few times. He reaches his hand out to shut his door, but the sound of gunfire makes him freeze. He looks at me, then back at Angus. "Somebody's in trouble."

Angus groans and I look back at him. He shakes his head. "Do we gotta save every prick we run into?"

Axl slams the door and rolls the window down as he starts the car. He doesn't answer Angus. He just puts the car in gear and speeds out of the parking lot, burning rubber as he races toward the sound of gunfire. I grip the dashboard while keeping an eye open. A mini mall with mostly abandoned shops comes into view. The horde of dead in front leaves no doubt that we've found the right place.

Axl jerks the wheel to the left and pulls into the parking lot, coming up behind the horde. There are a dozen or more bodies, all crowded around a woman who's pressed up against the building. She fires a gun over and over while the bodies close in, but she's surrounded. There's no way she has enough bullets to kill them all.

Where did I put my gun? I scan the car, and my eyes land on my knife. It's hanging out of the cup holder. I grab it and throw the door open almost before Axl has the car in park. I stumble when I jump down, almost falling, but manage to regain my footing as I scramble forward. Axl and Angus are right next to me, and we reach the horde just as the woman runs out of bullets. She lets out a cry of frustration and flips the gun around, using the handle to slam the bodies in the head.

I drive my knife into the skull of the nearest body. It falls and I jerk the blade out, turning to the next one. Our arrival distracts some of the dead from their current target and they converge on us.

While I stab at the bodies, the woman steps forward. I catch sight of a tuft of brown hair behind her. She isn't alone. There's a boy. The woman has him pressed up against the building with her body securely between him and the dead.

The knowledge that a child's life is at stake gives me a renewed sense of urgency. I stab the next body harder, driving my knife right into the eye socket of a dead woman and almost gag. The smell is overpowering, both from the scent of their decaying bodies and the putrid black goo that fills the pitiful creatures.

Axl reaches the last body just as it wraps its hands around the woman's throat. He drives his knife right into the base of the skull and up into its brain. It falls to the ground in a mangled pile of decay. We're all breathing heavily by then.

"Th-thank you," the woman says. She reaches behind her and pulls the boy forward, bending down so she can check him over. "Are you okay?"

He nods and looks over at us. He's tall and thin, with light brown hair and blue eyes. Cute, maybe seven or eight years old. He's terrified.

The woman smiles nervously. "I'm Anne. You're the first people I've seen in days, except for Jake here. I was beginning to think everyone had died except us."

Axl introduces us before looking down at the bodies on the ground. "That was close."

She nods. "They're getting more aggressive."

I stare at the bodies. "What are you talking about?"

Anne runs her hand through her hair and lets out a big sigh. "When they're first turned they're slower, not as smart. I've run into a few newly turned zombies and they don't do a whole lot. They respond to noise, but it takes them longer to decide to attack." She tilts her head forward, motioning toward the ground. "These guys were on me before I even made a sound. I thought they'd be like the others, that they wouldn't bother me if I stayed quiet. But they went after me right away."

Angus leans down, studying the bodies while he listens. His lips are pursed. What's going through his head?

The other cars pull into the parking lot behind us and Anne's eyes get big. "There are more of you?"

"Fifteen of us." My chest constricts. "I mean, fourteen."

She watches the others climb out and head our way. "Where are you from?"

"All over," Axl says. "Been pickin' people up as we go."

"Go where? You have some place special? Because as far as I can tell we're dead no matter where we go." Anne puts her hand on Jake's shoulder, like she's trying to protect him from her words.

"I don't think it's that bad. Most people died in their homes, and if they're trapped inside we should be okay," I say.

Everyone but Mitchell has come over to join us. He stays next to the cars and gives us an evil glare.

Anne lets out a small laugh. "That's what I thought at first, too. Then I noticed that every day there seemed to be more and more of them walking around on the streets. I saw a few houses with doors open and thought someone must be going around, searching homes for supplies and letting the zombies out in the process." She pauses and looks us all over. "Then I saw one open a door."

A few people gasp, and all the air whooshes out of my lungs. They can open doors? Anne was right. If Mitchell doesn't hold up his part of the bargain, we're dead for sure.

"Nowhere is safe," she says.

"We got a safe place." Axl tilts his head toward the cars. "You're welcome to come with us."

Anne shakes her head like she doesn't believe us. "Where?"

"Fallout shelter for rich folks," Angus says. "We found us a rich guy who was more than happy to take us along."

Mitchell must be able to hear us, because he turns and climbs into the car, slamming the door behind him.

"He seems happy about it," Anne says.

I stand outside Anne's house with a few people, waiting for her to get her things together. Mitchell stands five feet away from me. His arms are crossed over his chest while he continues to glare at everyone. There is no way in hell this guy intends to let us in that shelter. I'm sure of it.

"You think the Internet is still up?" Al asks. "It would be nice to get on a computer once we get to the shelter, see how the rest of the world has been affected by this."

I shrug. "I honestly don't know enough about the Internet to even take a guess. I didn't own a computer and I've only been on the Internet a few times."

Al looks at me like I'm insane. "Seriously?"

"My dad was poor and an ass. A computer wasn't on his list of priorities. When I got a job of my own I saved all my money for these." I grab my breasts and Al's eyes get huge. He turns red and looks away, making me laugh a little.

He clears his throat. "Well, I was on the computer every day for hours. I was the president of the computer club in school. Man, I'm going to miss it."

"What did you do in computer club?" Mitchell asks suddenly.

"Um, well the official answer would have been online games. But really we did a lot more hacking. I'm actually pretty excited to see the security system at the shelter. From what I read online, it seems pretty amazing."

"So you know all about that kind of stuff then?" Mitchell asks. "You could say, run the surveillance if you had to?"

"I don't know for sure until I see it, but I'd guess I could."

Why the hell is Mitchell suddenly so interested in Al? I'm about to ask when the others come out of the house.

Anne tosses her bag into the back of the Nissan and nods. "We're all set."

When I turn back, Mitchell has already climbed into the Explorer. I have no idea what he's thinking, but I'm sure I'm not going to like it.

Anne and Jake end up in the minivan with Mike, Sophia, and Ava. She seems nice. Guess we'll have years ahead of us to get to know one another.

Chapter Twenty-Seven

Angus is asleep less than ten minutes into the drive. The silence hanging between Axl and me is unnerving. Does he blame me for Emily or is he just upset? I want things to be okay between us.

"Thank you, Axl. For taking care of me." I have to blink back the tears that fill my eyes.

He his hands tighten on the steering wheel. "You snapped out of it mighty fast."

He does blame me. Or maybe he's just disappointed in me. Not that I can blame him, but I don't want him to think I don't care. That Emily's death meant nothing. "I just couldn't let someone else die. When I saw those things attacking Anne, I knew I couldn't let my own tragedy take over. It's not just me anymore. We need to look out for each other if we want to survive this."

"Not somethin' I'm used to."

"Me neither, believe me."

Axl takes a slow, deep breath. "None of this was your fault. You did the best you could. Not many people woulda thought to go check on her like you did. You tried. All you can do sometimes."

He won't look at me, but his words mean more than he can possibly know. I have no idea exactly when it happened, but Axl's opinion of me has become almost as important to my survival as air.

"You know, just yesterday I was thinking about how sad my life was," I say. "Everyone had lost someone except me, because I didn't have anyone to lose. Now here I am."

"Does it make you feel better?"

I laugh, but it's a short, bitter sound that almost chokes me. "Not even a little."

"It's better to have loved and lost, than to never love at all," Axl mutters. I twist in my seat so I'm facing him. He shrugs and his cheeks get red. "Had me a girlfriend in high school that liked poetry and shit. Knew right away it wasn't gonna last, but she was hot. She had big dreams 'bout goin' to college and gettin' outta the trailer park. Not like I could compete."

"Did you ever have any dreams?"

"Naw, guess I always thought the trailer park and construction was my only option. Don't think a guy like me can hope for much more."

"You sell yourself short."

"It ain't like I got brains like the Doc or Trey. They're smart. They had big lives 'head of 'em. I was goin' nowhere."

"You're smart in a different way. You're every bit as good as those guys," I say. "You've really been a leader here, helped to keep us all safe. You should be proud."

"This whole thing ain't natural for me. Watchin' out for somebody else. Weren't how I was raised."

"You think it is for me? You think my dad was out there in the trailer park helping others? No way. He only thought of himself."

Axl looks at me with narrowed eyes. "How'd you do it then? How do you only think of somebody else when you hear a man on the street callin' for help? Risk your life without a moment's hesitation?"

"Because I don't want to live the way my dad did. Even if it means I may die trying to help someone else. I spent the last two years of my life pushing people away, thinking that everyone was like my parents. That I wasn't worth being loved. This group we have here, it's a good thing. I don't want to screw that up."

Axl purses his lips. He looks so much like Angus when he does that, but he's so different than his brother. So much better.

We stop in Bakersfield. It's not quite the halfway point, but Axl refuses to go any further without getting the code. There's a small shopping center just off the interstate. He pulls into the parking lot. The dead are everywhere, so he pulls up next to the Explorer and rolls down the window. The air is thick with the scent of decay. I gag and cover my nose.

"We ain't going 'nother inch till you tell us the code," Axl says.

Mitchell's in the backseat. The corners of his mouth turn down and he crosses his arms over his chest. He reminds me of a kid, pouting because he didn't get his way. It makes my skin crawl.

"That's fine," Axl says. "We can let you out here. Ain't that right, Winston?"

Winston nods. "That was the agreement."

Mitchell's eyes get as big as golf balls and he sits up straighter, frantically looking around the parking lot. The dead lumber toward the cars from all directions. There are at least twenty of them coming at us, with more off in the distance.

"You wouldn't leave me here!"

"Why not? You wanted to leave Emily," I spit at him. "You didn't have any way of knowing for sure that she'd turn, but you were willing to just toss her aside. You're better equipped to take care of yourself than she was." I'm shaking, and I cram my nails back into my palms, digging them even deeper.

"But she was infected!"

"You didn't know that!"

Axl puts his hand on my leg, and I turn away from Mitchell. He disgusts me, but I need to shut up so he and Axl can talk about the code.

"What'd you say?" Axl asks.

Mitchell shakes his head, but droops back against his seat. "Rose. You could pick any alpha or numeric code you wanted, so I chose Rose. It was my mom's name."

Axl nods. His hand is still on my leg. "Alright, then."

He moves his hand and rolls the window up, then heads back out onto the interstate.

My leg tingles where his hand was. "You think we can trust him?"

"Nope. But we got no choice."

"I think that chick was right," Angus says from the backseat.

The sound of his voice makes me jump and I spin around to face him. I didn't even know he was awake.

"I was lookin' at them zombies we killed at the mini mall. They was a lot more rotted out than the ones we saw in the garage. Seems like they start off kinda slow and get more aggressive."

"Just our luck," Axl mutters. "If this prick don't let us in we'll have to find a place to hole up in Vegas, right when these bastards get feisty."

The swerve of the car jerks me awake and I squint from the bright sun. Axl is turning around.

"Shit," he mutters.

"What's wrong," I ask, looking around. We're on the highway and the landscape is even more brown and sandy then when I went to sleep. We must be getting close.

"Don't know. Mike pulled over back there."

"Car trouble, maybe," Angus says from the back.

I look down the street as we head back to the others. They're all climbing out. Angus must be right, there's no reason to stop in the middle of the road, and they had plenty of gas to make it into the desert.

"How much further do we have to go?" I ask as Axl pulls over next to the others.

"We still got 'bout three hours."

He turns the car off and we all hop out. By the time we make it over everyone is talking at once. I do my best to sort through the individual conversations and figure out what's going on, but it isn't easy.

"Check engine light just came on and the damn thing wouldn't accelerate," Mike grumbles.

"Let's just leave the stuff behind. I don't like being out here in the open," Sophia pleads. She's holding Ava in her arms and her eyes don't stop moving for a second.

There isn't much around, but we're right off an exit and there are a few signs in the distance. A gas station, a restaurant, stores. There's a small wooded area to our right and a huge housing development beyond that. It makes me squirm. All those houses so close to us. If Anne's right and these things really have learned how to open doors, we could be in trouble.

"We ain't leavin' our stuff." Axl walks to the back of the van, jerks open the door and start pulling boxes out. "We got guns and other stuff we need."

I run over to the Nissan and open the back so he can put it in, but it's pretty full.

"Shit." He puts the box on the ground. "We gotta rearrange all this shit. We gotta pull the third row up so more people can fit in and we gotta fit more of this gear in there."

He starts pulling boxes out and I help. We need to get it done as fast as possible. I glance over my shoulder. Everyone except Mitchell is unloading the van. Winston, Mike, and Trey are all busy moving things around in the other vehicles, trying to make room for more stuff and more people.

My heart pounds and I don't stop looking around while I work. Sophia was right. Being out here in the open sucks.

Once Axl has the back cleaned out, we both climb in and pull up the third row. It only takes a few minutes, but I'm on edge. We still have to load up before we can get out of here.

Angus and Axl start loading boxes and I stand back. They're faster than I would be and I want it done. From the looks of it, the others are getting close to having their cars packed up too. Just a few more minutes.

I tap my toe nervously and a soft breeze blows, bringing with it the scent of decay. My shoulders tense and my heart beats faster. I search the area around us. The road is clear and the exit ramp is clear. I don't see anything.

"You smell that?" I call to the brothers and pull my gun out.

"Yup," Axl says. "We're hurryin'."

I chew on my bottom lip and rush to the other car to see if there's anything I can do to help. They're almost done.

Sophia screams and my stomach clenches. I spin around. There's nothing by her, but she's pointing toward the woods. I turn just as two of the dead step out of the trees. They head right for us. Only two.

"Get in the car!" I tell her, aiming at their heads.

I pull the trigger and hit the first one between the eyes before turning to the second. He meets with an identical end. I exhale in relief just as dozens of bodies come racing from the woods.

Everything explodes. People yell, guns go off, the dead run toward us with their arms raised and their hands reaching out. Moans and unearthly screams come out of their rotting mouths. The stink of decomposing flesh is so overwhelming I have to hold my breath while I shoot into the horde.

Others fire and I lower my gun, running for Sophia. I grab her arm and yank her toward the Explorer. "Get in!"

Anne shoots at the bodies with Jake clinging to her legs. "Anne! Take Jake to the Nissan," I yell as a body stumbles toward me with raised arms.

She's fast. So much faster than any of the others we've encountered, and so much more decomposed. Her skin is gray and ripped in places. Black ooze seeps out of the wounds, giving off the putrid smell of decay. Her hands grab my arm and yank me toward her, but before she can sink her teeth into my flesh I put the barrel of my gun to her temple and pull the trigger. Instinctively I close my eyes and mouth, turning my face away as black goo explodes out of her skull, covering me in the stinking liquid.

"Vivian!" Axl yells.

I run, glancing over my shoulder to make sure everyone else is okay. Most people have climbed into the cars, but Mike is still firing his gun. There are too many of them. Bodies converge on him. They grab his limbs and pull him forward. He continues to fire, even as teeth sink into his skin and he screams in agony.

"Mike!" I stop in my tracks. My legs won't work.

But Axl is next to me. He pulls me toward the Nissan. I try to resist, but he's too strong.

"We have to help him!" I sob.

"Too late."

Axl pushes me behind him, back toward the car, and lifts his gun. He pulls the trigger. The bullet hits Mike in the head and he goes down, lost in a mass of dead bodies.

I stumble to the car and jump into the passenger seat, shutting the door just as Axl climbs in. The engine is already running and he hits the gas.

"Did everyone get out?" Anne asks anxiously from the back.

I clench my hands to stop them from shaking. "We lost Mike."

"Shit," Angus mutters. "Dead bastards."

We're all silent. I gasp and my heart pounds. I squeeze my eyes shut while I work hard to slow my breathing. But I can't stop shaking. Not with Mike's screams still ringing in my ears.

"Don't wanna be an ass," Axl says. "But you stink."

I open my eyes. What's he talking about? He nods toward my shirt and I look down. My clothes are covered in black goo.

I pull my shirt over my head and roll down window to toss it outside. Axl raises an eyebrow and Angus actually leans forward so he can get a better look. I give him the finger, then pull a fresh shirt out of my bag. Pervert.

When I have a clean shirt on I lean my head back and close my eyes. "What are we going to do if Mitchell doesn't let us in that shelter?"

"Hell if I know," Axl says. "Whatever we do, we ain't goin' near a city."

Chapter Twenty-Eight

We've been driving through the desert for almost an hour, passing nothing but sand and rocks. We have to be getting close.

Axl drums his fingers on the steering wheel. "We're runnin' low on gas."

"We're screwed if this guy leads us out there for nothin'," Angus grumbles.

Anne, who is sitting in the second row with Angus so Jake can sleep, leans forward. "We need a backup plan. Where do we go if this doesn't work out?"

I stare out at the passing desert. This conversation is getting old. And exhausting. Right now, I just want to pretend that Mitchell is a decent human being. That this shelter does exist and we'll be safely inside sometime in the next twenty minutes. That Emily is asleep in the back of the car.

"Farm," Axl says. "That's all we got so far."

"What about a hotel?" Anne asks. "We could clear it out and take over. It would have a generator and rooms for us. Could be okay."

"We did that in San Francisco. It was alright," I say.

"Problem is, it'd have to be a good-sized hotel to have a generator, and that means goin' into Vegas. Not ideal. Then you're gonna have to worry about runnin' outta fuel." Axl sighs and shakes his head. "A remote area would be better."

Anne sits back and exhales. She has even fewer answers than we do.

"So what did you do for a living?" I ask Anne. I need a distraction.

"I was a cop."

"No shit," Angus says. "I always loved me a lady cop."

I glance over my shoulder. He's raising his eyebrows suggestively, checking her out. I laugh and shake my head. One thing Angus is good for, comic relief when things get too tense.

Anne's probably his age, although she looks several years younger, but she's way too classy-looking for him. She's small and thin, with chin-length brown hair and brown eyes that crinkle in the corners when she talks. She isn't beautiful, but she is cute.

"So where's Jake's father?" Maybe if I keep her talking I can save her from more suggestive comments. Angus has to have quite a few bouncing around in that empty head of his.

"Both his parents are dead. He isn't mine. I found him wandering around the streets the day before you guys saved us. Poor kid, he's been through a lot."

The smile disappears from my lips. Emily. It's like someone has poured hot lava into my stomach.

"There it is," Axl says, saving me from torturing myself. For now.

There's a small square building in the distance, surrounded by a six foot chain link fence. The building is gray and plain. No windows, a flat roof, only one door. There's nothing remotely interesting or special about it. Next to the building is a concrete landing pad with a small helicopter sitting on it. That must have been what was supposed to go pick Mitchell up. Bet he'll be ticked it's sitting there.

Off in the distance is a wind turbine. It's outside the fence, probably about a football field's length away. The turbine's three blades spin at a rapid speed as the wind sweeps across the desert.

Axl pulls up to the fence, and once the car has come to a stop I hop out and run over. It's shut with just a simple latch. No lock or anything else to keep intruders out. I push it open and run back to the car, and Axl parks right next to the building. There are no other vehicles in sight. Either everyone hitched a ride on the helicopter before the pilot got too sick or ran out of fuel, or no one else is here.

Everyone gets out and butterflies start flapping around in my stomach. All eyes are on Mitchell as he walks to the door. He's holding his gun and he has a smug smile on his face.

"Thank you for getting me here safely," he says when he stops in front of the building. He smiles and scans the group. "I truly appreciate it. I only wish I could do more. Unfortunately, when I bought the condo I signed an agreement with the company that forbids me from allowing anyone else in."

"You son of a bitch!" Winston snarls.

"So that code was a bunch of bullshit?" Axl steps forward and pulls out his gun.

"Of course it was. You think I'm stupid?" Mitchell shakes his head. "I didn't become a billionaire by accident."

"You're nothing now," I say. "You think all that money you have in the bank means anything? You may as well use it to start a fire. It's worthless!"

"But it got me here when it was worth something, and that's all that matters." He sighs and shakes his head, trying to look sympathetic. He doesn't. "I'm willing to be reasonable, though. I'm sure some of the people who bought condos didn't show up. I'm willing to take in a few people who have proven that they'd be useful to have around. Joshua, you're more than welcome to come. Having a doctor would be helpful." He turns and looks at Al next. "The Asian kid seems like he'd be a good person to have around as well. We can always use someone in the control room. I'd take you," he says, tilting his head toward to Axl. "You've proven that you have some very useful skills, I just don't think you could take orders."

Axl clenches his hand tighter around his gun and takes a small step forward.

"Screw you," Al says. "I'm not going in there to live with you. I'd rather take my chance with the zombies!"

Joshua nods. "I agree."

Mitchell frowns. "I would consider it a personal favor to me. I really want to be sure there's a doctor in case I get sick."

"Are you for real?" Joshua says with a laugh. "Who cares what you want?"

I bite my lip and consider the situation. We don't have anything to bargain with. We could try to overpower him, but there's a good chance someone would get shot in the process. If Mitchell gets killed, we're all screwed. No one gets in if he dies. But if we let him go some of us will make it at least. That's better than nothing. Maybe someone can even convince whoever else is inside to let the rest of us in.

"You have to take Sophia and the kids," I say.

Mitchell laughs. "I'm not taking a woman and two kids. I want people who can help me survive, not burdens."

Anger builds up inside me, but I clench my jaw shut so I don't say something I'll regret. "Sophia's pregnant. You can't just leave a pregnant woman and two children in the desert to rot. Even you have to know that's wrong." I don't look at Sophia. I'm not sure whether or not she'll think it's a betrayal, but I had to take a chance. Maybe deep down Mitchell is human.

Mitchell swears, but before he can say anything Joshua steps forward. "I won't go unless she does. If you want a doctor, you'll have to let her in too."

"And Arthur," I say. "He's sick. He needs to be with a doctor."

Arthur tries to argue but I ignore him, looking everyone else over. There has to be someone else I can plead the case for. Someone who possesses a skill Mitchell would find useful. But I can't think of anyone. Unfortunately, most of us are useless in this kind of situation.

"Fine," Mitchell says. "They can come. I can always use a maid."

"I can't just leave you all out here," Sophia says. "It wouldn't be right."

"You have to go," Jessica tells her. "For the kids, for your baby. We'll be fine."

Sophia's eyes fill with tears as she looks us all over. No one looks at her with anger or malice.

"Okay," she whispers.

Mitchell lifts his gun. He turns it on Sophia. "No one else. If you try to stop me, I'll shoot her first."

"Bastard," Axl mutters.

"Get your shit, we're going," Mitchell barks at the others.

Sophia runs by me, and Joshua and Arthur follow. My chest is tight, but knowing they'll be going in helps ease the disappointment.

Mitchell looks at me with an evil sneer on his face. "I could always use a little entertainment. Strippers are useful even after the world has ended. What do you say?"

"Fuck you," Axl growls, stepping in front of me.

"What he said," I say.

Mitchell glares at us. "This is why I was rich and you were poor. I'm willing to do whatever it takes to get ahead. Do me a favor.

When a zombie bites your face off, remember that I offered."

I look away and bite my tongue. Literally. We can't piss him off. He could change his mind.

Sophia comes back with her things. She's crying and she stops briefly when she goes by me, leaning forward to kiss me on the cheek.

"Don't go. We will get you in," she whispers.

I want to tell her to be careful, but I'm afraid to give her away.

"I'm going through this door and into the building. If you follow me, if anyone even opens the door, I will kill little Ava." He gives us an evil smile and looks straight at me. "Don't think anyone wants to see another dead little girl today, do they?"

Axl swears and starts to step forward, but I grab his arm and stop him. I lace my fingers through his and stare up at him, shaking my head while the storm rages in his eyes.

Mitchell and the others go inside. My eyes are closed, so I don't see it. When the door clicks shut, it's like a punch in the stomach.

"Now what?" Jessica asks.

"We wait." I open my eyes. "For the night at least. Give them time to talk to whoever else is inside. Maybe there's someone with some decency, someone who will let us in."

"If not?" Parvarti asks.

I look over toward Angus and Axl. "We go back to our original plan."

"We got 'nough gas for one car to get back to Vegas," Axl says. "If it comes to that, we'll have to send a car out to get more before we can all go."

"In the meantime, let's rest and get something to eat. Maybe we can get a fire started," Winston says.

There isn't a lot around since we're out in the desert, but we manage to find enough sticks and tumbleweeds to use for firewood. It's still warm, but the sun will be going down soon, and then the temperature will drop.

I work quietly, lighting the fire without help from anyone while the men bring boxes of food out of the car. With nine of us, the food we have won't last long, but no one wants to wander too far away from the building. Just in case the door does open.

People sit around the fire or in the cars, too dejected to really talk. I sit next to Axl, staring into the flames and eating a peanut butter sandwich made from the last of the bread.

"How'd you learn to do that?" Axl asks, tilting his head toward the fire.

"My dad. Things were never good. He was always a hard ass, but before my mom left they weren't awful. That was before he started using me as a punching bag."

Axl purses his lips. "What was his weapon of choice?"

I shudder, remembering the dreams from when I was sick. Roger standing over me with a leather belt in his hand. "Belt, most of the time. If he couldn't find that, he'd just use his fists." I preferred the belt, but I don't say that out loud. The leather stung and it left huge welts on my body. But the feeling of bone hitting bone...I'll never be able to get that out of my mind.

"My mom liked to slap me around," Axl says. He frowns into the fire. "'Til I got bigger. Guess she thought a simple slap was too good for me. That's when she started chuckin' things at me. Books, plates, full beer cans." He points to the scar on his chin. "That there was an ashtray. Broke when it hit me, left a big gash."

"Why you talkin' 'bout that shit?" Angus asks.

Axl shrugs and sits back in his chair. "Just somethin' to do."

"God, this sucks," Al mutters, tossing an empty wrapper into the fire. The plastic sizzles and melts. It's gone in seconds.

"You coulda gone," Axl tells him. "Nobody woulda faulted you."

"No way. That guy was a prick. What if he's the only one in there? You think I want to be stuck with that guy for the rest of my life?" Al shakes his head.

I stare at a tiny piece of black plastic. All that's left of the wrapper. It looks how I feel. Burned and shriveled. Discarded. "At least Sophia and the kids are safe."

Axl gives me a half-smile. When he gives me that look of approval, it makes me feel like I'm ten feet tall. "Yeah, that was good thinkin' on your part."

A loud moan fills the night sky and everyone stops talking.

"Was that a zombie?" Jessica asks, jumping to her feet.

"It can't be," I say. "We're in the middle of nowhere."

We all sit quietly, huddled around the campfire as we stare out into the desert. The sun is setting and the sky just above the horizon is painted a brilliant shade of orange that gets darker as it reaches into the sky. Makes it difficult to see very far. My heartbeat echoes through my chest, a steady thumping that keeps me on edge. I strain my ears, hoping against hope that the sound was some kind of animal. Deep down, I know it wasn't.

"Maybe it's just a straggler," Winston says. "Someone who got sick while they were out hiking or something and couldn't make it back."

"Yeah, that's gotta be it." Angus spits into the fire. It sizzles and the fire crackles, and another moan breaks through the air. This time it's followed by more.

"Shit," Axl says, getting to his feet. "We gotta get that gate shut."

"It doesn't have a lock," I call. "What good is that going to do if they can open doors?"

"We gotta find somethin' to lock it with," Angus says. "Don't we got some zip ties in the car somewhere?"

Axl nods and the brothers run to the Nissan in search of them while Winston heads to the gate. I grab my gun and run after him with Al and Trey right behind me.

"Here they come!" Al yells.

It's so bright. How can he see them? He must have perfect vision, because it takes me a few seconds of searching the desert before I can make them out. But he's right. They're coming, and not slowly.

"You guys got those zip ties yet?" I call.

"Still lookin'!" Axl yells back.

I glance over at Al. He's unarmed. "Al, go get a gun!"

He smacks himself on the forehead and runs back toward the cars. Jessica and Parvati huddle together by the fire. Anne heads our way. She's loaded down with weapons.

"Look how many of them are out there," Winston says.

My heart pounds. I start counting and stop at thirty. We're fenced in, but this chain link isn't going to last long against a big mob.

"It looks like they're wearing military uniforms," Anne says.

"Area 51!" Al yells excitedly when he comes to a stop next to me. He waves his gun toward the desert. "I bet we're close to area 51!"

"That's a good thing?" I ask. Will military training make them more deadly? Probably won't hurt.

"Got 'em." Axl runs up behind us and slips a zip tie through the latch on the fence.

"Not sure if it's going to help," Winston says. "Many more of them show up and they'll probably be able to push this fence down.

"What do we do?" I ask. "Do we take cover in the cars and hope they don't spot us or do we start shooting?"

"I think it's too late to hide," Anne says.

Trey bounces around on the balls of his feet. He reminds me of a football player right before a big game. "So shoot, then?"

Winston looks at Axl and shrugs. "I don't think we have any other options."

They're closing in on us now, and judging by the moaning they know we're here. It's getting darker, but the fenced area is well lit—probably for the helicopter—making us an easy target.

"Wait till you're sure you got a good shot," Axl says. "We got plenty of ammo, but who knows how many more are out there."

My heart pounds. Every time the wind blows I catch a whiff of decay and my stomach lurches. "Shit," I mutter, trying to control my shaking hands. "I didn't think we were going to die today."

"It's as good a day as any." Axl aims his gun and takes the first shot.

Trey pulls the trigger next, taking a body down. "If they knock this fence down we're dead for sure."

We all start shooting after that. The gunfire echoing through the silent desert night is overwhelming. Like a freight train. Bodies fall and the dead scream, but more keep coming. Before long there's a pile of them just outside the fence.

"They're never-ending!" I yell, firing my last bullet. I dig in my back pocket for another clip.

Anne sweeps her sweaty hair off her forehead. "What do we do?"

"Keep shootin'!" Angus growls.

My heart jumps to my throat when the first body reaches the fence. He's only there for a second before someone shoots him in the face, but another replaces him. Then another.

"There must be hundreds!" Al yells.

Before I know it twenty bodies are at the fence. They clutch the chain link and shake it, filling the night with their agonizing screams. We fall back, shooting as we walk. I don't know where we're going, but I want to be as far away from that fence as I can when it collapses.

"I'm out!" Anne turns and runs back to the car.

It isn't long until others run back as well. Soon it's just me and Angus still firing into the bodies. When my gun clicks and nothing happens, I follow the others. They're outside the Nissan, getting more guns and ammo ready. Angus only fires three more times before he runs toward us too.

"We got 'nough fuel in the Explorer, that's it," Axl yells. His face is red and sweat drips down his forehead. He wipes it from his eyes and looks us all over. "What'd we do? Make a run for it or try an' fight 'em off?"

I don't know what to say. Leaving would mean giving up all of our supplies, going off into the desert and praying we could find more and make our way in Vegas. It doesn't sound appealing.

"We have plenty of ammo," Trey says. "I say we fight."

"Anyone have a problem with that?" Winston asks.

Moans fill the silence while we stare at each other. Staying could mean death, but so could running. Everyone is breathing heavily, sweating and shaking. Terrified. But no one argues. No one wants to leave our supplies behind. No one wants to run away like a coward.

Axl's eyes meet mine and everything in me constricts. There are so many things I want to say to him before the end, but there isn't time. Not with the bodies charging us and everyone around. If only we had a few minutes to ourselves.

"I'm not ready to give up," I say, loud enough that only he can hear.

Axl swallows and his gray eyes fill with regret. Like he wishes he had more time with me as well. "Then we fight."

We turn back toward the fence just as the door to the concrete building opens behind us.

Shattered World
Mad World
Lost World
Available Now on Amazon!

Look for *New World*, the fifth book in the *Broken World* series, coming Summer of 2015!

Stranded in the middle of the Mojave Desert, surrounded by zombies, Vivian and Axl's group are sure they're facing the end. The dead are closing in and the shelter they were promised is sealed tight, only they refuse to go down without a fight. Just when they think they've run out of time, the doors to the shelter are thrown open and they're given refuge. Five years in underground condos with all the provisions there for the taking. It's almost too good to be true. With the promise of security, Vivian hopes she'll finally able to take a deep breath and deal with everything that's happened. The loss of Emily, her growing feelings for Axl, and the terrifying new world they're facing.

But the group's sense of security is soon shattered when they learn the shelter isn't the utopia they thought it would be. It seems the company that built the shelter decided to solve their financial problems by selling off provisions, which means the group has to find a way to get their own food, fuel and medical supplies. Or face starvation.

And Vegas is the closest city.

With her feelings for Axl stronger than ever, Vivian volunteers to accompany him and a few others on a trip into one of the biggest tourist cities in the world to search for supplies. The city is overrun with the dead, but there are other survivors as well. Only not everyone they meet is a welcome sight. As the emotional baggage piles up, Vivian and Axl's bond grows stronger than ever, but it doesn't take long to realize the dead isn't the only thing they have to fear.

ABOUT THE AUTHOR

Kate L. Mary is a stay-at-home mother of four and an Air Force wife. She spent most of her life in a small town just north of Dayton, Ohio where she and her husband met at the age of twelve. Since their marriage in 2002, they have lived in Georgia, Mississippi, South Carolina, and California.

Kate's love of books and writing has helped her survive countless husbandless nights. She enjoys any post-apocalyptic story – especially if zombies are involved – as long as there is a romantic twist to give the story hope. Kate prefers nerdy, non-traditional heroes that can make you laugh to hunky pieces of man-meat, and her love of wine and chocolate is legendary among her friends and family. She currently resides in Oklahoma with her husband and children.

You can visit her website at http://KateLMary.com

Made in the USA
San Bernardino, CA
06 January 2016